Stopford A. Brooke, Percy Bysshe Shelley

Poems of Shelley

Stopford A. Brooke, Percy Bysshe Shelley

Poems of Shelley

ISBN/EAN: 9783337391096

Printed in Europe, USA, Canada, Australia, Japan

Cover: Foto ©Andreas Hilbeck / pixelio.de

More available books at **www.hansebooks.com**

POEMS

OF

SHELLEY

SELECTED AND ARRANGED

BY

STOPFORD A. BROOKE

NEW YORK: 46 EAST 14TH STREET

THOMAS Y. CROWELL & CO.

BOSTON: 100 PURCHASE STREET

I.

AH, DID YOU ONCE SEE SHELLEY PLAIN,
  AND DID HE STOP AND SPEAK TO YOU,
AND DID YOU SPEAK TO HIM AGAIN?
  HOW STRANGE IT SEEMS, AND NEW!

II.

BUT YOU WERE LIVING BEFORE THAT,
  AND ALSO YOU ARE LIVING AFTER;
AND THE MEMORY I STARTED AT —
  MY STARTING MOVES YOUR LAUGHTER!

III.

I CROSSED A MOOR, WITH A NAME OF ITS OWN,
  AND A CERTAIN USE IN THE WORLD, NO DOUBT,
YET A HAND'S-BREADTH OF IT SHINES ALONE
  'MID THE BLANK MILES ROUND ABOUT:

IV.

FOR THERE I PICKED UP ON THE HEATHER,
  AND THERE I PUT INSIDE MY BREAST;
A MOULTED FEATHER, AN EAGLE FEATHER!
  WELL, I FORGET THE REST.

ROBERT BROWNING.

PREFACE.

———◆———

SHELLEY, from whose poetry this book of Selections is made, can only, like all other poets, be judged justly, or fitly loved, when everything he wished to be published has been carefully studied. We can no more comprehend him in the right way by reading only his finest poems, supposing we could choose them, than we can receive a true impression of the character of the scenery of a country by visiting a selection of its most beautiful places. Through his weakness we know part of his strength; nor is it only for his power we love him.   This necessity of reading all a poet's work, if we wish to know him truly, or to receive from him his special gift of pleasure, is the main objection to *Selections*; but its weight is lessened when the intention of a book of this kind is not to represent Shelley fully, but to present, in a brief compass, enough of his poetry to induce those who are ignorant of it to read the whole. That is the only valid reason and excuse for Selections from a poet, and it is the object of this book. If the excuse be accepted, we may say that Shelley is more open to selection than many of the other poets.   His whole work is short, and a great deal of it can be included in a small book. It is especially lyrical, and lyrics are the best material for selections.

Some, too, of the longer poems, such as *Alastor* and *Adonais*, in which we can study his steadier and more ambitious effort, are brief enough to be inserted entire, and they break the lyrics pleasantly, and offer a more varied enjoyment to the reader. There is also one spirit in Shelley's work which fills and brings into unity all his poems. It is the spirit of youth. We are not troubled in reading these Selections, by such a change in the whole nature of the poet as age made in Wordsworth. Owing to this unity of spirit, I have been able to place together, without fear of their jarring with one another, poems written at different periods of Shelley's life on the same or kindred themes. To group such poems together is the method followed in this book, and its fitness seems to be supported by the fact that Shelley, being very fond of his ideas, and also of the forms he gave them, repeated them continually. The impression made by one poem is therefore strengthened by another on the same subject. Shelley is his own best illustrator.

When *Selections* from any poet appear rapidly, it may be said that he has taken his place, that time and its verdict have distinguished him in his own country. And Shelley is now at home with us, and his praise becomes greater day by day. Some of that praise, especially when it exalts him, without distinctiveness of criticism, above his brother poets, seems undeserved, but there is no longer any doubt, among those worthy to judge, that Shelley has assumed his own separate throne among the greater poets of England.

It is then somewhat strange to look back nearly sixty years, and to think that when Shelley died, scarcely fifty people cared to read his poetry, and even these did not understand it. Seven years after his death opinion began to change. He had so far influenced the young men of Cambridge, that its Union sent a deputation in November 1829 to the Oxford Union, to maintain Shelley's superiority over Byron. "At that time," said Lord Houghton — speaking in 1866 — "we, the Cambridge undergraduates, were all very full of Mr. Shelley. We had printed his *Adonais* in 1829 for the first time in England, and a friend of ours suggested that, as he had been expelled from Oxford, and very badly treated in that University, it would be a grand thing for us to defend him there." The young men, Arthur Hallam, Monckton Milnes, and Sunderland, were received by Gladstone, Francis Doyle, and Milnes Gaskell. Wilberforce of Oriel was in the Chair. Sir Francis Doyle (Christ Church) moved that Shelley was a greater poet than Lord Byron. He was supported by the three Cambridge men, and by Mr. Oldham of Oriel. The negative was defended by Mr. Manning; and on a division Byron was declared the greater poet by a majority of fifty-seven. This interesting story proves that some young men at Oxford and Cambridge were now awakened to Shelley's genius. They felt and loved him as the most ideal of the poets, and year by year he has increased the number of those who give him that special place and honor.

About 1832 his power over the minds of men

increased. At that time fresh political and theo-
logical elements began to excite England, and then
the other side of Shelley's work began to tell. The
poems he had written as the prophet of liberty, equal-
ity, fraternity, and a Golden Age, were eagerly read
by the more intelligent among the working classes,
and by many who felt that the ideas of the French
Revolution were again arising into activity after their
winter sleep. It is a part of his work which still
continues to do good.

Again, within the last few years, the sad, regretful,
unsatisfied, self-considering, indefinite elements in
the mind of educated English society have found
food and expression in a certain number of Shelley's
poems, and this has increased the extent of his influence. That which has been called the "lyrical cry"
belongs now to a whole section of society, and Shelley often echoes its regret and indefiniteness with
great beauty.

Moreover, a great number of persons who care for
Nature as Art cares for her, that is, as alive and not
dead, being revolted by the materialistic aspect in
which some scientific theories now present her, have
turned with new pleasure to the spiritual representations given of her by such poets as Wordsworth and
Shelley. That also has added a fresh impulse to the
study of Shelley.

It may also be said that the forms, and especially
the ideal forms of passionate love, have been, of late,
more minutely dwelt on in poetry, and with greater
curiosity, than they have been since the Elizabethan
period. It is natural, then, that a poet like Shelley,

who made ideal love his study, and the subject of so much of his work, should now receive and claim greater attention.

Shelley, reflecting and embodying these various phases, is then a much more comprehensive poet than the common judgment supposes. And he is all the more comprehensive because his nature and his work were twofold. The first thing to say of him is, that he lived in two worlds, thought in two worlds, and in both of these did work which was at once varied and distinct. One was the world of Mankind and its hopes, the other was the world of his own heart.

His poetic life was an alternate changing from one of these worlds to the other. He passed from poetry written for the sake of mankind, to poetry written for his own sake and to express himself; from the Shelley who was inspired by moral aims and wrote in the hope of a regeneration of the world, to that other Shelley who, inspired only by his own ideas and regrets, wrote without any ethical end, and absolutely apart from humanity. The passionate lover of man crosses over the stage, singing of mankind, and disappears. The passionate poet succeeds, singing of himself, and disappears in turn. The interchange continues, but both the figures are the same man.

Shelley began as the prophet of the ideas of the French Revolution. *Queen Mab*, written with the enthusiasm of a youth for the overthrow of the evils that he thought oppressed mankind, and in hope of its deliverance into a world of love and peace, is not,

as a poem, so "absolutely worthless" as he imagined
it to be. The verse is musical; there are two direct
pictures of nature, both of the sky; the journey
through the stars has some of the imaginative power
which realized the flight of Asia and the Hours in
the *Prometheus*, but all the polemical part is very
prosaic. It is like a sermon in verse, and it has just
the poetical quality we expect in a sermon. The
latter portion is naturally the best. The most remarkable element *Queen Mab* possesses is didactic
force. But, owing to its uncultivated rhetoric, that
force is likely to tell most on very young persons,
and on uneducated but intelligent working men,
who may sympathize with its opinions. The poem
had such an influence, and that influence was widely
extended.

Two years later, in 1815, all was changed. The
circumstances of his life, illness, expectation of death,
made him lose, in losing all vigor and joy, his interest in man, and *Alastor*, his next long poem, is
entirely occupied with his own solitary thought and
life. The preface he wrote explains the meaning of
the poem, and, contrasted with the poem, reveals
that double nature in Shelley of which I write. He
repudiates in it, with all the sternness of a moralist,
yet with self-pity, the life described in *Alastor*; and
the lines with which he closes the poem itself—"It
is a woe too deep for tears," etc., are a cry of sorrow
and reproach against one who desired to work for
man, but who wasted his life in pursuit of that
unattainable beauty his soul could dream of, but
not realize.

Of all Shelley's longer poems, *Alastor* leaves on the general reader the easiest impression of an artistic whole. The subject is one, and never varies from itself: it is closely clung to from beginning to end, and is deeply felt throughout. The poetry and its art, both imaginative and technical, are of course less great than they became in after work, but so far as unity of conception and steadiness of expression and form are concerned, even *Adonais* is less artistic than *Alastor*. Shelley's personality absorbs the poem. The extreme ideality of the treatment alone relieves the intensity of this personal revelation, and makes it not too overwhelming to give pleasure. The natural descriptions prove how deeply Shelley had felt some of the larger aspects of Nature, and the melody of their verse is at times like the harmonies we seem to hear among waters and woods; but Nature in this poem is never described for herself alone, never for pure joy in her. She is made to reflect the thoughts and passion of the wandering poet until the very last, when his life and that of the moon ebb away together. This is deliberately done, and nowhere in a finer way than in the description of the long walk down the glen. We follow step by step the interpenetration of the poet's dying soul and of the various changes of the scene. As the brook flows to the precipice, so does his life; as the valley alters its landscape, so does the landscape in his heart. The skill and intensity with which this is wrought out is the cause of the fascination that passage has for all who read it.

In the *Hymn to Intellectual Beauty* and to *Mont*

Blanc, written after *Alastor*, Shelley, though writing
only as the artist of his own thought, has recovered
some of his hopes for Man. He tries to connect his
worship of Beauty with the redemption of the race;
he speaks of the Power hidden in the great mountain
to "repeal large codes of fraud and woe." His Con-
tinental journey had brought him new health, and
his life, new happiness, and with them came back the
old longing and the old interest to play his part in
the movement of the world. The result was the *Revolt of Islam*. Its genesis and its aim are explained
in the preface with which he accompanied the poem.
It seemed to Shelley that the age of despair that followed the end of the French Revolution was over,
and that now, when the reaction from that trance of
failure had begun, the time had arrived for him to
speak. In that belief he composed this poem. It
strove to kindle afresh the flame of liberty, but it had
no effect on the exhausted Englishmen of 1818.
Nor, as poetry, did it deserve to have a great effect.
It is the most unbalanced of all his works. The
interest is human, but it is too frequently taken out
of the world of actual human life to awaken practical
emotion. Were the scenery of the poem all ideal, or
all real, we should not be so troubled while we read.
Were the poem supremely ethical or supremely emo-
tional, had it any unity at all, it might keep its power
over us. But it has no unity, not even in feeling.
Its emotion is unequal; we are continually changing
the atmosphere, and are overchilled or overheated.
There is no artistic fusion of the poetry which aims
at giving a high pleasure with that which aims at

awakening man to his duties. That fusion was made in the *Prometheus Unbound*, but here it was not made.

And now another of these changes took place. Shelley fell ill again, the threatened loss of his children preyed upon him, and he left England for ever in 1818. He lost again for a time his enthusiasm for man, and the characteristic of the work of this year is sadness deepening into misery. With very few exceptions the poems are personal. One, however, differs from all that preceded it. *Julian and Maddalo*, composed at the end of the year, is personal, but still not so much so as to prevent Shelley from painting, with a firm hand, another character than his own. It is the first instance of that power of losing himself in the creation of distinct personages which enabled him to write the drama of the *Cenci*. *Julian and Maddalo* has unity, and the materials are carefully woven together. The style is subdued to a quiet level, and the imagination, which ran riot in the *Revolt of Islam*, is curbed to do its work, and only its special work, by the will of the poet. Reading it, we should predict that if again the enthusiasm for man should awaken in Shelley's heart, the work he would do on the subject would be more worthy of his power. It did awaken, and in how different a form it came ! It was no longer hampered by his notion that he must directly attack evil. It rose at once and easily, taking with it all the subjects of the *Revolt of Islam*, into the region of pure art, and there, in the world of passion and beauty and fire, he wrote the *Prometheus Unbound*. That poem is the marriage of Shelley's double nature, the fusion for creative work of the lover of man and the poet. He reaches in it that culminating point at which the thinker on man gives his best-loved materials to the artist, and the artist breathes into them life and beauty.

The same vivid interest in humanity was then made special in the *Cenci*, a tragedy wrought out with so much temperance of imagination, directness of emotion, and closeness of thought, that it is the strangest contrast to the *Prometheus*. The range of power implied in the production of these two dramas within twelve months, each so great, and so unlike, is rarely to be paralleled among the poets below those of the highest order. It is all the more wonderful when we think that about the same time such poems were also created as the *Sensitive Plant*, the *Skylark*, the *Cloud*, *Arethusa*, and the *Ode to the West Wind*. The last alone is enough to place Shelley apart from the other lyrical poets of England. In it, as in the *Prometheus*, and still more splendidly, all his powers and his poetic subjects are wrought into a whole. The emotion awakened by the approaching storm sets on fire other sleeping emotions in his heart, and the whole of his being bursts into flame around the first emotion. This is the manner of the genesis of all the noblest lyrics. He passes from magnificent union of himself with Nature and magnificent realization of her storm and peace, to equally great self-description, and then mingles all nature and all himself together, that he may sing of the restoration of mankind. There is no song in the whole of our literature more passionate, more penetrative, more full of the force by which the idea and its form are united into one creation.

This time, during which Shelley's twofold being was married for creative work, did not last long. The two elements always tended to separate, and now the special Shelley element, which fled from man into the recesses of his own heart, or communed with the ideal Nature which he made for himself out of the apparent world, began to absorb him, and finally drove out the other.

At the beginning of this reaction he was still gay, often bright; and the *Letter to Maria Gisborne* is one of the rare poems in which Shelley is at peace. An air of home and happiness flows through its familiar and melodious verse. *The Witch of Atlas* also belongs to this time; a poem in which he sent his imagination out, like a child into a meadow, without any aim save to enjoy itself. Now and again Shelley himself, as it were from a distance, alters or arranges the manner of the sport, as if with some intention, but never so much as to spoil the natural wildness of the Imagination's play. Enough is done to suggest that there may be a meaning in it all, but not enough to tell that meaning. " I mean nothing," Shelley would have said; " I did not write the poem. My imagination made it of her own accord." Nor was he so self-absorbed at first as wholly to neglect the cause of man. The *Ode to Liberty*, the *Ode to Naples*, belong to this summer and autumn of 1820.

We pass into the isolated poet with the *Sensitive Plant*, the companionless flower; and from this time forth the old Shelley, who loved Mankind, is dead. The only exception is the choral drama of *Hellas*, written in a transient enthusiasm for the cause of Greece. "I try to be what I might have been," he says, "but am not successful. It was written without much care, and in one of those few moments of enthusiasm which now seldom visit me, and which make me pay dear for their visits." Two poems, however, preceded *Hellas*; *Epipsychidion* and *Adonais*. Both are written by the lonely artist; nor is there any trace in them of the Shelley who prophesied for Man. Of *Epipsychidion* I have spoken in the notes of this book. The ideal passion, in which it originated, hid him in the light of thought, far away from humanity, and he never quite got back again.

Adonais, awakened in him not only by his sympathy with Keats, but also by the resemblance of the fate of Keats to his own, is almost as much concerned with Shelley as with its subject. There is nothing in English poetry so steeped in passionate personality as the description of himself in stanzas xxxi–iv. It is almost too close, too unveiled, too intense to have been written. The only other poet — for Byron's self-description is written with a view to effect — who has approached the wild self-sorrow of it, is Cowper, and he uses the same simile of the stricken stag. The poem is, as Shelley said, "a highly wrought piece of art." Its abstract spirituality, and its philosophy, remove it from the ordinary apprehension, and are the cause why it is less read than *Alastor*. But, in truth, Shelley himself, and the scenery and personages he creates in this abstract realm, are more real in this poem than in others which have to do with the actual world. It suited him to write about a spirit, and he wrote as he were himself a spirit. The Dreams which hover around Adonais, the Splendors and Glooms, Morning with the tears in her hair, Spring wild with grief, Echo singing in the hills, Urania flying to mourn beside the bier — Shelley has succeeded in giving them all being. While we read, we believe in the reality of this world as we believe in our dreams while we dream. The power of doing this is unique, and is due not only to imagination at its height, but also to keenness of abstract' intellect. His grip of these impalpable personages is quite certain. He creates them, and then he sees and hears them. Owing to this the conduct of the poem is clear. The unremitting beauty of the lines so engages attention as at first to forbid an analysis of the arrangement, but when that analysis is made, the pleasure *Adonais* gives is not disturbed, but doubled. And how passionate it is throughout, more passionate than most of his love poems! It is unceasingly strange, and the strangeness adds, from outside, to the charm of Shelley's poetry, to find him writing with a far greater intensity of feeling about the sorrow of Urania and the Dreams, about the Spirit of Love in the Universe, about Keats in the spiritual world, and about his own wearied and solitary heart, than he ever writes about men or women, about human love, or about the personal suffering of others.

A new element of isolation, that created by a passion which circumstances forbade him to pursue, separated him now, at the close of his life, still more from Mankind, and in that temper he died. But there are some proofs, to which I shall afterwards draw attention, that he would, as before, have passed out of this lonely inner life, and found himself again in sympathy with the external. Had he lived, he would have once more appeared as the Singer of Man, and in the cause of men. But the swift wind and the mysterious sea, the things he loved, slew their lover — a common fate — and we hear no more his singing. His work was done, and its twofold nature may well be imaged by the Sea that received into its uninhabited breast his uncompanioned spirit; for, while its central depths know only solitude, over its surface are always passing to and fro the life and fortunes of humanity.

But the sea gave up its dead, and all of Shelley's body that was rescued from flood and fire lies now where the rise of the ground ends, in a dark nook of the Aurelian wall. So deep is that resting-place in shadow that the violets blossom later there than on "the slope of green access" where, seen from Shelley's grave, the flowers grow over the dust of Adonais. We may be glad that both were buried in Italy rather than in England, for, though no Italian could have written their poetry, yet it was, — in all things else different, — of that spirit which Italy awakens in Englishmen who love her, rather than of the purely English spirit. The Italian air, the sentiment of Italy, fled and dreamed through their poems, but most through those of Shelley. It was but fitting, then, that Shelley, whose fame was England's, should be buried in the city which is the heart of

Italy. But he was born far away from this peaceful and melancholy spot, and grew up to manhood under the gray skies of England, until its Universities, its Church, its Society, its Law and its dominant policy became inhospitable to him, nay, even his own father cast him out. They all had, in the opinion of sober men of that time, good cause to make him a stranger, for he attacked them all, and it would be neither wise or true, nor grateful to Shelley himself, were he to be put forward as a genius unjustly treated, or as one who deserved or asked for pity. Those who separate themselves from society, and war against its dearest maxims, if they are as resolute in their choice, and as firm in their beliefs as Shelley, count the cost, and do not or rarely complain when the penalty is exacted. He was exiled, and it was no wonder. The opinion of the world did not trouble him, nor was that a wonder. But as this exile is the most prominent fact of his life, its influence is sure to underlie his work. The second question that any one who writes of Shelley has to ask, is, How did this exile from the Education, Law, Religion, and Society of his country, and from the soil of his country itself, affect his poetry?

It had a very great influence, partly for good and partly for evil. The good it did is clear. It deepened his individuality and the power which issued from that source. It set him free from the poetic conventions to which his art might have yielded too much obedience in England — a good which the obscurity of Keats also procured for him — it prevented him from being worried too much by the blind worms

of criticism, it enabled him to develop himself more
freely, and it placed him in contact with a natural
scenery, fuller and sunnier than he could ever have
had in England, in which his love of beauty found so
happy and healthy a food that it came to perfect
flower.   In Italy also, where impulse even more than
reason urges intelligence and inspires genius, lyrical
poetry, which is born of impulse, is more natural and
easy, though not better, than elsewhere, and the very
inmost spirit of Shelley, deeper than his metaphysics
or his love of Man and inspiring both, deeper even
than any personal passion, was the lyrical longing
of his whole body, soul, and spirit — "O that I had
wings like a dove; then would I flee away, and be
at rest."

But the good this exile did his art was largely
counterbalanced by its harm.   Shelley's individuality, unchecked by that of others, grew too great,
and tended not only to isolate him from men, but to
prevent his art from becoming conversant enough
with human life.   The absence of critical sympathy
of a good kind, such as that which flows from one
poet to another in a large society, left some of his
work, as it left some of Keats's, more formless, more
intemperate, more impalpable, more careless, more
apart from the realities of life, than it ought to have
been in the most poetical of poets since the days of
Elizabeth.   Even in his lyric work, the impassioned
impulse would have failed less often to fulfil its form
perfectly; there would not have been so many fragments thrown aside for want of patience or power to
complete them, had he been less personal, less sub-

ject to individual freakishness, more subject to the
unexpressed criticism which floats, as it were, in the
air of a large literary society, and constrains the art
of the poet into measured act and power. And as to
Nature, we should perhaps have had, with his genius,
a much wider and less ideal representation of her,
had he not been so enthralled by the vastness and
homelessness of Swiss, and by the ideality of Italian,
scenery. Even when he did write in England itself,
the recollected love of Switzerland and the Rhine
mingled with the impressions he received from the
Thames, and produced a scenery, as in certain passages in *Alastor* and the *Revolt of Islam*, which is not
directly studied from anything in heaven or earth.
It is none the worse for that, but it is not Nature, it
is Art.

These are general considerations, but there were
some more particular results, partly good and partly
evil, of this separation of Shelley from the ordinary
religious and political views of English society.

A good deal of his poetry became polemical, and
polemical, like satiric poetry, is apart from pure art.
It attacks evil directly, and the poet, his mind being
then fixed not on the beautiful but on the base, writes
prosaically. Or it embodies a creed in verse, and,
being concerned with doctrine, becomes dull. In both
cases the poet misses, as Shelley did, that inspiration
of the beautiful which arises from the seeing of truth,
not from the seeing of a lie; from the love of true
ideas, not from their intellectual perception. The
verses, for example, in the *Ode to Liberty*, which
directly attack kingcraft and priestcraft, however

gladly one would see their sentiments in prose, are inferior as poetry to all the rest; and it is the same throughout all Shelley's poetry of direct attack on evil. This polemical element in the *Revolt of Islam*, and the endeavor to lay down in it his revolutionary creed, are additional causes of the wastes of prosiac poetry which make it so unreadable. The very splendor and passion of the passages devoted to Nature and Love contrast so sharply, like burning spaces of sunlight on a gray sea, with the wearisome whole, that they lose half their value, and disturb, like so much else, the unity of the poem. The same things seem true of *Rosalind and Helen*, and of those political poems which are direct attacks on abuses in England. On the other hand, when Shelley wrote on these evils indirectly, inspired by the opposing truths, concerned with their beauty, and borne upwards by delight in them, his work entered the realm of art, and his poetry became magnificent. There is no finer example of this than *Prometheus Unbound*. The subject is at root the same as that of the *Revolt of Islam*, the things opposed are the same, the doctrine is the same, but the whole method of approaching his idea and fulfilling its form is changed, and all the questions are brought into that artistic representation which stirs around them inspiring and enduring emotion.

The good Shelley did in this way was very great. At a time when England, still influenced by its abhorrence of the Reign of Terror, by its fear of France and Napoleon, was most dead to the political ideas that had taken form in 1789, Shelley gave voice, through art, to these ideas, and encouraged that hope of a golden age which, however vague, does so much for human progress. He threw around these things imaginative emotion, and added all its power to the struggle for freedom.

Still greater is the unrecognized work he did in the same way for theology in England. That theology was no better than all theology had become under the influence of the imperial and feudal ideas of Europe. Its notion of God, and of man in relation to God, partly Hebraic, and therefore sacerdotal and sacrificial, partly deeply dyed with asceticism and other elements derived from the Oriental notion of the evil of matter, was further modified by the political views of the Roman Empire, transferred to God by the Roman Church. And when the universal ideas regarding mankind, and a return to nature, were put forth by France, they clashed instantly with this limited, sacerdotal, ascetic, aristocratic, and feudal theology. The sovereign right of God, because He was omnipotent, to destroy the greater part of His subjects, the right of a caste of priests to impose their doctrines on all, and to exile from religion all who did not agree with them; the view that whatever God was represented to do was right, though it might directly contradict the nature, the conscience, and the heart of Man; these, and other related views had been brought to the bar of humanity, and condemned from the intellectual point of view by a whole tribe of thinkers. But if a veteran theology is to be disarmed and slain, it needs to be brought not only into the arena of thought and argument, but into the arena of poetic emotion. A great part of that latter work was done in England by Shelley. He indirectly made, as time went on, an ever-increasing number of men feel that the will of God could not be in antagonism to the universal ideas concerning Man, that His character could not be in contradiction to the moralities of the heart, and that the destiny He willed for mankind must be as universal and as just and loving as Himself. There are more clergymen, and more religious laymen than we imagine, who trace to the emotion Shelley awakened in them when they were young, their wider and better views of God. Many men, also, who were quite careless of religion, yet cared for poetry, were led, and are still led, to think concerning the grounds of a true worship, by the moral enthusiasm which Shelley applied to theology. He made emotion burn around it, and we owe to him a great deal of its nearer advance to the teaching of Christ. But we owe it, not to those portions of his poetry which denounced what was false and evil, but to those which represented and revealed, in delight in its beauty, what was good and true. Had he remained in England, I do not think he would have worked on this matter in the ideal way of *Prometheus Unbound*, because continual contact with the reigning theology would have driven his easily wrought anger into direct violence. In Italy, in exile, it was different. The polemical temper in which he wrote the *Revolt of Islam* changed into the poetical temper in which he wrote *Prometheus Unbound*.

Connected with this, but not with his exile, is the

question, in what way his belief as to a Source of Nature influenced his art. He was not an atheist or a materialist. If he may be said to have occupied any theoretical position, it was that of an Ideal Pantheist; the position which, with regard to Nature, a modern poet who cares for the subject, naturally — whatever may be his personal view — adopts in the realm of his art. Wordsworth, a plain Christian at home, wrote about Nature as a Pantheist: the artist, as I said, loves to conceive of the Universe, not as dead, but as alive. Into that belief Shelley, in hours of inspiration, continually rose, and his work is seldom more impassioned and beautiful than in the passages where he feels and believes in this manner. The finest example is towards the close of the *Adonais*. In his mind, however, the living spirit which, in its living, made the Universe, was not conceived of as Thought, as Wordsworth conceived it, but as Love operating into Beauty; and there is a passage on this idea in the fragment of the *Coliseum*, which is as beautiful in prose as that in *Adonais* is in verse. But it is only in higher poetic hours that Shelley seems or cares to realise this belief. In the quieter realms of poetry, in daily life, he confessed no such creed plainly; he had little or no belief in a thinking or loving existence behind the phenomenal universe. It is infinitely improbable, he says, that the cause of mind is similar to mind. Nothing can be more characteristic of him — and he has the same temper in other matters — than that he should have a faith with regard to a Source of Nature, into which he could soar when he pleased, in which he could live for a time, but which he did not choose to live in, to define, or to realize, continuously. When, in the *Prometheus Unbound*, he is forced, as it were, to realize a central cause, he creates Demogorgon, the dullest of all his impersonations. It is scarcely an impersonation. Once he calls it a "living spirit," but it has neither form nor outline in his mind. He keeps it before him as an "awful Shape."

The truth is, the indefinite was a beloved element of his life. "Lift not the painted veil," he cries, "which those who live call Life." His worst pain was when he thought he had lifted it, and seemed to know the reality. But he did not always believe that he had done so, or he preferred to deny his conclusion. Not as a thinker in prose, but as a poet, he frequently loved the vague with an intensity which raised it almost into an object of worship. The speech of the Third Spirit, in the *Ode to Heaven*, is a wonderful instance of what I may call the rapture in indefiniteness. But this rapture had its other side, and when he was depressed by ill-health, the sense of a voiceless, boundless abyss, which for ever held its secret, and in which he floated, deepened his depression. The horror of a homeless and centreless heart which then beset him, is passionately expressed in the *Cenci*. Beatrice is speaking —

"Sweet Heaven, forgive weak thoughts, if there should be
No God, no Heaven, no Earth, in the void world;
The wide, gray, lampless, deep, unpeopled world."

But, on the whole, whether it brought him pain or joy, he preferred to be without a fixed belief with regard to a source of Nature. Could he have done otherwise, could he have given continuous substance in his thoughts to the great conception of ideal Pantheism in which Wordsworth rested, Shelley's whole work on Nature and his description of her would have been more direct, palpable, and homely. He would have loved Nature more, and made us love it more.

The result of all this is that a great deal of his poetry of Nature has no ground in thought, and consequently wants power. It is not that he could not have had this foundation and its strength. Both are his when he chooses. But, for the most part, he did not choose. Such was his temperament that he liked better to live with Nature and be without a centre for her. He would be

Dizzy, lost — but unbewailing.

But I am not sure whether the love of the undefined did not, in the first instance, arise out of his love of the constantly changing, and that itself out of the very character of his intellect, and the temper of his heart. His intellect, incessantly shaken into movement by his imagination, continually threw into new shapes the constant ideas he possessed. His heart, out of which are the issues of imagination, loved deeply a few great conceptions, but wearied almost immediately of any special form in which he embodied them, and changed it for another. In the matter of human love, he was uncontent with all the earthly images he formed of the ideal he had loved and continued to love in his own soul, and he could not but tend to change the images. In the ordinary life of feeling, the moment any emotion arose in his heart, a hundred others came rushing from every quarter into the original feeling, and mingled with it, and changed its outward expression. Sometimes they all clamored for expression, and we see that Shelley often tried to answer their call. It is when he does this that he is most obscure — obscure through abundance of feelings and their forms. His intellect, heart, and imagination were in a kind of Heraclitean flux, perpetually evolving fresh images, and the new, in swift succession, clouding the old; and then, impatient weariness of rest or of any one thing whatever, driving forward within him this incessant movement, he sank, at last and for the time, exhausted — "As summer clouds disburthened of their rain."

There is no need to illustrate this from his poetry. The huddling rush of images, the changeful crowd of thoughts are found on almost every page. It is often only the oneness of the larger underlying emotion or idea which makes the work clear. We strive to grasp a Proteus as we read. In an instant the thought or the feeling Shelley is expressing becomes impalpable, vanishes, reappears in another form, and then in a multitude of other forms, each in turn eluding the grasp of the intellect, until at last we seize the god himself, and know what Shelley meant, or Shelley felt. In all this he resembles, at a great distance, Shakspere; and has, at that distance, and in this aspect of his art, a strength and a weakness similar to, but not identical with, that which Shakspere possessed, — the strength of changeful activity of imagination, the weakness of being unable, through eagerness, to omit, to select, to co-ordinate his images. Yet, at his highest, when the full force of genius is urged by full and dominant emotion, what poetry it is ! How magnificent is the impassioned unity of the whole in spite of the diversity of the parts ! But this lofty height is reached in only a few of Shelley's lyrics, and in a few passages in his longer poems.

At almost every point, the scenery of the sky he drew so fondly images this temper of Shelley's mind, this incessant building and unbuilding, this cloud-changefulness of his imagination.

> I silently laugh at my own cenotaph,
>   And out of the caverns of rain,
> Like a child from the womb, like a ghost from the tomb
>   I arise and unbuild it again.

That is a picture of Shelley himself at work on a feeling or on a thought. " I change, but I cannot die."

I might illustrate this love of the changing from the history of his life, of his affections, of his theories; from his varied nature, and way of work, as the prose thinker and the poet; from the variety of the subjects on which he wrote, and which he half attempted — for he naturally fell into the fragmentary — from the eagerness with which he searched for new thought, new experiences of feeling, new literatures, even from his love of the strange and sometimes of the horrible; from that uncontent he had in the doctrines of others, until he had added to them, as he did to Plato's doctrine of Love, something of his own in order to make them new, — were there any necessity to enlarge on that which stands so clear. In all these things, what was said of Shelley's movements to and fro in the house at Lerici is true of his movement through the house of thought or of feeling. "Oh, he comes and goes like a spirit, no one knows when or where." But it remains to be said, that all through this secondary changefulness, he held fast to certain primary ideas of life, of morality, and of his art, which no one who cares for him can fail to discover.

There was, then, in Shelley this love of indefiniteness, and this love of changefulness. Which of the two was the cause of the other I cannot tell, but I am inclined to think that the latter was the first. It is better, however, to keep them both equally in view in the study of Shelley's art, and they are both well illustrated in his poetry of Nature.

I have said that his love of the indefinite with regard to a source of Nature weakened his work on Nature. His love of changefulness also weakened it by luring the imagination away from a direct sight of the thing into the sight of a multitude of images suggested by the thing.

But in the case of those who have great genius, that which enfeebles one part of their work often gives strength to another, and in three several ways these elements in Shelley's mind made his work on Nature of great value.

1. His love of that which is indefinite and changeful made him enjoy and describe better than any other English poet that scenery of the clouds and sky which is indefinite owing to infinite change of appearance.

The incessant forming and unforming of the vapors which he describes in the last verse of *The Cloud*, is that which he most cared to paint. Wordsworth often draws, and with great force, the aspect of the sky, and twice with great elaboration in the *Excursion ;* but it is only a momentary aspect, and it is mixed up with illustrations taken from the works of men, with the landscape of the earth below where men are moving, with his own feelings about the scene, and with moral or imaginative lessons. Shelley, when he is at work on the sky, troubles it with none of these human matters, and he describes not only the momentary aspect, but also the change and progress of the sunset or the storm. And he does this with the greatest care, and with a characteristic attention to those delicate tones and half-tones of color which resemble the subtle imaginations and feelings he liked to discover in human Nature, and to which he gave form in poetry.

In his very first poem, in *Queen Mab* (Part II.), there is one of these studies of Sunset. It is splendidly eclipsed by that in the beginning of *Julian and Maddalo*, where the Euganean Hills are lifted away from the earth and made a portion of the scenery of the sky. A special moment of sunset, with the moon and the evening-star in a sky reddened with tempest, is given in *Hellas*, but here, being in a drama, it is mingled with the fate of an empire. The Dawns are drawn with the same care as the sunsets, but with less passion. There are many of them, but the most beautiful perhaps is that in the beginning of the second Act of the *Prometheus*. The changes of color, as the light increases in the spaces of pure sky and in the clouds, are watched and described with precise truth ; the slow progress of the dawn, during a long time, is noted down line by line, and all the movement of the mists and of the clouds " shepherded by the slow unwilling wind." Nor is that minuteness of observation wanting which is the proof of careful love.   Shelley's imaginative study of beauty is revealed in the way the growth of the dawn is set before us by the waxing and waning of the light of the star, as the vapors rise and melt before the morn.

The Storms are even better than the sunsets and dawns.   I have drawn attention in the notes to the finest of these in the first canto of the *Revolt of Islam.*   There is another description at the beginning of the eleventh canto of the same poem (p. 83 of this book), in which the vast wall of blue cloud before which gray mists are flying is cloven by the wind, and the sunbeams, like a river of fire flowing between lofty banks, pour through the chasm across the sea, while the shattered vapors which the coming storm has driven forth to make the opening, are tossed, all crimson, into the sky.   This is a favorite picture of Shelley's.   In the *Vision of the Sea* it is transferred from sunset to sunrise.   The fierce wind coming from the west rushes like a flooded river upon the dense clouds which are piled in the east, and rends them asunder, and through the gorge thus cleft

> the beams of the sunrise flow in,
> Unimpeded, keen, golden and crystalline,
> Banded armies of light and air.

The description is a little over-wrought, but criticism has no voice when it thinks that no other poet has ever attempted to render, with the same absolute loss of himself, the successive changes, minute by minute, of such an hour of tempest and of sunrise. We are alone with Nature; I might even say, We see Nature alone with herself. Still greater, more poetic, less sensational, is the approach of the gale in the *Ode to the West Wind*, where the wind itself is the river on which the forest of the sky shakes down its foliage of clouds, and these are tossed upwards like a Mænad's "uplifted hair," or trail downwards, like the "locks" of Typhon,[1] the vanguard of the tempest. In gathered mass behind, the congregated might of vapors is rising to vault the heaven like a sepulchral dome. Nothing can be closer than the absolute truth to the working of the clouds that fly before the main body of a storm, which is here kept in the midst of these daring comparisons of the imagination.

The same delight in the indefinite and changeful aspects of Nature appears in Shelley's power of describing vast landscapes, such as that seen at noontide from the Euganean Hills, or that which the poet in *Alastor* looks upon from the edge of the mountain precipice. Both swim in the kind of light that makes all objects undefined, deep noon, and sunset light.

Kindred to this is Shelley's pleasure in the intricate, changeful, and incessant weaving and unweaving of nature's life in a great forest. In the *Recollection* it is the Pisan Pineta he describes, and that is a painting directly after Nature. But he has his own

---

[1] I wonder that Mr. Ruskin has not quoted this verse in the *Angel of the Sea* (*Modern Painters*, vol. v.). Shelley's lines might well form a text for that chapter.

ideal forest, of which he tells in *Alastor*, in *Rosalind and Helen*, in the *Triumph of Life*, and again and again in the *Prometheus*.   It is no narrow wood, but a universe of forest; full of all trees and flowers, in which are streams, and pools, and lakes, and lawny glades, and hills, and caverns; and in whose multitudinous scenery Shelley's imagination could lose and find itself without an end.   The special love of caverns, with their dim recesses, adds another characteristic touch.   These then, — The scenery of the sky, of the forest, of the vast plain, — are the aspects of nature Shelley loved the most, and out of the weakness that elsewhere made him too indefinite, and too uncertain through desire of change, for Wordsworth's special kind of descriptive power, arose the force with which he realized them.

2.   Again, just because Shelley had no wish to conceive of Nature as involved in one definite thought, he had the power of conceiving the life of separate things in Nature with astonishing individuality.   When he wrote of the Cloud, or of Arethusa, or of the Moon, or of the Earth, as distinct existences, he was not led away from their solitary personality by any universal existence in which they were merged, or by the necessity of adding to these any tinge of humanity, any elements of thought or love, such as the Pantheist is almost sure to add.   His imagination was free to realise pure Nature, and the power by which he does this, as well as the work done, are quite unique in modern poetry.   Theology, with its one Creator of the Universe; Pantheism, with its "one spirit's plastic stress;" Science with its one Energy, forbid

the modern poet, whose mind is settled into any one of these three views, to see anything in Nature as having a separate life of its own. He cannot, as a Greek could do, divide the life of the Air from that of the Earth. of the cloud from that of the stream. But Shelley, able to loosen himself from all these modern conceptions which unite the various universe, could and did, when he pleased, divide and subdivide the life of Nature in the same way as a Greek — and this is the cause why even in the midst of wholly modern imagery and a modern manner, one is conscious of a Greek note in many passages of his poetry of Nature. The little poem on the Dawn might be conceived by a primitive Aryan. It is [1] a Nature myth. But Shelley's conceptions of the life of these natural things are less human than even the Homeric Greek or early Indian poet would have made them. They described the work of Nature in terms of human act. Shelley's spirits of the Earth and Moon are utterly apart from our world of thought and from our life. Of this class of poems *The Cloud* is the most perfect example. It describes the life of the Cloud as it might have been a million years before man came on earth. The "sanguine Sunrise" and the "orbed Maiden," the moon, who are the playmates of the cloud, are pure elemental beings.

The same observation is true if we take a poem on a living thing in Nature, like *The Skylark*, into which human sentiment is introduced. The sentiment belongs to Shelley, not to the lark. The bird has joy, but it is not our joy. It is "unbodied joy," nor "can

---

[1] See p. 15**⊙**

we come near it." Wordsworth's *Skylark* is truer,
perhaps, to the everyday life of the bird, and the poet
remembers, because he loves his own home, that the
singer will return to its nest; but Shelley sees and
hears the bird who, in its hour of inspired singing,
will not recollect that it has a home. Wordsworth
humanizes the whole spirit of "the pilgrim of the
sky" — "True to the kindred points of heaven and
home." Shelley never brings the bird into contact
with us at all. It is left in the sky, singing; it will
never leave the sky. It is the archetype of the lark
we seem to listen to, and yet we cannot conceive it,
we have no power — "What thou art we know not."
The flowers in the *Sensitive Plant* have the same
apartness from humanity, and are wholly different
beings and in a different world from the Daisy or the
Celandine of Wordsworth. It is only the Sensitive
Plant, and that is Shelley himself, which has an inner
sympathy with the Lady of the garden.

Shelley, then, could isolate and perceive distinct
existences in Nature as if he were himself one of these
existences. It was a strange power, and we naturally
cannot love with a human love things so represented.
In Wordsworth's poems we touch the human heart
of flowers and birds. In Shelley's we touch " Shapes
that haunt Thought's wildernesses." Yet it is quite
possible, though we cannot feel affection for Shelley's
Cloud or Bird, that they are both truer to the actual
fact of things than Wordsworth made his birds and
clouds. Strip off the imaginative clothing from *The
Cloud*, and Science will support every word of it.
Let the Skylark sing, let the flowers grow, for their

own joy alone. In truth, what sympathy have they, what sympathy has Nature with Man? We may not like to think of Nature in this way; we are left quite cold by *The Cloud*, and by the spirits of the Earth and Moon in the *Prometheus*; and if we are not left as cold by *The Skylark*, it is because we are made to think of our own sorrow, not because we care for the bird. But whether we like or no to see Nature in this fashion, we should be grateful for these unique representations, and to the poet who was able to make them. In this matter also Shelley's want of a central and uniting Thought in Nature made his strength.

The other side of Shelley's relation to Nature is a remarkable contrast to this statement. When he was absorbed in his own being, and writing poems which concerned himself alone, he makes Nature the mere image of his own feelings, the creature of his mood. In his "life alone doth Nature live." This was the natural result, at these times, of his intellectual rejection of such Pantheism as enabled Wordsworth always to distinguish between himself and the Nature he perceived. The Nature Wordsworth saw we can love well, because it is not ourselves — never a reflection of ourselves. The Nature such as Shelley saw in *Alastor* is not easy to love, because it is ourselves in other form. For this reason also we are not able to love Nature, when thus represented by Shelley, so well as we love her in Wordsworth.[1]

[1] Shelley's love of the undefined and changing is still further illustrated by the fact that we see Nature in his poetry in these three ways — on all of which I have dwelt. We some-

3. Lastly, on this subject, the vagueness and changefulness of Shelley's feeling and view of Nature, except in the instances mentioned, the dreams and shadows of it in his poetry that incessantly form and dissolve like the upper clouds of the sky, each fleeting while its successor is being born, and few living long enough to be outlined, are the only images we possess in art, save perhaps in music, of the many hours we ourselves pass with Nature when we neither think nor feel, but drift and dream incessantly from one impression to another, enjoying, but never defining our enjoyment, receiving moment by moment, but never caring to say to any single impression, " Stay and keep me company." In this thing also, Shelley's weakness made his power.

This want of definite belief and of its force belongs also to his conception of the ideal state of mankind. He does not see quite clearly what he desires for man, and describes the golden age chiefly by negatives of wrong. At times he rises into a passionate realization of his Utopia, as he rises into Pantheism, but he cannot long remain in it. The high-wrought prophecy, too weak to keep the height it has gained, sinks down again and again into an abyss of seeming hopelessness. The last stanza of the *Ode to Liberty* is the type of many an hour of his life, and of the close of many a poem. But he never let hopelessness or depression master him. Shelley is full of resurrec-

times look on her as the ideal Pantheist beholds her; we look on her again as the mere reflection of the poet's moods; we look on her often as she may be in herself, apart from theories about her, apart from man.   .

tion power, and the fall from the peak of prophecy is more the result of reaction after impassioned excitement, than the result of any unbelief in his hopes for men, or in that on which they were grounded.

These hopes, that belief, had their strong foundation. There was one thing at least that Shelley grasped and realized with force in poetry — the moralities of the heart in their relation to the progress of Mankind. Love and its eternity; mercy, forgiveness, and endurance, as forms of love; joy and freedom, justice and truth as the results of love; the sovereign right of Love to be the ruler of the Universe, and the certainty of its victory, — these were the deepest realities, the only absolute certainty, the only centre in Shelley's mind; and whenever, in behalf of the whole Race, he speaks of them, and of the duties and hopes that follow from them, strength is then instinctive and vital in his imagination. Neither now nor hereafter can men lose this powerful and profound impression. It is Shelley's great contribution to the progress of humanity.

But he could not combine with this large view and this large sympathy with the interests of Man, personal sympathy with personal human life. That is absent from his poetry, and his want of it was confirmed by his exile. Confined to a small circle of which he was the centre, among foreigners, feeling himself repudiated by the society of his own country, and incapable of such quiet association with the lives of men and women as Wordsworth loved and enjoyed, it is no wonder that large spaces of human life are entirely unreflected and unidealized in his poetry.

The common human heart was not his theme, nor did he care to write of it. And, so far, he is less universal than Wordsworth, and less the great poet. But on the other hand he did two things, in his work on human nature, that Wordsworth could not do. First, he realized in song, so far as it was possible, the impalpable dreams of the poetic temperament, those which, when they arise in happiness, he expresses in the little poem, *On a poet's lips I slept*, and others also less joyous — the lonely wanderings of regretful thought, the imagination in its hours of childlike play with images, the moments when we are on the edge where emotion and thought incessantly change into one another, the visions of Nature which we compose but which are not Nature, the sorrows and depressions which have no name and to which we allot no cause, the depths of passionate fancy when we have not only no relation to mankind, but hate to feel that relation. Of all this Wordsworth gives us nothing; and though what he does give us is of more use and worth to us as men who have to do with men, yet Shelley's work in this is dear to our personal life, and has in fact as much to do with one realm of humanity as the sorrow of Michael, or the daily life of the dalesmen have with another. English poetry needed the expression of these things; Shelley's expression of them is unique, but I doubt whether he would ever have expressed them in so complete a way had he not been thrown into isolation.

Secondly, there is an element almost altogether wanting in Wordsworth, the absence of which forbids us to class him as a poet who has touched all the important sides of human life — the element of passionate love. A few of his poems, such as *Barbara*, or in another kind, *Laodameia*, solemnly glide into it and retreat, but on the whole, this, the most universal subject of lyric poetry, was not felt by Wordsworth. It was felt by Shelley, but not quite naturally, not as Burns, or even Byron felt it. Love, in his poetry, sometimes dies into dreams, sometimes likes its imagery better than itself. It is troubled with a philosophy ; it seems now and again to be even bored, if I may be allowed the word, by its own ideality. As Shelley soared but rarely into definite Pantheism, so he rose but rarely into definite passion, nor does he often care to realize it. It was frequently his deliberate choice to celebrate the love which did not " deal with flesh and blood," and as frequently, when he writes directly of love, he prefers to touch the lip of the cup, but not to drink, lest in the reality he should lose the charm of indefiniteness, of ignorance, of pursuit. Of course he was therefore fickle.

For this very reason, however, two realms in this aspect of his art belong to him. Neither of them is the realm of joyous passion, but one is the realm of its ideal approaches, and the other the realm of its ideal regret. No one has expressed so well the hopes, and fears, and fancies, and dreams, which the heart creates for its own pleasure and sorrow, when it plays with love which it realizes within itself, but which it never means to realize without ; and this is a realm which is so much lived in by many that they ought to be grateful to Shelley for his expression of it. No one else has done it, and it is perfectly done.

But still more perfect, and perhaps more beautiful than any other work of his, are the poems written in the realm of ideal Regret. Whenever he came close to earthly love, touched it, and then of his own will passed it by, it became, as he looked back upon it, ideal, and a part of that indefinite world he loved. The ineffable regret of having lost that which one did not choose to take, is most marvellously, most passionately expressed by Shelley. Song after song records it. The music changes from air to air, but the theme is the same, and so is the character of the music. And, like all the rest of his work, it is unique.

But in this matter, a change passed over Shelley before he died. It is impossible not to feel that the poems written for Mrs. Williams, a whole chain of which exist, are different from the other love poems. They have the same imaginative qualities as the previous songs, and they belong also to the two realms of which I have written above, but there is a new note in them, the beginning of the unmistakable directness of passion. It is, of course, modified by the circumstances, but there it is. And it is from the threshold of this actual world that he looks back on *Epipsychidion* and feels that it belonged to "a part of him that was already dead." The philosophy which made Emilia the shadow of a spiritual Beauty is conspicuous by its total absence from all these later love poems. Moreover, they are not, like the others, all written in the same atmosphere. The atmosphere of ideal love, however varied its cloud-imagery, is always the same thin ether. But these poems breathe in the changing atmosphere of the Earth, and they one and all possess reality. Every one feels that *Ariel to Miranda*, *The Invitation*, *The Recollection*, have the variety of true passion. But none of them reach the natural joy of Burns in passionate love. Two exceptions, however, exist, both dating from this time, and both written away from his own life — the *Bridal Song*, and the song *To Night*. These seem to prove that, had Shelley lived, we might have had from him vivid, fresh, and natural songs of passion.

Had he lived! Had not the sea been too envious, what might we not have possessed and loved! It were too curious perhaps to speculate, but Shelley seems to have been recovering the power of working on subjects beyond himself, in the quiet of those last days at Lerici. He was always capable of rising again, and the extreme clearness and positive element of his intellect acted, like a sharp physician, on his passion-haunted heart and freed it, when it was outwearied with its own feeling, from self-slavery.

While still at Pisa, at the beginning of 1822, Shelley set to work on a Drama, *Charles I.*, the motive of which was to be the ruin of the king through pride and its weakness, the same motive as *Coriolanus*. It was to be "the birth of severe and high feelings," and to transcend the *Cenci* as a work of art. But severe feeling was not then the temper of his mind, nor could he at that time lose himself enough to create an external world. He laid the play aside, saying that he had not sufficient interest in English history to continue it. Yet it is plain, even from the fragments we possess, how great was the effort Shelley then made to realize, even more than in the *Cenci*, other characters than his own. There is not a trace in it of his own self. It is full of steady power, power more at its ease than in the *Cenci*. The characters stand clear, and are carefully distinguished, so as not only to represent the various elements in England which brought about, in their clashing together, the ruin of monarchy, but also to show the forces and weaknesses in each of the greater personages which led to their personal ruin or success. The unconscious movement of Shelley's imagination — within the speeches set to each character — in vivid illustration, in quick invention of changes of feeling, and in its harmonizing of the whole and the parts, is, like the excellence just mentioned, in the manner of Shakspere's art, and approaches his strength. Archy, the fool, is made perhaps too imaginative in phrase, yet he is much nearer than any other poet's creation of the same kind to the fools of Shakspere, so wise because they are half mad. Yet neither in this, nor in the rest, does Shelley directly imitate Shakspere here, as he sometimes does in the *Cenci*. The principles of Shakspere's art are followed ; the work itself is quite original. The same thing is true of the blank verse. It is built on the model of Shakspere's, but it is Shelley's own, and its movement, sure to be beautiful in the hands of this master of all melody in all kinds of verse, is more free, more fitted to the changing moods of the speakers, and more delightful than it is in the *Cenci*. The noble speech of Hampden, with which this fragment concludes, illustrates and confirms all I have said. It is quite plain that it cannot be said of the artist who did this piece of work that he had exhausted his vein.

It becomes still more clear that Shelley would have done more for us when we consider the *Triumph of Life*, the gravest of his poems. Its personal interest is as great as its interest for this generation. He may have been composing it when the sea overwhelmed him. Over it gathers, then, all the tenderness which belongs to last words, and all the power they possess to awaken love, pity, and enthusiasm. Its somewhat morbid view of life is not to be wondered at, so much as to be forgiven for the sake of the strength which rises through the dim allegory, like a fountain which will become a river. It proves that, had he lived, he would have filled his poetry and his life with new intention. And it is worthy of the cry which, closing the last poem in this book, is prophetic of that unconquerable hope for mankind which, underlying the greater part of Shelley's poetry, has made half its influence upon the world —

> O wind,
> If winter comes, can spring be far behind ?

NOTE ON THE TRIUMPH OF LIFE.

THIS poem is so difficult to understand that I have ventured to make the following analysis : —

It opens with a noble picture of sunrise, filled with solemn and stately images, and more disengaged from self than any of Shelley's previous work. He then describes himself passing into a waking trance, in which he is conscious that in some previous existence he has been in the same place, and heard and seen the same things. And in that trance he sees a Vision.

He finds himself on a dusty and flowerless road, on either side of which is a forest full of sweet streams and flowers and lawns, and on the road a multitude of folk, old age and youth, and manhood and infancy, all hastening onward like a torrent. This represents, under the common allegory, the ordinary life of men. What kind of life that now seemed to Shelley is described in the lines which begin —

"Some flying from the thing they feared,"

but of all this crowd, none, so hurried and so serious was their folly, could hear the sweetness of the stream or know the beauty of the wood. Nor did any understand — and this was the universal condition — "whither he went or whence he came, or why he made one of the multitude." Life is an inexplicable secret, and in the terrible attraction this secret has for men and in their failure to solve it, lies the reason of the victory Life wins over its victims. In the midst of this crowd the Triumph passes by. As the throng grew wilder, a cold glare, that obscured the sun with a false light, came, and in the glare a chariot, and in the chariot, Life, the Conqueror. None could see its incommunicable face, double-hooded, double-caped, over its head a cloud-like crape; nor its form, crouching like age within the car, as one who sat in the shadow of a tomb; while the ethereal gloom that poured forth from this dread Shape tempered the fierce light in which the chariot moved. Every image in this allegorical representation tells of the mystery of life, the unfathomable riddle that none could penetrate, but which conquered and led all captive. It is this thought which is the foundation of the Poem. The deep concealment is doubled by the further imagery. The Charioteer is a four-faced Shadow — Time itself, perhaps, with its three faces that look into the present, the past, and the future ; but its eyes are banded so that it cannot see while in the service of Life. The winged shapes that draw the car are lost to sight in thick lightnings. And the Charioteer guides the car blindly, so that its course is aimless. Life itself knows not where it is conducted. Before the car is the wild dance of youth, seeking in tempestuous pleasure to find the secret of Life, and outspeeding Life ; behind it, the foul and impotent dance of age, still cleaving to Life, still limping to reach the glare of Life's light; and the youths and maidens are overtaken and trampled by the car of Life into foam like the barren sea-foam, and the old sink into corrupted dust.[1] These are the common crew who have only sought to live according to impulse and desires.

There are others, however, who do not belong to the two bands before and behind, but are dragged, chained captives, along with the triumphal car. These are they who tried to know what Life was, or

---

[1] The whole of this may be compared with Tennyson's *Vision of Sin.*

to conquer it; who labored, but in vain; who died
and never knew the secret.

> All those who had grown old in power
> Or misery, all who had their age subdued
> By action or by suffering,

alike the famous and the infamous. Only a few are
not seen there, are not captives — the Prophets of
Mankind, who touched the world with flame, and
then fled back to their native noon; who put aside
the diadem; who were not victims of Life, because
they despised all that Life could offer; who conquered its secret by not caring to penetrate it, of
whom the types were they of Athens and Jerusalem
— Socrates and Christ.

In his trance Shelley asks, What is this? And a
Shape, like an old root by the wayside, who is
Rousseau, answers him that it is the pageantry of
Life's Triumph, and that if Shelley can forbear to
join the dance — as he does forbear — he will unfold
that to which this deep scorn — this thing worthy of
deep scorn — has led him and his companions.
"Then, if you want further knowledge, follow the
car; for me, I am weary, nor would corruption now
inherit so much of Rousseau

> " if the spark with which Heaven lit my spirit
> Had been with purer sentiment supplied."

Who are those chained to the car? Shelley asks.
"The wise, the great, the unforgotten," who were
wise, but did not know themselves. Their love,
their might, that won for them empire, " could not

repress the mystery within." For at the last, that fierce mystery shrouded in the car, Life, and the question what it is, arose in their soul and conquered them, and deep night swallowed them.

Napoleon is then seen, and all the conquerors of the world by force of arms or intellect, chained to Life's car and vanquished by its scornful secret. I myself, speaks Rousseau, was overcome by my own heart alone. that nothing in the world *could temper to its object.*[1]

The course of the vision is here interrupted by two speeches of Shelley's, and both of them are meant to mark his present apartness from the throng of Life and his disdain of those who, through desire of conquest or fame, were slaves to Life. The last of these speeches, and Rousseau's answer to it, are steeped in Shelley's passionate sense that humanity was but an imagery of an eternal Oneness behind it, which, reflected in the ever-changing mirror of circumstance and nature, made its infinite variety. But all the reflections are reflections, nothing more. The same thought is in *Adonais*, lii. Here, it is —

> Figures ever new
> Rise on the bubble, paint them as you may;
> We have but thrown, as those before us threw,
> Our shadows on it as it passed away.

Then he sees, captives also, "the mighty phantoms of an elder day." Plato expiating his too great feeling of joy and of sorrow, not his own master, whom Life conquered at last by love ; Aristotle, Alexander,

---

[1] How close to truth !

whose conquests the Life of the world finally made
nought; the Elder Bards, "who quelled

> " The passions which they sung, as by their strain
> May well be known : their living melody
> Tempers its own contagion to the vein
> Of those who are infected with it."

Even these, who quelled passions, are captive to Life,
because they were too curious of the passions, and
because they knew their work would stir in others
the passions they themselves subdued.   But they are
of a higher cast than Rousseau, who, like Shelley,
"suffered what he wrote," and whose words have
seeds of misery.

Then the dreamer sees the Emperors of Rome
and her great Bishops, whose power was given but
to destroy; and, sick at heart, turns again to Rousseau (if, as I think, there is no long break here in the
poem, and the "leader" mentioned is still Rousseau
and not another), and asks him how his course began
and why.   Rousseau then tells his tale and that of
the pageant; and portions of the story are so like
what Shelley has at other times said of his own life,
that it seems as if he would have partly told his own
story in the tale that Rousseau tells.   Rousseau
thinks that if Shelley would become actor or victim
instead of spectator in this wretchedness, and follow
the Conqueror —

> What thou wouldst be taught I then may learn
> From thee.

That is, he would learn from Shelley's fate to understand his own.

A new phase of the allegory now begins ; the story
of a single life and its overthrow by Life. Rousseau
describes himself asleep at the portals of this and
of the antenatal world, a place here imaged as a
cavern, through which flows a stream in which all
things are forgotten. All those who are in the
pageant of life have also been, as we understand at
the end, asleep in this oblivious valley. When he
arose into being. in infancy. he says that all things
around kept the trace of some diviner light than that
of earth, and melodies that confused the sense of
earthly things were heard. This is the half Platonic
conception of reminiscence. Boyhood comes, imaged
by the brightness of morning that floods the cavern,
and then, a Shape all light stood before him, flinging
freshness, and in her hand a cup of nepenthe. It is
the Spirit of the aspirations and dreams of youth, the
vision of Beauty Shelley saw, the Vision which, in
different forms, all the creators see. She leads the
youth forth out of the cave, and as he follows her all
his thoughts were strewn under her feet like embers,
and, thought by thought, she quenched them, and
all that was, seemed, as he gazed, as if it had been
not. That is the swift succession of aspiration,
thought, and feeling. each dying as its successor is
born, which we know when we are young, and the
sense, then also ours, of all the outward world becoming, in the pursuit of the ideal, as if it had no real
being. At last the mystery of life which cannot be
repressed, begins to stir within the youth. He can
no longer resist the fatal question all must ask, and
— "Show whence I came, he cries, and where I am,

and why." "Arise and quench thy thirst," the Shape
replies; and as he drank the cup, this Dream of
youth grew dim, and her light — a light of heaven
that hereafter glimmered only, forever sought again,
forever lost — waned in the glare of the Masque of
Life that now rushed through the forest. It is the
entrance into manhood, life as it is in the world of
action. He sees — and it seems the answer to his
question — the car in which Life itself is borne, its
captives, and those who played, or gazed; or followed, or out-speeded the car — all as yet young.
He himself plunges into "the thickest billows of
that living storm," but before the chariot had begun to climb the steep of middle age a new wonder
grew.

The weariness, the cruel working of life's secret,
begins to exhaust and destroy all the pleasure, all the
eagerness, with which men at the first follow the
chariot of Life. The way in which Shelley images
this change, and the cause he assigns for it are as
imaginative as they are original. Shadows began to
people the grove, dense flocks of phantoms, of various quality and shape, who hid in the capes of kings,
and rode across the tiara of popes; and some were
old anatomies that hatched broods, and whose dead
eyes took power and gave it to those who ruined
earth; and some fell like flashes of discolored snow
on the bosoms of the young and were melted by the
glow which they extinguished; and others, like small
gnats, thronged about the brows of lawyer, states-
man, priest, and theorist. Shelley invents all kinds
of them, and each has its meaning. These are the

thoughts, written or spoken, the work and the passions of men; all that men have poured forth from
their hearts or impressed upon the world; the old
theologies, the old doctrines of kingcraft whose dead
eyes have power; the political theories, poetry, phil-
osophies, which have been sent forth from the beginning of humanity, but which poured forth so fast and
furious before the Revolution. Rousseau knows
whence they came. "Each one

> "Of that great crowd sent forth incessantly
> These shadows."

Shadows as they were, form was given them by the
creative rays of the car, for all the thoughts and feelings of men are moulded by the mystery of life. And
so moulded, and darkening all the ways of the pageant
with the sense of the deep mystery that gave them
shape, they did their work, and hour by hour the
unconquerable secret, embodied in the forms given
to it by the infinite questioning of men, destroyed
its victims.

> From every form the beauty slowly waned;
> From every firmest limb and fairest face
> The strength and freshness fell like dust —

And long before the day of life

> Was old, the joy which waked like heaven's glance
> The sleepers in the oblivious valley died;
> And some grew weary of the ghastly dance,
> And fell as I have fallen, by the wayside; —

And those fell soonest who had done most creative
work; who had thought and felt and expressed the

most — the more passionate, whether for good or evil, the worse off.

> Those soonest from whose forms most shadows passed,
> And least of strength and beauty did abide.
> " Then what is Life? " I cried.

. And with that cry all that Shelley wrote 's ended.

CONTENTS.

lviii   *CONTENTS.*

PAGE

POEMS FROM SHELLEY

HYMN TO INTELLECTUAL BEAUTY.

THE awful shadow of some unseen Power
  Floats tho' unseen amongst us, — visiting
  This various world with as inconstant wing
As summer winds that creep from flower to flower, —
Like moonbeams that behind some piny mountain
    shower,
    It visits with inconstant glance
    Each human heart and countenance;
Like hues and harmonies of evening, —
    Like clouds in starlight widely spread, —
    Like memory of music fled, —
    Like aught that for its grace may be
Dear, and yet dearer for its mystery.

Spirit of BEAUTY, that dost consecrate
  With thine own hues all thou dost shine upon
  Of human thought or form, — where art thou gone?
Why dost thou pass away and leave our state,
This dim vast vale of tears, vacant and desolate?
    Ask why the sunlight not for ever
    Weaves rainbows o'er yon mountain river,
Why aught should fail and fade that once is shown,
    Why fear and dream and death and birth
    Cast on the daylight of this earth
    Such gloom, — why man has such a scope
For love and hate, despondency and hope?

No voice from some sublimer world hath ever
  To sage or poet these responses given —
  Therefore the names of Demon, Ghost, and
    Heaven,
Remain the records of their vain endeavor,
Frail spells — whose uttered charm might not avail to
    sever,
    From all we hear and all we see,
    Doubt, chance, and mutability.
Thy light alone — like mist o'er mountains driven,
    Or music by the night wind sent,
    Thro' strings of some still instrument,
    Or moonlight on a midnight stream,
Gives grace and truth to life's unquiet dream.

Love, Hope, and Self-esteem, like clouds depart
  And come, for some uncertain moments lent.
  Man were immortal, and omnipotent,
Didst thou, unknown and awful as thou art,
Keep with thy glorious train firm state within his
    heart.
    Thou messenger of sympathies,
    That wax and wane in lovers' eyes —
Thou — that to human thought art nourishment,
    Like darkness to a dying flame!
    Depart not as thy shadow came,
    Depart not — lest the grave should be,
Like life and fear, a dark reality.

While yet a boy I sought for ghosts, and sped
  Thro' many a listening chamber, cave and ruin,
  And starlight wood, with fearful steps pursuing
Hopes of high talk with the departed dead.

I called on poisonous names with which our youth is
    fed,
    I was not heard — I saw them not —
    When musing deeply on the lot
Of life, at that sweet time when winds are wooing
    All vital things that wake to bring
    News of birds and blossoming, —
    Sudden, thy shadow fell on me ;
I shrieked, and clasped my hands in ecstasy!

I vowed that I would dedicate my powers
    To thee and thine — have I not kept the vow?
    With beating heart and streaming eyes, even
    now
I call the phantoms of a thousand hours
Each from his voiceless grave : they have in visioned
    bowers
    Of studious zeal or love's delight
    Outwatched with me the envious night —
They know that never joy illumed my brow
    Unlinked with hope that thou wouldst free
    This world from its dark slavery,
    That thou — O awful LOVELINESS,
Wouldst give whate'er these words cannot express.

The day becomes more solemn and serene
    When noon is past — there is a harmony
    In autumn, and a lustre in its sky,
Which thro' the summer is not heard or seen,
As if it could not be, as if it had not been!
    Thus let thy power, which like the truth
    Of nature on my passive youth

Descended, to my onward life supply
    Its calm — to one who worships thee,
    And every form containing thee,
    Whom, SPIRIT fair, thy spells did bind
To fear himself, and love all human kind.

1816.

—◦◦◦—

THE POET'S PHILOSOPHY.

[WE] look on that which cannot change — the One,
The unborn and the undying.   Earth and Ocean,
Space, and the isles of life or light that gem
The sapphire floods of interstellar air,
This firmament pavilioned upon chaos,
With all its cressets of immortal fire,
Whose outwall, bastionèd impregnably
Against the escape of boldest thoughts, repels them
As Calpe the Atlantic clouds — this Whole
Of suns, and worlds, and men, and beasts, and flowers,
With all the silent or tempestuous workings
By which they have been, are, or cease to be,
Is but a vision ; all that it inherits
Are motes of a sick eye, bubbles and dreams ;
Thought is its cradle and its grave, nor less
The future and the past are idle shadows
Of thought's eternal flight — they have no being :
Nought is but that which feels itself to be.

    .   .   .   .   .

Hellas.

THE POET'S WORLD.

On a poet's lips I slept
Dreaming like a love-adept
In the sound his breathing kept;
Nor seeks nor finds he mortal blisses,
But feeds on the aërial kisses
Of shapes that haunt thought's wildernesses.
He will watch from dawn to gloom
The lake-reflected sun illume
The yellow bees in the ivy bloom,
Nor heed nor see what things they be;
But from these create he can
Forms more real than living man,
Nurslings of immortality!

Prometheus Unbound.

𝔄lastor.

"Nondum amabam, et amare amabam, quærebam quid amarem, amans amare." — *Confess. St. Augustine.*

THE poem entitled "ALASTOR" may be considered as allegorical of one of the most interesting situations of the human mind. It represents a youth of uncorrupted feelings and adventurous genius, led forth, by an imagination inflamed and purified through familiarity with all that is excellent and majestic, to the contemplation of the universe. He drinks deep of the fountains of knowledge, and is still insatiate. The magnificence and beauty of the external world sinks profoundly into the frame of his conceptions, and affords to their modifications a variety not to be exhausted. So long as it is possible for his desires to point towards objects thus infinite and unmeasured, he is joyous and tranquil and self-possessed. But the period arrives when these objects cease to suffice. His mind is at length suddenly awakened, and thirsts for intercourse with an intelligence similar to itself. He images to himself the Being whom he loves. Conversant with speculations of the sublimest and most perfect natures, the vision in which he embodies his own imaginations unites all of wonderful or wise or beautiful which the poet, the philosopher, or the lover, could depicture. The intellectual faculties, the imagination, the functions of sense, have their respective requisitions on the sympathy of corresponding powers in other human beings. The Poet is represented as uniting these requisitions, and attaching them to a single image. He seeks in vain for a prototype of his conception. Blasted by his disappointment, he descends to an untimely grave.

The picture is not barren of instruction to actual men. The

6

Poet's self-centred seclusion was avenged by the Furies of an irresistible passion pursuing him to speedy ruin. But that power which strikes the luminaries of the world with sudden darkness and extinction, by awakening them to too exquisite a perception of its influences, dooms to a slow and poisonous decay those meaner spirits that dare to abjure its dominion. Their destiny is more abject and inglorious, as their delinquency is more contemptible and pernicious. They who, deluded by no generous error, instigated by no sacred thirst of doubtful knowledge, duped by no illustrious superstition, loving nothing on this earth, and cherishing no hopes beyond, yet keep aloof from sympathies with their kind, rejoicing neither in human joy nor mourning with human grief; these, and such as they, have their apportioned curse. They languish, because none feel with them their common nature. They are morally dead. They are neither friends, nor lovers, nor fathers, nor citizens of the world, nor benefactors of their country. Among those who attempt to exist without human sympathy, the pure and tender-hearted perish, through the intensity and passion of their search after its communities when the vacancy of their spirit suddenly makes itself felt. All else, selfish, blind, and torpid, are those unforeseeing multitudes who constitute, together with their own, the lasting misery and loneliness of the world. Those who love not their fellow-beings live unfruitful lives, and prepare for their old age a miserable grave.

> " The good die first,
> And those whose hearts are dry as summer dust,
> Burn to the socket! "

EARTH, ocean, air, belovèd brotherhood !
If our great Mother has imbued my soul
With aught of natural piety to feel
Your love, and recompense the boon with mine;
If dewy morn, and odorous noon, and even,
With sunset and its gorgeous ministers,

And solemn midnight's tingling silentness;
If autumn's hollow sighs in the sere wood,
And winter robing with pure snow and crowns
Of starry ice the gray grass and bare boughs;
If spring's voluptuous pantings when she breathes
Her first sweet kisses, have been dear to me;
If no bright bird, insect, or gentle beast
I consciously have injured, but still loved
And cherished these my kindred; then forgive
This boast, belovèd brethren, and withdraw
No portion of your wonted favor now!

Mother of this unfathomable world!
Favor my solemn song, for I have loved
Thee ever, and thee only; I have watched
Thy shadow, and the darkness of thy steps,
And my heart ever gazes on the depth
Of thy deep mysteries. I have made my bed
In charnels and on coffins, where black death
Keeps record of the trophies won from thee,
Hoping to still these obstinate questionings
Of thee and thine, by forcing some lone ghost
Thy messenger, to render up the tale
Of what we are. In lone and silent hours,
When night makes a weird sound of its own stillness,
Like an inspired and desperate alchymist
Staking his very life on some dark hope,
Have I mixed awful talk and asking looks
With my most innocent love, until strange tears
Uniting with those breathless kisses, made
Such magic as compels the charmèd night
To render up thy charge: . . . . and, though ne'er yet

Thou hast unveiled thy inmost sanctuary,
Enough from incommunicable dream,
And twilight phantasms, and deep noonday thought,
Has shone within me, that serenely now
And moveless, as a long-forgotten lyre
Suspended in the solitary dome
Of some mysterious and deserted fane,
I wait thy breath, Great Parent, that my strain
May modulate with murmurs of the air,
And motions of the forests and the sea,
And voice of living beings, and woven hymns
Of night and day, and the deep heart of man.

There was a Poet whose untimely tomb
No human hands with pious reverence reared,
But the charmed eddies of autumnal winds
Built o'er his mouldering bones a pyramid
Of mouldering leaves in the waste wilderness : —
A lovely youth, — no mourning maiden decked
With weeping flowers, or votive cypress wreath,
The lone couch of his everlasting sleep : —
Gentle, and brave, and generous, no lorn bard
Breathed o'er his dark fate one melodious sigh :
He lived, he died, he sung, in solitude.
Strangers have wept to hear his passionate notes,
And virgins, as unknown he past, have pined
And wasted for fond love of his wild eyes.
The fire of those soft orbs has ceased to burn,
And Silence, too enamoured of that voice,
Locks its mute music in her rugged cell.

By solemn vision, and bright silver dream,
His infancy was nurtured.   Every sight

And sound from the vast earth and ambient air,
Sent to his heart its choicest impulses.
The fountains of divine philosophy
Fled not his thirsting lips, and all of great,
Or good, or lovely, which the sacred past
In truth or fable consecrates, he felt
And knew.   When early youth had past, he left
His cold fireside and alienated home
To seek strange truths in undiscovered lands.
Many a wide waste and tangled wilderness
Has lured his fearless steps; and he has bought
With his sweet voice and eyes, from savage men,
His rest and food.   Nature's most secret steps
He like her shadow has pursued, where'er
The red volcano overcanopies
Its fields of snow and pinnacles of ice
With burning smoke, or where bitumen lakes
On black bare pointed islets ever beat
With sluggish surge, or where the secret caves
Rugged and dark, winding among the springs
Of fire and poison, inaccessible
To avarice or pride, their starry domes
Of diamond and of gold expand above
Numberless and immeasurable halls,
Frequent with crystal column, and clear shrines
Of pearl, and thrones radiant with chrysolite.
Nor had that scene of ampler majesty
Than gems or gold, the varying roof of heaven
And the green earth lost in his heart its claims
To love and wonder; he would linger long
In lonesome vales, making the wild his home,
Until the doves and squirrels would partake

From his innocuous hand his bloodless food,
Lured by the gentle meaning of his looks,
And the wild antelope, that starts whene'er
The dry leaf rustles in the brake, suspend
Her timid steps to gaze upon a form
More graceful than her own.

      His wandering step
Obedient to high thoughts, has visited
The awful ruins of the days of old :
Athens, and Tyre, and Balbec, and the waste
Where stood Jerusalem, the fallen towers
Of Babylon, the eternal pyramids,
Memphis and Thebes, and whatsoe'er of strange
Sculptured on alabaster obelisk,
Or jasper tomb, or mutilated sphynx,
Dark Æthiopia in her desert hills
Conceals. Among the ruined temples there,
Stupendous columns, and wild images
Of more than man, where marble dæmons watch
The Zodiac's brazen mystery, and dead men
Hang their mute thoughts on the mute walls around,
He lingered, poring on memorials
Of the world's youth, through the long burning day
Gazed on those speechless shapes, nor, when the
    moon
Filled the mysterious halls with floating shades
Suspended he that task, but ever gazed
And gazed, till meaning on his vacant mind
Flashed like strong inspiration, and he saw
The thrilling secrets of the birth of time.

Meanwhile an Arab maiden brought his food,
Her daily portion, from her father's tent.
And spread her matting for his couch, and stole
From duties and repose to tend his steps : —
Enamored, yet not daring for deep awe
To speak her love : — and watched his nightly sleep,
Sleepless herself, to gaze upon his lips
Parted in slumber, whence the regular breath
Of innocent dreams arose : then, when red morn
Made paler the pale moon, to her cold home
Wildered, and wan, and panting, she returned.

The Poet wandering on, through Arabie
And Persia, and the wild Carmanian waste,
And o'er the aërial mountains which pour down
Indus and Oxus from their icy caves,
In joy and exultation held his way;
Till in the vale of Cashmire, far within
Its loneliest dell, where odorous plants entwine
Beneath the hollow rocks a natural bower,
Beside a sparkling rivulet he stretched
His languid limbs.   A vision on his sleep
There came, a dream of hopes that never yet
Had flushed his cheek.   He dreamed a veilèd maid
Sate near him, talking in low solemn tones.
Her voice was like the voice of his own soul
Heard in the calm of thought; its music long,
Like woven sounds of streams and breezes, held
His inmost sense suspended in its web
Of many-colored woof and shifting hues.
Knowledge and truth and virtue were her theme,
And lofty hopes of divine liberty,

Thoughts the most dear to him, and poesy,
Herself a poet.   Soon the solemn mood
Of her pure mind kindled through all her frame
A permeating fire; wild numbers then
She raised, with voice stifled in tremulous sobs
Subdued by its own pathos: her fair hands
Were bare alone, sweeping from some strange harp
Strange symphony, and in their branching veins
The eloquent blood told an ineffable tale.
The beating of her heart was heard to fill
The pauses of her music, and her breath
Tumultuously accorded with those fits
Of intermitted song.   Sudden she rose,
As if her heart impatiently endured
Its bursting burthen: at the sound he turned,
And saw by the warm light of their own life
Her glowing limbs beneath the sinuous veil
Of woven wind, her outspread arms now bare,
Her dark locks floating in the breath of night,
Her beamy bending eyes, her parted lips
Outstretched, and pale, and quivering eagerly.
His strong heart sunk and sickened with excess
Of love.   He reared his shuddering limbs and quelled
His gasping breath, and spread his arms to meet
Her panting bosom: . . . she drew back a while,
Then, yielding to the irresistible joy,
With frantic gesture and short breathless cry
Folded his frame in her dissolving arms.
Now blackness veiled his dizzy eyes, and night
Involved and swallowed up the vision; sleep,
Like a dark flood suspended in its course,
Rolled back its impulse on his vacant brain.

Roused by the shock he started from his trance —
The cold white light of morning, the blue moon
Low in the west, the clear and garish hills,
The distinct valley and the vacant woods,
Spread round him where he stood. Whither have fled
The hues of heaven that canopied his bower
Of yesternight? The sounds that soothed his sleep,
The mystery and the majesty of Earth,
The joy, the exultation? His wan eyes
Gaze on the empty scene as vacantly
As ocean's moon looks on the moon in heaven.
The spirit of sweet human love has sent
A vision to the sleep of him who spurned
Her choicest gifts. He eagerly pursues
Beyond the realms of dream that fleeting shade;
He overleaps the bound. Alas! alas!
Were limbs, and breath, and being intertwined
Thus treacherously? Lost, lost, for ever lost,
In the wide pathless desert of dim sleep,
That beautiful shape! Does the dark gate of death
Conduct to thy mysterious paradise,
O Sleep? Does the bright arch of rainbow clouds,
And pendent mountains seen in the calm lake,
Lead only to a black and watery depth,
While death's blue vault, with loathliest vapors hung,
Where every shade which the foul grave exhales
Hides its dead eye from the detested day,
Conduct, O Sleep, to thy delightful realms?
This doubt with sudden tide flowed on his heart,
The insatiate hope which it awakened, stung
His brain even like despair.

While day-light held
The sky, the Poet kept mute conference
With his still soul. At night the passion came,
Like the fierce fiend of a distempered dream,
And shook him from his rest, and led him forth
Into the darkness. — As an eagle grasped
In folds of the green serpent, feels her breast
Burn with the poison, and precipitates
Through night and day, tempest, and calm, and cloud,
Frantic with dizzying anguish, her blind flight
O'er the wide aëry wilderness : thus driven
By the bright shadow of that lovely dream,
Beneath the cold glare of the desolate night,
Through tangled swamps and deep precipitous dells,
Startling with careless step the moon-light snake,
He fled. Red morning dawned upon his flight,
Shedding the mockery of its vital hues
Upon his cheek of death. He wandered on
Till vast Aornos seen from Petra's steep
Hung o'er the low horizon like a cloud ;
Through Balk, and where the desolated tombs
Of Parthian kings scatter to every wind
Their wasting dust, wildly he wandered on,
Day after day, a weary waste of hours,
Bearing within his life the brooding care
That ever fed on its decaying flame.
And now his limbs were lean ; his scattered hair
Sered by the autumn of strange suffering
Sung dirges in the wind ; his listless hand
Hung like dead bone within its withered skin ;
Life, and the lustre that consumed it, shone
As in a furnace burning secretly

From his dark eyes alone.   The cottagers,
Who ministered with human charity
His human wants, beheld with wondering awe
Their fleeting visitant.   The mountaineer,
Encountering on some dizzy precipice
That spectral form. deemed that the Spirit of wind
With lightning eyes, and eager breath, and feet
Disturbing not the drifted snow, had paused
In its career : the infant would conceal
His troubled visage in his mother's robe
In terror at the glare of those wild eyes,
To remember their strange light in many a dream
Of after-times ; but youthful maidens, taught
By nature, would interpret half the woe
That wasted him, would call him with false names
Brother, and friend, would press his pallid hand
At parting, and watch, dim through tears, the path
Of his departure from their father's door.

At length upon the lone Chorasmian shore
He paused, a wide and melancholy waste
Of putrid marshes.   A strong impulse urged
His steps to the sea-shore.   A swan was there,
Beside a sluggish stream among the reeds.
It rose as he approached, and with strong wings
Scaling the upward sky, bent its bright course
High over the immeasurable main.
His eyes pursued its flight. — " Thou hast a home,
Beautiful bird ; thou voyagest to thine home,
Where thy sweet mate will twine her downy neck
With thine, and welcome thy return with eyes
Bright in the lustre of their own fond joy.

And what am I that I should linger here,
With voice far sweeter than thy dying notes,
Spirit more vast than thine, frame more attuned
To beauty, wasting these surpassing powers
In the deaf air, to the blind earth, and heaven
That echoes not my thoughts?" A gloomy smile
Of desperate hope wrinkled his quivering lips.
For sleep, he knew, kept most relentlessly
Its precious charge, and silent death exposed,
Faithless perhaps as sleep, a shadowy lure,
With doubtful smile mocking its own strange charms.

Startled by his own thoughts he looked around.
There was no fair fiend near him, not a sight
Or sound of awe but in his own deep mind.
A little shallop floating near the shore
Caught the impatient wandering of his gaze.
It had been long abandoned, for its sides
Gaped wide with many a rift, and its frail joints
Swayed with the undulations of the tide.
A restless impulse urged him to embark
And meet lone Death on the drear ocean's waste;
For well he knew that mighty Shadow loves
The slimy caverns of the populous deep.

The day was fair and sunny, sea and sky
Drank its inspiring radiance, and the wind
Swept strongly from the shore, blackening the waves.
Following his eager soul, the wanderer
Leaped in the boat, he spread his cloak aloft
On the bare mast, and took his lonely seat,

And felt the boat speed o'er the tranquil sea
Like a torn cloud before the hurricane.

   As one that in a silver vision floats
Obedient to the sweep of odorous winds
Upon resplendent clouds, so rapidly
Along the dark and ruffled waters fled
The straining boat. — A whirlwind swept it on,
With fierce gusts and precipitating force,
Through the white ridges of the chafèd sea.
The waves arose.   Higher and higher still
Their fierce necks writhed beneath the tempest's
    scourge
Like serpents struggling in a vulture's grasp.
Calm and rejoicing in the fearful war
Of wave ruining on wave, and blast on blast
Descending, and black flood on whirlpool driven
With dark obliterating course, he sate:
As if their genii were the ministers
Appointed to conduct him to the light
Of those belovèd eyes, the Poet sate
Holding the steady helm.   Evening came on,
The beams of sunset hung their rainbow hues
High 'mid the shifting domes of sheeted spray
That canopied his path o'er the waste deep;
Twilight, ascending slowly from the east,
Entwined in duskier wreaths her braided locks
O'er the fair front and radiant eyes of day;
Night followed, clad with stars.   On every side
More horribly the multitudinous streams
Of ocean's mountainous waste to mutual war
Rushed in dark tumult thundering, as to mock

The calm and spangled sky.   The little boat
Still fled before the storm; still fled, like foam
Down the steep cataract of a wintry river;
Now pausing on the edge of the riven wave;
Now leaving far behind the bursting mass
That fell, convulsing ocean: safely fled —
As if that frail and wasted human form,
Had been an elemental god.

                 At midnight
The moon arose: and lo ! the ethereal cliffs
Of Caucasus, whose icy summits shone
Among the stars like sunlight, and around
Whose caverned base the whirlpools and the waves
Bursting and eddying irresistibly
Rage and resound for ever. — Who shall save? —
The boat fled on, — the boiling torrent drove,
The crags closed round with black and jaggèd arms,
The shattered mountain overhung the sea,
And faster still, beyond all human speed,
Suspended on the sweep of the smooth wave,
The little boat was driven.   A cavern there
Yawned, and amid its slant and winding depths
Ingulfed the rushing sea.   The boat fled on
With unrelaxing speed. — "Vision and love !"
The Poet cried aloud, "I have beheld
The path of thy departure.   Sleep and death
Shall not divide us long !"

                 The boat pursued
The windings of the cavern.   Day-light shone
At length upon that gloomy river's flow;

Now, where the fiercest war among the waves
Is calm, on the unfathomable stream
The boat moved slowly. Where the mountain, riven,
Exposed those black depths to the azure sky,
Ere yet the flood's enormous volume fell
Even to the base of Caucasus, with sound
That shook the everlasting rocks, the mass
Filled with one whirlpool all that ample chasm;
Stair above stair the eddying waters rose,
Circling immeasurably fast, and laved
With alternating dash the gnarlèd roots
Of mighty trees, that stretched their giant arms
In darkness over it.   I' the midst was left,
Reflecting, yet distorting every cloud,
A pool of treacherous and tremendous calm.
Seized by the sway of the ascending stream,
With dizzy swiftness, round, and round, and round,
Ridge after ridge the straining boat arose,
Till on the verge of the extremest curve,
Where, through an opening of the rocky bank,
The waters overflow, and a smooth spot
Of glassy quiet mid those battling tides
Is left, the boat paused shuddering. — Shall it sink
Down the abyss ? — Shall the reverting stress
Of that resistless gulf embosom it ?
Now shall it fall ? — A wandering stream of wind,
Breathed from the west, has caught the expanded sail,
And, lo ! with gentle motion, between banks
Of mossy slope, and on a placid stream,
Beneath a woven grove it sails, and, hark !
The ghastly torrent mingles its far roar,
With the breeze murmuring in the musical woods.

Where the embowering trees recede, and leave
A little space of green expanse, the cove
Is closed by meeting banks, whose yellow flowers
For ever gaze on their own drooping eyes,
Reflected in the crystal calm.   The wave
Of the boat's motion marred their pensive task,
Which nought but vagrant bird, or wanton wind,
Or falling spear-grass, or their own decay
Had e'er disturbed before.   The Poet longed
To deck with their bright hues his withered hair,
But on his heart its solitude returned,
And he forbore.   Not the strong impulse hid
In those flushed cheeks, bent eyes, and shadowy frame
Had yet performed its ministry : it hung
Upon his life, as lightning in a cloud
Gleams, hovering ere it vanish, ere the floods
Of night close over it.

                   The noonday sun
Now shone upon the forest, one vast mass
Of mingling shade, whose brown magnificence
A narrow vale embosoms.   There, huge caves,
Scooped in the dark base of their aëry rocks
Mocking its moans, respond and roar for ever.
The meeting boughs and implicated leaves
Wove twilight o'er the Poet's path, as led
By love, or dream, or god, or mightier Death,
He sought in Nature's dearest haunt, some bank,
Her cradle, and his sepulchre.   More dark
And dark the shades accumulate.   The oak,
Expanding its immense and knotty arms,
Embraces the light beech.   The pyramids

Of the tall cedar overarching, frame
Most solemn domes within, and far below,
Like clouds suspended in an emerald sky,
The ash and the acacia floating hang
Tremulous and pale.   Like restless serpents, clothed
In rainbow and in fire, the parasites,
Starred with ten thousand blossoms, flow around
The gray trunks, and, as gamesome infants' eyes,
With gentle meanings, and most innocent wiles,
Fold their beams round the hearts of those that love,
These twine their tendrils with the wedded boughs
Uniting their close union ; the woven leaves
Make net-work of the dark blue light of day,
And the night's noontide clearness, mutable
As shapes in the weird clouds.   Soft mossy lawns
Beneath these canopies extend their swells,
Fragrant with perfumed herbs, and eyed with blooms
Minute yet beautiful.   One darkest glen
Sends from its woods of musk-rose, twined with
          jasmine,
A soul-dissolving odor, to invite
To some more lovely mystery.   Through the dell,
Silence and Twilight here, twin-sisters, keep
Their noonday watch, and sail among the shades,
Like vaporous shapes half seen ; beyond, a well,
Dark, gleaming, and of most translucent wave,
Images all the woven boughs above,
And each depending leaf, and every speck
Of azure sky, darting between their chasms ;
Nor aught else in the liquid mirror laves
Its portraiture, but some inconstant star
Between one foliaged lattice twinkling fair,

Or, painted bird, sleeping beneath the moon,
Or gorgeous insect floating motionless,
Unconscious of the day, ere yet his wings
Have spread their glories to the gaze of noon.

Hither the Poet came. His eyes beheld
Their own wan light through the reflected lines
Of his thin hair, distinct in the dark depth
Of that still fountain ; as the human heart,
Gazing in dreams over the gloomy grave,
Sees its own treacherous likeness there. He heard
The motion of the leaves, the grass that sprung
Startled and glanced and trembled even to feel
An unaccustomed presence, and the sound
Of the sweet brook that from the secret springs
Of that dark fountain rose. A Spirit seemed
To stand beside him — clothed in no bright robes
Of shadowy silver or enshrining light,
Borrowed from aught the visible world affords
Of grace, or majesty, or mystery ; —
But, undulating woods, and silent well,
And leaping rivulet, and evening gloom
Now deepening the dark shades, for speech assuming,
Held commune with him, as if he and it
Were all that was, — only . . . when his regard
Was raised by intense pensiveness, . . . two eyes,
Two starry eyes hung in the gloom of thought,
And seemed with their serene and azure smiles
To beckon him.

                        Obedient to the light
That shone within his soul, he went, pursuing
The windings of the dell. — The rivulet

Wanton and wild, through many a green ravine
Beneath the forest flowed. Sometimes it fell
Among the moss with hollow harmony
Dark and profound. Now on the polished stones
It danced; like childhood laughing as it went:
Then, through the plain in tranquil wanderings crept,
Reflecting every herb and drooping bud
That overhung its quietness. — " O stream !
Whose source is inaccessibly profound,
Whither do thy mysterious waters tend?
Thou imagest my life. Thy darksome stillness,
Thy dazzling waves, thy loud and hollow gulfs,
Thy searchless fountain, and invisible course
Have each their type in me : and the wide sky,
And measureless ocean may declare as soon
What oozy cavern or what wandering cloud
Contains thy waters, as the universe
Tell where these living thoughts reside, when stretched
Upon thy flowers my bloodless limbs shall waste
I' the passing wind! "

                              Beside the grassy shore
Of the small stream he went; he did impress
On the green moss his tremulous step, that caught
Strong shuddering from his burning limbs. As one
Roused by some joyous madness from the couch
Of fever, he did move; yet, not like him,
Forgetful of the grave, where, when the flame
Of his frail exultation shall be spent,
He must descend. With rapid steps he went
Beneath the shade of trees, beside the flow
Of the wild babbling rivulet; and now

The forest's solemn canopies were changed
For the uniform and lightsome evening sky.
Gray rocks did peep from the spare moss, and stemmed
The struggling brook : tall spires of windlestrae
Threw their thin shadows down the rugged slope,
And nought but gnarlèd roots of ancient pines
Branchless and blasted, clenched with grasping roots
The unwilling soil.   A gradual change was here,
Yet ghastly.   For, as fast years flow away,
The smooth brow gathers, and the hair grows thin
And white, and where irradiate dewy eyes
Had shone, gleam stony orbs : — so from his steps
Bright flowers departed, and the beautiful shade
Of the green groves, with all their odorous winds
And musical motions.   Calm, he still pursued
The stream, that with a larger volume now
Rolled through the labyrinthine dell ; and there
Fretted a path through its descending curves
With its wintry speed.   On every side now rose
Rocks, which, in unimaginable forms,
Lifted their black and barren pinnacles
In the light of evening, and its precipice
Obscuring the ravine, disclosed above,
'Mid toppling stones, black gulfs and yawning caves,
Whose windings gave ten thousand various tongues
To the loud stream.   Lo! where the pass expands
Its stony jaws, the abrupt mountain breaks,
And seems, with its accumulated crags,
To overhang the world : for wide expand
Beneath the wan stars and descending moon
Islanded seas, blue mountains, mighty streams,
Dim tracts and vast, robed in the lustrous gloom

Of leaden-colored even, and fiery hills
Mingling their flames with twilight, on the verge
Of the remote horizon.   The near scene,
In naked and severe simplicity,
Made contrast with the universe.   A pine,
Rock-rooted, stretched athwart the vacancy
Its swinging boughs, to each inconstant blast
Yielding one only response, at each pause
In most familiar cadence, with the howl,
The thunder and the hiss of homeless streams
Mingling its solemn song, whilst the broad river,
Foaming and hurrying o'er its rugged path,
Fell into that immeasurable void
Scattering its waters to the passing winds.

Yet the gray precipice and solemn pine
And torrent, were not all; one silent nook
Was there.   Even on the edge of that vast mountain,
Upheld by knotty roots and fallen rocks,
It overlooked in its serenity
The dark earth, and the bending vault of stars.
It was a tranquil spot, that seemed to smile
Even in the lap of horror.   Ivy clasped
The fissured stones with its entwining arms,
And did embower with leaves for ever green,
And berries dark, the smooth and even space
Of its inviolated floor, and here
The children of the autumnal whirlwind bore,
In wanton sport, those bright leaves, whose decay,
Red, yellow, or ethereally pale,
Rivals the pride of summer.   'Tis the haunt
Of every gentle wind, whose breath can teach

The wilds to love tranquillity.   One step,
One human slep alone, has ever broken
The stillness of its solitude : — one voice
Alone inspired its echoes ; — even that voice
Which hither came, floating among the winds,
And led the loveliest among human forms
To make their wild haunts the depository
Of all the grace and beauty that endued
Its motions, render up its majesty,
Scatter its music on the unfeeling storm,
And to the damp leaves and blue cavern mould,
Nurses of rainbow flowers and branching moss,
Commit the colors of that varying cheek,
That snowy breast, those dark and drooping eyes.

    The dim and hornèd moon hung low, and poured
A sea of lustre on the horizon's verge
That overflowed its mountains.   Yellow mist
Filled the unbounded atmosphere, and drank
Wan moonlight even to fulness : not a star
Shone, not a sound was heard ; the very winds,
Danger's grim playmates, on that precipice
Slept, clasped in his embrace. — O, storm of death !
Whose sightless speed divides this sullen night :
And thou, colossal Skeleton, that, still
Guiding its irresistible career
In thy devastating omnipotence,
Art king of this frail world, from the red field
Of slaughter, from the reeking hospital,
The patriot's sacred couch, the snowy bed
Of innocence, the scaffold and the throne,
A mighty voice invokes thee.   Ruin calls

His brother Death.   A rare and regal prey
He hath prepared, prowling around the world;
Glutted with which thou mayst repose, and men
Go to their graves like flowers or creeping worms,
Nor ever more offer at thy dark shrine
The unheeded tribute of a broken heart.

    When on the threshold of the green recess
The wanderer's footsteps fell, he knew that death
Was on him.   Yet a little, ere it fled,
Did he resign his high and holy soul
To images of the majestic past,
That paused within his massive being now,
Like winds that bear sweet music, when they breathe
Through some dim latticed chamber.   He did place
His pale lean hand upon the rugged trunk
Of the old pine.   Upon an ivied stone
Reclined his languid head, his limbs did rest
Diffused and motionless, on the smooth brink
Of that obscurest chasm; — and thus he lay,
Surrendering to their final impulses
The hovering powers of life.   Hope and despair,
The torturers, slept; no mortal pain or fear
Marred his repose, the influxes of sense,
And his own being unalloyed by pain,
Yet feebler and more feeble, calmly fed
The stream of thought, till he lay breathing there
At peace, and faintly smiling: — his last sight
Was the great moon, which o'er the western line
Of the wide world her mighty horn suspended,
With whose dun beams inwoven darkness seemed
To mingle.   Now upon the jaggèd hills

It rests, and still as the divided frame
Of the vast meteor sunk, the Poet's blood,
That ever beat in mystic sympathy
With nature's ebb and flow, grew feebler still :
And when two lessening points of light alone
Gleamed through the darkness, the alternate gasp
Of his faint respiration scarce did stir
The stagnate night : — till the minutest ray
Was quenched, the pulse yet lingered in his heart.
It paused — it fluttered. But when heaven remained
Utterly black, the murky shades involved
An image, silent, cold, and motionless,
As their own voiceless earth and vacant air.
Even as a vapor fed with golden beams
That ministered on sunlight, ere the west
Eclipses it, was now that wondrous frame —
No sense, no motion, no divinity —
A fragile lute, on whose harmonious strings
The breath of heaven did wander — a bright stream
Once fed with many-voicèd waves — a dream
Of youth, which night and time have quenched for
    ever,
Still, dark, and dry, and unremembered now.

    O, for Medea's wondrous alchemy,
Which wheresoe'er it fell made the earth gleam
With bright flowers, and the wintry boughs exhale
From vernal blooms fresh fragrance ! O, that God,
Profuse of poisons, would concede the chalice
Which but one living man has drained, who now,
Vessel of deathless wrath, a slave that feels
No proud exemption in the blighting curse

He bears, over the world wanders for ever,
Lone as incarnate death !   O, that the dream
Of dark magician in his visioned cave,
Raking the cinders of a crucible
For life and power, even when his feeble hand
Shakes in its last decay, were the true law
Of this so lovely world !   But thou art fled
Like some frail exhalation ; which the dawn
Robes in its golden beams, — ah ! thou hast fled !
The brave, the gentle, and the beautiful,
The child of grace and genius.   Heartless things
Are done and said i' the world, and many worms
And beasts and men live on. and mighty Earth
From sea and mountain, city and wilderness,
In vesper low or joyous orison,
Lifts still its solemn voice : — but thou art fled —
Thou canst no longer know or love the shapes
Of this phantasmal scene, who have to thee
Been purest ministers. who are, alas !
Now thou art not.   Upon those pallid lips
So sweet even in their silence, on those eyes
That image sleep in death. upon that form
Yet safe from the worm's outrage, let no tear
Be shed — not even in thought.   Nor, when those
      hues
Are gone, and those divinest lineaments,
Worn by the senseless wind, shall live alone
In the frail pauses of this simple strain,
Let not high verse, mourning the memory
Of that which is no more, or painting's woe
Or sculpture, speak in feeble imagery
Their own cold powers.   Art and eloquence,

And all the shows o' the world are frail and vain
To weep a loss that turns their lights to shade.
It is a woe too " deep for tears," when all
Is reft at once, when some surpassing Spirit,
Whose light adorned the world around it, leaves
Those who remain behind, not sobs or groans,
The passionate tumult of a clinging hope :
But pale despair and cold tranquillity,
Nature's vast frame, the web of human things,
Birth and the grave, that are not as they were.

1815.

THE TWO SPIRITS.

An Allegory.

FIRST SPIRIT.

O THOU, who plumed with strong desire
  Wouldst float above the earth. beware !
A Shadow tracks thy flight of fire —
    Night is coming !
Bright are the regions of the air,
  And among the winds and beams
It were delight to wander there —
    Night is coming !

SECOND SPIRIT.

The deathless stars are bright above ;
  If I would cross the shade of night,
Within my heart is the lamp of love,
    And that is day !
And the moon will smile with gentle light
On my golden plumes where'er they move ;
  The meteors will linger round my flight,
    And make night day.

FIRST SPIRIT.

But if the whirlwinds of darkness waken
  Hail, and lightning, and stormy rain;
See, the bounds of the air are shaken —
      Night is coming!
The red swift clouds of the hurricane
Yon declining sun have overtaken,
  The clash of the hail sweeps over the plain —
      Night is coming!

SECOND SPIRIT.

I see the light, and I hear the sound;
  I'll sail on the flood of the tempest dark,
With the calm within and the light around
      Which makes night day:
And thou, when the gloom is deep and stark,
Look from thy dull earth, slumber-bound,
  My moon-light flight thou then may'st mark
      On high, far away.

———

Some say there is a precipice
  Where one vast pine is frozen to ruin
O'er piles of snow and chasms of ice
      'Mid Alpine mountains;
And that the languid storm pursuing
That wingèd shape, for ever flies
  Round those hoar branches, aye renewing
      Its aëry fountains.

Some say when nights are dry and clear,
  And the death-dews sleep on the morass,
Sweet whispers are heard by the traveller,
      Which make night day:
And a silver shape like his early love doth pass
Upborne by her wild and glittering hair,
  And when he awakes on the fragrant grass,
      He finds night day.
                  1820.

LINES.

THE cold earth slept below;
  Above the cold sky shone;
    And all around,
    With a chilling sound,
From caves of ice and fields of snow,
The breath of night like death did flow
  Beneath the sinking moon.

The wintry hedge was black,
  The green grass was not seen,
    The birds did rest
    On the bare thorn's breast,
Whose roots, beside the pathway track,
Had bound their folds o'er many a crack
  Which the frost had made between.

Thine eyes glowed in the glare
  Of the moon's dying light;
    As a fen-fire's beam,
    On a sluggish stream,
Gleams dimly — so the moon shone there,
And it yellowed the strings of thy tangled hair
  That shook in the wind of night.

The moon made thy lips pale, beloved;
  The wind made thy bosom chill;
    The night did shed
    On thy dear head
Its frozen dew, and thou didst lie
Where the bitter breath of the naked sky
  Might visit thee at will.

1815.

— • ■ • —

A SUMMER EVENING CHURCHYARD.

LECHLADE, GLOUCESTERSHIRE.

THE wind has swept from the wide atmosphere
Each vapor that obscured the sunset's ray;
And pallid evening twines its beaming hair
In duskier braids around the languid eyes of day:
Silence and twilight, unbeloved of men,
Creep hand in hand from yon obscurest glen.

They breathe their spells towards the departing day,
Encompassing the earth, air, stars, and sea;
Light, sound, and motion own the potent sway,
Responding to the charm with its own mystery.
The winds are still, or the dry church-tower grass
Knows not their gentle motions as they pass.

Thou too, aërial Pile! whose pinnacles
Point from one shrine like pyramids of fire,
Obeyest in silence their sweet solemn spells,
Clothing in hues of heaven thy dim and distant spire,
Around whose lessening and invisible height
Gather among the stars the clouds of night.

The dead are sleeping in their sepulchres:
And, mouldering as they sleep, a thrilling sound

36

Half sense, half thought, among the darkness stirs,
Breathed from their wormy beds all living things
    around,
And mingling with the still night and mute sky
Its awful hush is felt inaudibly.

Thus solemnized and softened, death is mild
And terrorless as this serenest night :
Here could I hope, like some enquiring child
Sporting on graves, that death did hide from human
    sight
Sweet secrets, or beside its breathless sleep
That loveliest dreams perpetual watch did keep.

                                    1815.

SONNET.

Ye hasten to the dead ! What seek ye there,
Ye restless thoughts and busy purposes
Of the idle brain, which the world's livery wear?
O thou quick Heart which pantest to possess
All that anticipation feigneth fair !
Thou vainly curious mind which wouldest guess
Whence thou didst come, and whither thou mayst go,
And that which never yet was known wouldst know —
Oh, whither hasten ye that thus ye press
With such swift feet life's green and pleasant path,
Seeking alike from happiness and woe
A refuge in the cavern of gray death?
O heart, and mind, and thoughts ! What thing do y⁓ⁿ
Hope to inherit⸰in the grave below?

                                  182

SONNET.

LIFT not the painted veil which those who live
Call Life : though unreal shapes be pictured there,
And it but mimic all we would believe
With colors idly spread, — behind, lurk Fear
And Hope, twin destinies ; who ever weave
Their shadows, o'er the chasm, sightless and drear.
I knew one who had lifted it — he sought,
For his lost heart was tender, things to love,
But found them not, alas ! nor was there aught
The world contains, the which he could approve.
Through the unheeding many he did move,
A splendor among shadows, a bright blot
Upon this gloomy scene, a Spirit that strove
For truth, and like the Preacher found it not.

1818?

PEACE.

THE rude wind is singing,
The dirge of the music dead,
The cold worms are clinging
Where kisses were lately fed.

THE babe is at peace within the womb,
The corpse is at rest within the tomb,
We begin in what we end.

THE DIRGE OF GINEVRA.

OLD winter was gone
In his weakness back to the mountains hoar,
    And the spring came down
From the planet that hovers upon the shore
  Where the sea of sunlight encroaches
On the limits of wintry night; —
If the land, and the air, and the sea
  Rejoice not when spring approaches,
We did not rejoice in thee,
     Ginevra!

She is still, she is cold
    On the bridal couch,
One step to the white death-bed,
    And one to the bier,
And one to the charnel — and one, O where?
    The dark arrow fled
    In the noon.

Ere the sun through heaven once more has rolled,
The rats in her heart
Will have made their nest,
And the worms be alive in her golden hair,
While the spirit that guides the sun,
Sits throned in his flaming chair,
     She shall sleep.

                  1821.

THE DIRGE OF BEATRICE.

FALSE friend, wilt thou smile or weep
When my life is laid asleep?
Little cares for a smile or a tear,
The clay-cold corpse upon the bier !
      Farewell ! Heigho !
      What is this whispers low?
There is a snake in thy smile, my dear;
And bitter poison within thy tear.

Sweet sleep, were death like to thee,
Or if thou couldst mortal be,
I would close these eyes of pain;
When to wake?   Never again.
      O, World ! Farewell !
      Listen to the passing bell !
It says, thou and I must part,
With a light and a heavy heart.
                 Cenci.

SLEEP AND DEATH.

They. WE strew these opiate flowers
      On thy restless pillow, —
   They were stript from Orient bowers,
      By the Indian billow
        Be thy sleep
        Calm and deep,
Like theirs who fell — not ours who weep !

She.　Away, unlovely dreams !
　　　Away, false shapes of sleep !
　　Be his, as Heaven seems,
　　　Clear, and bright, and deep !
　Soft as love, and calm as death,
　Sweet as a summer night without a breath.

They.　Sleep, sleep ! our song is laden
　　　With the soul of slumber ;
　　It was sung by a Samian maiden,
　　　Whose lover was of the number
　　　　Who now keep
　　　　That calm sleep
　Whence none may wake, where none shall weep.

She.　I touch thy temples pale !
　　　I breathe my soul on thee !
　　And could my prayers avail,
　　　All my joy should be
　Dead, and I would live to weep,
　So thou might'st win one hour of quiet sleep.
　　　　　　　　　　　Hellas.

"Songs Consecrate to Liberty."

TO WORDSWORTH.

POET of Nature, thou hast wept to know
That things depart which never may return :
Childhood and youth, friendship and love's first glow,
Have fled like sweet dreams, leaving thee to mourn.
These common woes I feel.   One loss is mine
Which thou too feel'st, yet I alone deplore.
Thou wert as a lone star, whose light did shine
On some frail bark in winter's midnight roar :
Thou hast like to a rock-built refuge stood
Above the blind and battling multitude :
In honored poverty thy voice did weave
Songs consecrate to truth and liberty, —
Deserting these, thou leavest me to grieve,
Thus having been, that thou shouldst cease to be.

1815.

THE SNAKE AND EAGLE.

WHEN the last hope of trampled France had failed
Like a brief dream of unremaining glory,
From visions of despair I rose, and scaled
The peak of an aërial promontory,

Whose caverned base with the vext surge was
    hoary;
And saw the golden dawn break forth, and waken
Each cloud, and every wave : — but transitory
The calm : for sudden, the firm earth was shaken,
As if by the last wreck its frame were overtaken.

So as I stood, one blast of muttering thunder
Burst in far peals along the waveless deep,
When, gathering fast, around, above and under,
Long trains of tremulous mist began to creep,
Until their complicating lines did steep
The orient sun in shadow : — not a sound
Was heard; one horrible repose did keep
The forests and the floods, and all around
Darkness more dread than night was poured upon
    the ground.

Hark ! 'tis the rushing of a wind that sweeps
Earth and the ocean. See ! the lightnings yawn
Deluging Heaven with fire, and the lashed deeps
Glitter and boil beneath : it rages on,
One mighty stream, whirlwind and waves upthrown,
Lightning, and hail, and darkness eddying by.
There is a pause — the sea-birds, that were gone
Into their caves to shriek, come forth, to spy
What calm has fall'n on earth, what light is in the
    sky.

For, where the irresistible storm had cloven
That fearful darkness, the blue sky was seen
Fretted with many a fair cloud interwoven
Most delicately, and the ocean green,

Beneath that opening spot of blue serene,
Quivered like burning emerald : calm was spread
On all below ; but far on high, between
Earth and the upper air, the vast clouds fled,
Countless and swift as leaves on autumn's tempest
    shed.

For ever, as the war became more fierce
Between the whirlwinds and the rack on high,
That spot grew more serene ; blue light did pierce
The woof of those white clouds, which seemed to
    lie
Far, deep, and motionless ; while thro' the sky
The pallid semicircle of the moon
Past on, in slow and moving majesty ;
Its upper horn arrayed in mists, which soon
But slowly fled, like dew beneath the beams of noon.

I could not choose but gaze ; a fascination
Dwelt in that moon, and sky, and clouds, which
    drew
My fancy thither, and in expectation
Of what I knew not, I remained : — the hue
Of the white moon, amid that heaven so blue,
Suddenly stained with shadow did appear ;
A speck, a cloud, a shape, approaching grew,
Like a great ship in the sun's sinking sphere
Beheld afar at sea, and swift it came anear.

Even like a bark, which from a chasm of mountains,
Dark, vast, and overhanging, on a river
Which there collects the strength of all its fountains,
Comes forth, whilst with the speed its frame doth
    quiver,

Sails, oars, and stream, tending to one endeavor;
So, from that chasm of light a wingèd Form
On all the winds of heaven approaching ever
Floated, dilating as it came: the storm
Pursued it with fierce blasts, and lightnings swift and
    warm.

A course precipitous, of dizzy speed,
Suspending thought and breath; a monstrous
    sight!
For in the air do I behold indeed
An Eagle and a Serpent wreathed in fight:—
And now relaxing its impetuous flight,
Before the aërial rock on which I stood,
The Eagle, hovering, wheeled to left and right,
And hung with lingering wings over the flood,
And startled with its yells the wide air's solitude.

A shaft of light upon its wings descended,
And every golden feather gleamed therein—
Feather and scale inextricably blended.
The Serpent's mailed and many-colored skin
Shone thro' the plumes its coils were twined within
By many a swollen and knotted fold, and high
And far, the neck receding lithe and thin,
Sustained a crested head, which warily
Shifted and glanced before the Eagle's stedfast eye.

Around, around, in ceaseless circles wheeling
With clang of wings and scream, the Eagle sailed
Incessantly—sometimes on high concealing
Its lessening orbs, sometimes as if it failed,

Drooped thro' the air; and still it shrieked and
    wailed,
And casting back its eager head, with beak
And talon unremittingly assailed
The wreathèd Serpent, who did ever seek
Upon his enemy's heart a mortal wound to wreak.

What life, what power was kindled and arose
Within the sphere of that appalling fray !
For, from the encounter of those wondrous foes,
A vapor like the sea's suspended spray
Hung gathered: in the void air, far away,
Floated the shattered plumes; bright scales did
    leap,
Where'er the Eagle's talons made their way,
Like sparks into the darkness; — as they sweep,
Blood stains the snowy foam of the tumultuous deep.

Swift chances in that combat — many a check,
And many a change, a dark and wild turmoil;
Sometimes the Snake around his enemy's neck
Locked in stiff rings his adamantine coil,
Until the Eagle, faint with pain and toil,
Remitted his strong flight, and near the sea
Languidly fluttered, hopeless so to foil
His adversary, who then reared on high
His red and burning crest, radiant with victory.

Then on the white edge of the bursting surge,
Where they had sunk together, would the Snake
Relax his suffocating grasp, and scourge
The wind with his wild writhings; for to break

That chain of torment, the vast bird would shake
The strength of his unconquerable wings
As in despair, and with his sinewy neck,
Dissolve in sudden shock those linkèd rings, ‑
Then soar — as swift as smoke from a volcano springs.

Wile baffled wile, and strength encountered strength,
Thus long, but unprevailing : — the event
Of that portentous fight appeared at length :
Until the lamp of day was almost spent
It had endured, when lifeless, stark, and rent,
Hung high that mighty Serpent, and at last
Fell to the sea, while o'er the continent,
With clang of wings and scream the Eagle past,
Heavily borne away on the exhausted blast.

    .   .   .   .   .   .

Such is this conflict — when mankind doth strive
With its oppressors in a strife of blood,
Or when free thoughts, like lightnings are alive ;
And in each bosom of the multitude
Justice and truth, with custom's hydra brood
Wage silent war ; — when priests and kings dis-
    semble
In smiles or frowns their fierce disquietude,
When round pure hearts, a host of hopes assemble,
The Snake and Eagle meet — the world's foundations
    tremble !

Revolt of Islam, canto i.   1817.

THE MASK OF ANARCHY.

WRITTEN ON THE OCCASION OF THE MASSACRE AT
MANCHESTER.

As I lay asleep in Italy
There came a voice from over the Sea,
And with great power it forth led me
To walk in the visions of Poesy.

I met Murder on the way —
He had a mask like Castlereagh ;
Very smooth he looked, yet grim ;
Seven blood-hounds followed him :

All were fat ; and well they might
Be in admirable plight,
For one by one, and two by two,
He tossed them human hearts to chew
Which from his wide cloak he drew.

Next came Fraud, and he had on,
Like Eldon, an ermined gown ;
His big tears, for he wept well,
Turned to mill-stones as they fell.

And the little children, who
Round his feet played to and fro,
Thinking every tear a gem,
Had their brains knocked out by them.

Clothed with the Bible, as with light,
And the shadows of the night,
Like Sidmouth, next, Hypocrisy
On a crocodile rode by.

And many more Destructions played
In this ghastly masquerade,
All disguised, even to the eyes,
Like Bishops, lawyers, peers or spies.

Last came Anarchy: he rode
On a white horse, splashed with blood;
He was pale even to the lips,
Like Death in the Apocalypse.

And he wore a kingly crown;
And in his grasp a sceptre shone;
On his brow this mark I saw —
" I AM GOD, AND KING, AND LAW ! "

With a pace stately and fast,
Over English land he past,
Trampling to a mire of blood
The adoring multitude.

And a mighty troop around,
With their trampling shook the ground,
Waving each a bloody sword,
For the service of their Lord.

And with glorious triumph, they
Rode thro' England proud and gay,
Drunk as with intoxication
Of the wine of desolation.

O'er fields and towns, from sea to sea,
Past the Pageant swift and free,
Tearing up, and trampling down;
Till they came to London town.

And each dweller, panic-stricken,
Felt his heart with terror sicken
Hearing the tempestuous cry
Of the triumph of Anarchy.

For with pomp to meet him came,
Clothed in arms like blood and flame,
The hired murderers, who did sing
"Thou art God, and Law, and King.

"We have waited, weak and lone
For thy coming, Mighty One!
Our purses are empty, our swords are cold,
Give us glory, and blood, and gold."

Lawyers and priests, a motley crowd,
To the earth their pale brows bowed;
Like a bad prayer not over loud,
Whispering — " Thou art Law and God." —

Then all cried with one accord,
"Thou art King, and God, and Lord;
Anarchy, to thee we bow,
Be thy name made holy now ! "

And Anarchy, the Skeleton,
Bowed and grinned to every one,
As well as if his education
Had cost ten millions to the nation.

For he knew the Palaces
Of our Kings were nightly his;
His the sceptre, crown, and globe,
And the gold-inwoven robe.

So he sent his slaves before
To seize upon the Bank and Tower,
And was proceeding with intent
To meet his pensioned Parliament

When one fled past, a maniac maid,
And her name was Hope, she said:
But she looked more like Despair,
And she cried out in the air:

"My father Time is weak and gray
With waiting for a better day;
See how idiot-like he stands,
Fumbling with his palsied hands!

" He has had child after child,
And the dust of death is piled
Over every one but me —
Misery, oh, Misery!"

Then she lay down in the street,
Right before the horses' feet,
Expecting, with a patient eye,
Murder, Fraud, and Anarchy.

When between her and her foes
A mist, a light, an image rose,
Small at first, and weak, and frail
Like the vapor of a vale:

Till as clouds grow on the blast,
Like tower-crowned giants striding fast,
And glare with lightnings as they fly,
And speak in thunder to the sky,

It grew — a Shape arrayed in mail
Brighter than the viper's scale,
And upborne on wings whose grain
Was as the light of sunny rain.

On its helm, seen far away,
A planet, like the Morning's, lay;
And those plumes its light rained thro'
Like a shower of crimson dew.

With step as soft as wind it past
O'er the heads of men — so fast
That they knew the presence there,
And looked, — and all was empty air.

As flowers beneath May's footstep waken,
As stars from Night's loose hair are shaken,
As waves arise when loud winds call,
Thoughts sprung where'er that step did fall.

And the prostrate multitude
Looked — and ankle-deep in blood,
Hope, that maiden most serene,
Was walking with a quiet mien:

And Anarchy, the ghastly birth,
Lay dead earth upon the earth;
The Horse of Death tameless as wind
Fled, and with his hoofs did grind
To dust, the murderers thronged behind.

A rushing light of clouds and splendor,
A sense awakening and yet tender
Was heard and felt — and at its close
These words of joy and fear arose

As if their own indignant Earth
Which gave the sons of England birth
Had felt their blood upon her brow,
And shuddering with a mother's throe

Had turnèd every drop of blood
By which her face had been bedewed
To an accent unwithstood, —
As if her heart had cried aloud :

"Men of England, heirs of Glory,
Heroes of unwritten story,
Nurslings of one mighty Mother,
Hopes of her, and one another ;

" Rise like Lions after slumber
In unvanquishable number —
Shake your chains to earth like dew
Which in sleep had fallen on you —
Ye are many — they are few."

1819.

SONG

TO THE MEN OF ENGLAND.

MEN of England, wherefore plough
For the lords who lay ye low?
Wherefore weave with toil and care
The rich robes your tyrants wear?

Wherefore feed, and clothe, and save,
From the cradle to the grave,
Those ungrateful drones who would
Drain your sweat — nay, drink your blood?

Wherefore, Bees of England, forge
Many a weapon, chain and scourge,
That these stingless drones may spoil
The forced produce of your toil?

Have ye leisure, comfort, calm,
Shelter, food, love's gentle balm?
Or what is it ye buy so dear
With your pain and with your fear?

The seed ye sow, another reaps;
The wealth ye find, another keeps;
The robes ye weave, another wears;
The arms ye forge, another bears.

Sow seed, — but let no tyrant reap;
Find wealth, — let no impostor heap;
Weave robes, — let not the idle wear;
Forge arms, — in your defence to bear.

Shrink to your cellars, holes, and cells ;
In halls ye deck another dwells.
Why shake the chains ye wrought?   Ye see
The steel ye tempered glance on ye.

With plough and spade, and hoe and loom,
Trace your grave, and build your tomb,
And weave your winding sheet, till fair
England be your sepulchre.

1819.

———•◦•———

SONNET:

ENGLAND IN 1819.

AN old, mad, blind, despised, and dying king, —
Princes, the dregs of their dull race, who flow
Through public scorn, — mud from a muddy spring, —
Rulers who neither see, nor feel, nor know,
But leech-like to their fainting country cling,
Till they drop, blind in blood, without a blow, —
A people starved and stabbed in the untilled field, —
An army, which liberticide and prey
Makes as a two-edged sword to all who wield
Golden and sanguine laws which tempt and slay ;
Religion Christless, Godless — a book sealed ;
A Senate, — Time's worst statute unrepealed, —
Are graves, from which a glorious Phantom may
Burst, to illumine our tempestuous day.

SONNET:

POLITICAL GREATNESS.

NOR happiness, nor majesty, nor fame,
Nor peace, nor strength, nor skill in arms or arts,
Shepherd those herds whom tyranny makes tame;
Verse echoes not one beating of their hearts,
History is but the shadow of their shame,
Art veils her glass, or from the pageant starts
As to oblivion their blind millions fleet,
Staining that Heaven with obscene imagery
Of their own likeness.   What are numbers knit
By force or custom?   Man who man would be,
Must rule the empire of himself; in it
Must be supreme, establishing his throne
On vanquished will, quelling the anarchy
Of hopes and fears, being himself alone.

                                        1821.

ODE TO LIBERTY.

Yet, Freedom, yet thy banner torn but flying,
Streams like a thunder-storm against the wind.
                                        BYRON.

A GLORIOUS people vibrated again:
   The lightning of the nations, Liberty,
From heart to heart, from tower to tower, o'er Spain,
   Scattering contagious fire into the sky,
Gleamed.   My soul spurned the chains of its dismay,
      And, in the rapid plumes of song,
      Clothed itself, sublime and strong;

As a young eagle soars the morning clouds among,
  Hovering in verse o'er its accustomed prey;
    Till from its station in the heaven of fame
    The spirit's whirlwind rapt it, and the ray
    Of the remotest sphere of living flame
Which paves the void was from behind it flung,
  As foam from a ship's swiftness, when there came
  A voice out of the deep: I will record the same.

The Sun and the serenest Moon sprang forth:
  The burning stars of the abyss were hurled
Into the depths of heaven. The dædal earth,
  That island in the ocean of the world,
Hung in its cloud of all-sustaining air:
      But this divinest universe
      Was yet a chaos and a curse,
For thou wert not: but power from worst producing
    worse,
  The spirit of the beasts was kindled there,
    And of the birds, and of the watery forms,
  And there was war among them, and despair
    Within them, raging without truce or terms:
The bosom of their violated nurse
    Groaned, for beasts warred on beasts, and worms
      on worms,
    And men on men; each heart was as a hell of
      storms.

Man, the imperial shape, then multiplied
  His generations under the pavilion   ·
Of the Sun's throne: palace and pyramid,
    Temple and prison, to many a swarming million,

Were, as to mountain-wolves their ragged caves.
    This human living multitude
    Was savage, cunning, blind, and rude,
For thou wert not; but o'er the populous solitude,
  Like one fierce cloud over a waste of waves
    Hung Tyranny; beneath, sate deified
  The sister-pest, congregator of slaves;
    Into the shadow of her pinions wide
Anarchs and priests who feed on gold and blood,
  Till with the stain their inmost souls are dyed,
  Drove the astonished herds of men from every side.

The nodding promontories, and blue isles,
  And cloud-like mountains, and dividuous waves
Of Greece, basked glorious in the open smiles
  Of favoring heaven: from their enchanted caves
Prophetic echoes flung dim melody.
    On the unapprehensive wild
    The vine, the corn, the olive mild,
Grew savage yet, to human use unreconciled;
  And, like unfolded flowers beneath the sea,
    Like the man's thought dark in the infant's brain,
  Like aught that is which wraps what is to be,
    Art's deathless dreams lay veiled by many a vein
Of Parian stone; and yet a speechless child,
  Verse murmured, and Philosophy did strain
  Her lidless eyes for thee; when o'er the Ægean
    main

Athens arose: a city such as vision
  Builds from the purple crags and silver towers
Of battlemented cloud, as in derision
  Of kingliest masonry: the ocean-floors

Pave it; the evening sky pavilions it;
 Its portals are inhabited
 By thunder-zonèd winds, each head
Within its cloudy wings with sunfire garlandrd,
 A divine work ! Athens diviner yet
  Gleamed with its crest of columns, on the will
Of man, as on a mount of diamond, set;
  For thou wert, and thine all-creative skill
Peopled with forms that mock the eternal dead
 In marble immortality, that hill
 Which was thine earliest throne and latest oracle.

Within the surface of Time's fleeting river
 Its wrinkled image lies, as then it lay
Immovably unquiet, and for ever
 It trembles, but it cannot pass away !
The voices of thy bards and sages thunder
  With an earth-awakening blast
  Through the caverns of the past;
Religion veils her eyes; Oppression shrinks aghast :
 A wingèd sound of joy, and love, and wonder,
  Which soars where Expectation never flew,
 Rending the veil of space and time asunder !
  One ocean feeds the clouds, and streams, and dew;
One sun illumines heaven; one spirit vast
  With life and love makes chaos ever new,
 As Athens doth the world with thy delight renew.

Then Rome was, and from thy deep bosom fairest,
 Like a wolf-cub from a Cadmæan Mænad,
She drew the milk of greatness, though thy dearest
 From that Elysian food was yet unweanèd;

And many a deed of terrible uprightness
  By thy sweet love was sanctified;
  And in thy smile, and by thy side,
Saintly Camillus lived, and firm Atilius died.
  But when tears stained thy robe of vestal whiteness,
   And gold profaned thy Capitolian throne,
  Thou didst desert, with spirit-wingèd lightness,
   The senate of the tyrants: they sunk prone
Slaves of one tyrant: Palatinus sighed
  Faint echoes of Ionian song; that tone
  Thou didst delay to hear, lamenting to disown.

From what Hyrcanian glen or frozen hill,
  Or piny promontory of the Arctic main,
  Or utmost islet inaccessible,
  Didst thou lament the ruin of thy reign,
Teaching the woods and waves, and desert rocks,
   And every Naiad's ice-cold urn,
   To talk in echoes sad and stern,
Of that sublimest lore which man had dared unlearn?
  For neither didst thou watch the wizard flocks
   Of the Scald's dreams, nor haunt the Druid's sleep.
  What if the tears rained through thy shattered locks
   Were quickly dried? for thou didst groan, not
    weep,
  When from its sea of death, to kill and burn,
   The Galilean serpent forth did creep,
  And made thy world an undistinguishable heap.

A thousand years the Earth cried, Where art thou?
  And then the shadow of thy coming fell
On Saxon Alfred's olive-cinctured brow:
  And many a warrior-peopled citadel,

Like rocks which fire lifts out of the flat deep,
   Arose in sacred Italy,
   Frowning o'er the tempestuous sea
Of kings, and priests, and slaves, in tower-crowned
   majesty;
   That multitudinous anarchy did sweep,
   And burst around their walls, like idle foam,
Whilst from the human spirit's deepest deep
   Strange melody with love and awe struck dumb
Dissonant arms; and Art, which cannot die,
   With divine wand traced on our earthly home
Fit imagery to pave heaven's everlasting dome.

Thou huntress swifter than the Moon! thou terror
   Of the world's wolves! thou bearer of the quiver,
Whose sunlike shafts pierce tempest-wingèd Error,
   As light may pierce the clouds when they dissever
In the calm regions of the orient day!
   Luther caught thy wakening glance,
   Like lightning, from his leaden lance
Reflected, it dissolved the visions of the trance
   In which, as in a tomb, the nations lay;
   And England's prophets hailed thee as their
     queen,
   In songs whose music cannot pass away,
   Though it must flow for ever: not unseen
Before the spirit-sighted countenance
   Of Milton didst thou pass, from the sad scene
Beyond whose night he saw, with a dejected mien.

The eager hours and unreluctant years
   As on a dawn-illumined mountain stood,
Trampling to silence their loud hopes and fears,

Darkening each other with their multitude,
And cried aloud, Liberty ! Indignation
    Answered Pity from her cave ;
    Death grew pale within the grave,
And Desolation howled to the destroyer, Save !
  When like heaven's sun girt by the exhalation
    Of its own glorious light, thou didst arise,
  Chasing thy foes from nation unto nation
    Like shadows : as if day had cloven the skies
At dreaming midnight o'er the western wave,
  Men started, staggering with a glad surprise,
  Under the lightnings of thine unfamiliar eyes.

Thou heaven of earth ! what spells could pall thee
    then,
  In ominous eclipse ? a thousand years
Bred from the slime of deep oppression's den,
  Dyed all thy liquid light with blood and tears,
Till thy sweet stars could wipe the stain away ;
    How like Bacchanals of blood
    Round France, the ghastly vintage, stood
Destruction's sceptred slaves, and Folly's mitred
    brood !
  When one, like them, but mightier far than they,
    The Anarch of thine own bewildered powers
  Rose : armies mingled in obscure array,
    Like clouds with clouds, darkening the sacred
    bowers
Of serene heaven. He, by the past pursued,
  Rests with those dead, but unforgotten hours,
  Whose ghosts scare victor kings in their ancestral
    towers.

England yet sleeps: was she not called of old?
  Spain calls her now, as with its thrilling thunder
Vesuvius wakens Ætna, and the cold
  Snow-crags by its reply are cloven in sunder:
O'er the lit waves every Æolian isle
    From Pithecusa to Pelorus
    Howls, and leaps, and glares in chorus:
They cry, " Be dim, ye lamps of heaven suspended
    o'er us."
  Her chains are threads of gold, she need but smile
    And they dissolve; but Spain's were links of steel,
  Till bit to dust by virtue's keenest file.
    Twins of a single destiny! appeal
To the eternal years enthroned before us,
  In the dim West; impress us from a seal,
  All ye have thought and done! Time cannot dare
    conceal.

Tomb of Arminius! render up thy dead,
  Till, like a standard from a watch-tower's staff,
His soul may stream over the tyrant's head;
  Thy victory shall be his epitaph,
Wild Bacchanal of truth's mysterious wine,
    King-deluded Germany,
    His dead spirit lives in thee.
Why do we fear or hope? thou art already free!
  And thou, lost Paradise of this divine
    And glorious world! thou flowery wilderness!
  Thou island of eternity! thou shrine
    Where desolation clothed with loveliness,
Worships the thing thou wert! O Italy,

Gather thy blood into thy heart; repress
The beasts who make their dens thy sacred palaces.

O, that the free would stamp the impious name
  Of King into the dust ! or write it there,
So that this blot upon the page of fame
  Were as a serpent's path, which the light air
Erases, and the flat sands close behind !
      Ye the oracle have heard :
      Lift the victory-flashing sword,
And cut the snaky knots of this foul gordian word,
   Which weak itself as stubble, yet can bind
    Into a mass, irrefragably firm,
  The axes and the rods which awe mankind ;
    The sound has poison in it, 'tis the sperm
Of what makes life foul, cankerous, and abhorred ;
  Disdain not thou, at thine appointed term,
  To set thine armèd heel on this reluctant worm.

O, that the wise from their bright minds would
      kindle
Such lamps within the dome of this dim world,
That the pale name of Priest might shrink and
      dwindle
Into the hell from which it first was hurled,
A scoff of impious pride from fiends impure ;
    Till human thoughts might kneel alone
    Each before the judgment-throne
Of its own aweless soul, or of the power unknown !
  O, that the words which make the thoughts ob-
    scure

From which they spring, as clouds of glimmer-
    ing dew
From a white lake blot heaven's blue portraiture,
    Were stript of their thin masks and various hue
And frowns and smiles and splendors not their own,
    Till in the nakedness of false and true
    They stand before their Lord, each to receive its
       due.

He who taught men to vanquish whatsoever
    Can be between the cradle and the grave
Crowned him the King of Life. O vain endeavor!
    If on his own high will a willing slave,
He has enthroned the oppression and the oppressor.
      What if earth can clothe and feed
      Amplest millions at their need,
And power in thought be as the tree within the seed?
    O, what if Art, an ardent intercessor,
      Driving on fiery wings to Nature's throne,
    Checks the great mother stooping to caress her,
      And cries: "Give me, thy child, dominion
Over all height and depth?" if Life can breed
    New wants, and wealth from those who toil and
      groan
    Rend of thy gifts and hers a thousand fold for one.

Come Thou, but lead out of the inmost cave
    Of man's deep spirit, as the morning-star
Beckons the Sun from the Eoan wave,
    Wisdom. I hear the pennons of her car
Self-moving, like cloud charioted by flame ;

Comes she not, and come ye not,
Rulers of eternal thought,
To judge, with solemn truth, life's ill-apportioned
lot ?
Blind Love, and equal Justice, and the Fame
Of what has been, the Hope of what will be ?
O, Liberty ! if such could be thy name
Wert thou disjoined from these, or they from
thee :
If thine or theirs were treasures to be bought
By blood or tears, have not the wise and free
Wept tears, and blood like tears ?   The solemn
harmony

Paused, and the spirit of that mighty singing
To its abyss was suddenly withdrawn ;
Then, as a wild swan, when sublimely winging
Its path athwart the thunder-smoke of dawn,
Sinks headlong through the aërial golden light
On the heavy sounding plain,
When the bolt has pierced its brain ;
As summer clouds dissolve, unburdened of their
rain ;
As a far taper fades with fading night,
As a brief insect dies with dying day,
My song, its pinions disarrayed of might,
Drooped ; o'er it closed the echoes far away
Of the great voice which did its flight sustain,
As waves which lately paved his watery way
Hiss round a drowner's head in their tempestuous
play.

1820.

OZYMANDIAS.

I MET a traveller from an antique land
Who said: "Two vast and trunkless legs of stone
Stand in the desert. Near them, on the sand,
Half sunk, a shattered visage lies, whose frown,
And wrinkled lip, and sneer of cold command,
Tell that its sculptor well those passions read
Which yet survive, stamped on these lifeless things,
The hand that mocked them and the heart that fed:
And on the pedestal these words appear:
'My name is Ozymandias, king of kings:
Look on my works, ye Mighty, and despair!'
Nothing beside remains. Round the decay
Of that colossal wreck, boundless and bare
The lone and level sands stretch far away."

1817.

TIME.

UNFATHOMABLE Sea! whose waves are years,
Ocean of Time, whose waters of deep woe
Are brackish with the salt of human tears!
Thou shoreless flood, which in thy ebb and flow

Claspest the limits of mortality !
And sick of prey, yet howling on for more,
Vomitest thy wrecks on its inhospitable shore ;
Treacherous in calm, and terrible in storm,
Who shall put forth on thee,
Unfathomable Sea ?

1821.

———◦◦◦———

THE SEASONS.

THE blasts of Autumn drive the wingèd seeds
Over the earth, — next come the snows, and
rain,
And frosts, and storms, which dreary Winter leads
Out of his Scythian cave, a savage train ;
Behold ! Spring sweeps over the world again,
Shedding soft dews from her etherial wings ;
Flowers on the mountains, fruits over the plain,
And music on the waves and woods she flings,
And love on all that lives, and calm on lifeless
things.

O Spring ! of hope and love and youth and glad-
ness
Wind-wingèd emblem ! brightest, best, and fair-
est !
Whence comest thou, when, with dark Winter's
sadness
The tears that fade in sunny smiles thou sharest ;
Sister of joy, thou art the child who wearest

Thy mother's dying smile, tender and sweet;
  Thy mother Autumn, for whose grave thou bear-
    est
Fresh flowers, and beams like flowers, with gentle
    feet,
Disturbing not the leaves which are her winding-
    sheet.

Revolt of Islam, Canto ix.

SPRING.

'TWAS at the season when the Earth upsprings
From slumber, as a spherèd angel's child,
Shadowing its eyes with green and golden wings,

Stands up before its mother bright and mild,
Of whose soft voice the air expectant seems —
So stood before the sun, which shone and smiled .

To see it rise thus joyous from its dreams,
The fresh and radiant Earth. The hoary grove
Waxed green — and flowers burst forth like starry
    beams : —

The grass in the warm sun did start and move,
And sea-buds burst beneath the waves serene : —
How many a one, though none be near to love,

Loves then the shade of his own soul, half seen
In any mirror — or the spring's young minions,
The wingèd leaves amid the copses green ; —

How many a spirit then puts on the pinions
Of fancy, and outstrips the lagging blast,
And his own steps — and over wide dominions

Sweeps in his dream-drawn chariot, far and fast,
More fleet than storms — the wide world shrinks
      below,
When winter and despondency are past.
              Prince Athanase. 1817.

JUNE.

IT was the azure time of June,
When the skies are deep in the stainless noon,
    And the warm and fitful breezes shake
    The fresh green leaves of the hedgerow briar,
    And there were odors then to make
    The very breath we did respire
A liquid element, whereon
Our spirits, like delighted things
That walk the air on subtle wings,
Floated and mingled far away,
Mid the warm winds of the sunny day.
And when the evening star came forth
    Above the curve of the new-bent moon,
And light and sound ebbed from the earth,
Like the tide of the full and weary sea
To the depths of its own tranquillity,
Our natures to its own repose
    Did the Earth's breathless sleep attune.
              Rosalind and Helen.

SUMMER AND WINTER.

IT was a bright and cheerful afternoon,
Towards the end of the sunny month of June,
When the north wind congregates in crowds
The floating mountains of the silver clouds
From the horizon — and the stainless sky
Opens beyond them like eternity.
All things rejoiced beneath the sun; the weeds,
The river, and the corn-fields, and the reeds;
The willow leaves that glanced in the light breeze
And the firm foliage of the larger trees.

It was a winter such as when birds die
In the deep forests; and the fishes lie
Stiffened in the translucent ice, which makes
Even the mud and slime of the warm lakes
A wrinkled clod as hard as brick; and when,
Among their children, comfortable men
Gather about great fires, and yet feel cold:
Alas then for the homeless beggar old !

1820.

AUTUMN.

A DIRGE.

THE warm sun is failing, the bleak wind is wailing,
The bare boughs are sighing, the pale flowers are
 dying,

And the year
On the earth her death-bed, in a shroud of leaves
  dead,
      Is lying.
   Come, months, come away,
   From November to May,
   In your saddest array;
   Follow the bier
   Of the dead cold year,
And like dim shadows watch by her sepulchre.

The chill rain is falling, the nipt worm is crawling,
The rivers are swelling, the thunder is knelling
      For the year;
The blithe swallows are flown, and the lizards each
  gone
      To his dwelling;
   Come, months, come away;
   Put on white, black, and gray;
   Let your light sisters play —
   Ye, follow the bier
   Of the dead cold year,
And make her grave green with tear on tear.
                1820.

DIRGE FOR THE YEAR.

ORPHAN hours, the year is dead,
  Come and sigh, come and weep!
Merry hours, smile instead,
  For the year is but asleep.
See, it smiles as it is sleeping,
Mocking your untimely weeping.

As an earthquake rocks a corse
  In its coffin in the clay,
So White Winter, that rough nurse,
  Rocks the death-cold year to-day;
Solemn hours! wail aloud
For your mother in her shroud.

As the wild air stirs and sways
  The tree-swung cradle of a child,
So the breath of these rude days
  Rocks the year: — be calm and mild,
Trembling hours, she will arise
With new love within her eyes.

January gray is here,
  Like a sexton by her grave;
February bears the bier,
  March with grief doth howl and rave,
And April weeps — but, O, ye hours,
Follow with May's fairest flowers.

1821.

MUTABILITY.

THE flower that smiles to-day
    To-morrow dies;
All that we wish to stay
    Tempts and then flies.
What is this world's delight?
Lightning that mocks the night,
    Brief even as bright.

Virtue, how frail it is !
    Friendship how rare ! .
Love, how it sells poor bliss
    For proud despair !
But we, though soon they fall,
Survive their joy, and all
    Which ours we call.

Whilst skies are blue and bright,
    Whilst flowers are gay,
Whilst eyes that change ere night
    Make glad the day ;
Whilst yet the calm hours creep,
Dream thou — and from thy sleep
    Then wake to weep.

                1821.

TO-MORROW.

WHERE art thou, beloved To-morrow?
    When young and old and strong and weak,
Rich and poor, through joy and sorrow,
    Thy sweet smiles we ever seek, —
In thy place — ah ! well-a-day !
We find the thing we fled — To-day.

                1821.

LINES.

IF I walk in Autumn's even
   While the dead leaves pass,
If I look on Spring's soft heaven, —
   Something is not there which was.
Winter's wondrous frost and snow,
Summer's clouds, where are they now?

1821.

——◦◦◦——

THE PAST.

WILT thou forget the happy hours
Which we buried in Love's sweet bowers,
Heaping over their corpses cold
Blossoms and leaves, instead of mould?
   Blossoms which were the joys that fell,
      And leaves, the hopes that yet remain.

Forget the dead, the past? O yet
There are ghosts that may take revenge for it,
Memories that make the heart a tomb,
Regrets which glide through the spirit's gloom,
   And with ghastly whispers tell
      That joy, once lost, is pain.

1818.

——◦◦◦——

TIME LONG PAST.

LIKE the ghost of a dear friend dead
      Is time long past.
A tone which is now forever fled,

A hope which is now forever past,
A love so sweet it could not last,
      Was time long past.

There were sweet dreams in the night
      Of time long past:
And, was it sadness or delight,
Each day a shadow onward cast
Which made us wish it yet might last —
      That time long past.

There is regret, almost remorse,
      For time long past.
'Tis like a child's belovèd corse
A father watches, till at last
Beauty is like remembrance cast
      From time long past.

                            1820.

LINES.

THAT time is dead forever, child,
Drowned, frozen, dead forever!
    We look on the past
    And stare aghast
At the spectres wailing, pale and ghast,
Of hopes which thou and I beguiled
    To death on life's dark river.

The stream we gazed on then, rolled by ;
Its waves are unreturning ;
    But we yet stand
    In a lone land,
Like tombs to mark the memory
Of hopes and fears, which fade and flee
In the light of life's dim morning.

                1817.

Songs of Love.

LOVE'S PHILOSOPHY.

THE fountains mingle with the river,
    And the rivers with the ocean;
The winds of heaven mix for ever
    With a sweet emotion;
Nothing in the world is single;
    All things by a law divine
In one another's being mingle;—
Why not I with thine?

See the mountains kiss high heaven,
    And the waves clasp one another;
No sister flower would be forgiven,
    If it disdained its brother;
And the sunlight clasps the earth,
    And the moonbeams kiss the sea:
What are all these kissings worth,
    If thou kiss not me?

                                    1819.

FROM THE ARABIC.

AN IMITATION.

MY faint spirit was sitting in the light
    Of thy looks, my love;
It panted for thee like the hind at noon

For the brooks, my love.
Thy barb whose hoofs outspeed the tempest's flight
    Bore thee far from me ;
My heart, for my weak feet were weary soon,
    Did companion thee.

Ah! fleeter far than fleetest storm or steed,
    Or the death they bear,
The heart which tender thought clothes like a dove
    With the wings of care ;
In the battle, in the darkness, in the need,
    Shall mine cling to thee,
Nor claim one smile for all the comfort, love,
    It may bring to thee.

                         1821.

THE INDIAN SERENADE.

I ARISE from dreams of thee
In the first sweet sleep of night,
When the winds are breathing low,
And the stars are shining bright :
I arise from dreams of thee,
And a spirit in my feet
Hath led me — who knows·how?
To thy chamber window, Sweet!

The wandering airs they faint
On the dark, the silent stream —
And the champak-odors fail
Like sweet thoughts in a dream ;

The nightingale's complaint,
It dies upon her heart; —
As I must on thine,
O! belovèd as thou art!

O lift me from the grass!
I die! I faint! I fail!
Let thy love in kisses rain
On my lips and eyelids pale.
My cheek is cold and white, alas!
My heart beats loud and fast; —
Oh! press it close to thine again,
Where it will break at last.

1819.

TO ——.

I FEAR thy kisses, gentle maiden,
  Thou needest not fear mine;
My spirit is too deeply laden
  Ever to burden thine.

I fear thy mien, thy tones, thy motion,
  Thou needest not fear mine;
Innocent is the heart's devotion
  With which I worship thine.

1820

SONG FOR "TASSO."

I LOVED — alas! our life is love;
But when we cease to breathe and move
I do suppose love ceases too.

I thought, but not as now I do,
Keen thoughts and bright of linkèd lore,
Of all that men had thought before,
And all that nature shows, and more.

And still I love and still I think,
But strangely, for my heart can drink
The dregs of such despair, and live,
And love ;
And if I think, my thoughts come fast,
I mix the present with the past,
And each seems uglier than the last.

Sometimes I see before me flee
A silver spirit's form, like thee,
O Leonora, and I sit
Still watching it,
Till by the grated casement's ledge
It fades, with such a sigh, as sedge
Breathes o'er the breezy streamlet's edge.

1818.

LOVE LEFT ALONE.

I LOVED, I love, and when I love no more,
Let joys and grief perish, and leave despair
To ring the knell of youth.   He stood beside me,
The embodied vision of the brightest dream,
Which like a dawn heralds the day of life ;
The shadow of his presence made my world
A paradise.   All familiar things he touched,

All common words he spoke, became to me
Like forms and sounds of a diviner world.
He was as is the sun in his fierce youth,
As terrible and lovely as a tempest;
He came, and went, and left me what I am.

Alas! Why must I think how oft we two
Have sate together near the river springs,
Under the green pavilion which the willow
Spreads on the floor of the unbroken fountain,
Strewn by the nurslings that linger there,
Over that islet paved with flowers and moss,
While the musk-rose leaves, like flakes of crimson
    snow,
Showered on us, and the dove mourned in the pine,
Sad prophetess of sorrows not her own?
The crane returned to her unfrozen haunt,
And the false cuckoo bade the spray good morn;
And on a wintry bough the widowed bird,
Hid in the deepest night of ivy-leaves,
Renewed the vigils of a sleepless sorrow.
             An Unfinished Drama.   1822.

————◆◆◆————

A SONG.

A WIDOW bird sate mourning for her love
    Upon a wintry bough;
The frozen wind crept on above,
    The freezing stream below.

There was no leaf upon the forest bare,
  No flower upon the ground,
And little motion in the air
  Except the mill-wheel's sound.

———◆◇◆———

LOVE AND PARTING.

SHE saw me not — she heard me not — alone
Upon the mountain's dizzy brink she stood;
She spake not, breathed not, moved not — there
    was thrown
Over her look, the shadow of a mood
Which only clothes the heart in solitude,
A thought of voiceless depth ; — she stood alone,
Above, the Heavens were spread ; — below, the
    flood
Was murmuring in its caves ; — the wind had
    blown
Her hair apart, thro' which her eyes and forehead
    shone.

A cloud was hanging o'er the western mountains ;
Before its blue and moveless depth were flying
Gray mists poured forth from the unresting foun-
    tains
Of darkness in the North : — the day was dying : —
Sudden, the sun shone forth, its beams were lying
Like boiling gold on Ocean, strange to see,
And on the shattered vapors, which defying
The power of light in vain, tossed restlessly
In the red Heaven, like wrecks in a tempestuous sea.

It was a stream of living beams, whose bank
On either side by the cloud's cleft was made;
And where its chasms that flood of glory drank,
Its waves gushed forth like fire, and as if swayed
By some mute tempest, rolled on *her;* the shade
Of her bright image floated on the river
Of liquid light, which then did end and fade —
Her radiant shape upon its verge did shiver;
Aloft, her flowing hair like strings of flame did quiver.

I stood beside her, but she saw me not —
She looked upon the sea, and skies, and earth;
Rapture, and love, and admiration wrought
A passion deeper far than tears, or mirth,
Or speech, or gesture, or whate'er has birth
From common joy; which, with the speechless
      feeling
That led her there united, and shot forth
From her far eyes, a light of deep revealing,
All but her dearest self from my regard concealing.

Her lips were parted, and the measured breath
Was now heard there; — her dark and intricate
      eyes
Orb within orb, deeper than sleep or death,
Absorbed the glories of the burning skies,
Which, mingling with her heart's deep ecstasies,
Burst from her looks and gestures; — and a light
Of liquid tenderness like love, did rise
From her whole frame, an atmosphere which quite
Arrayed her in its beams, tremulous and soft and
      bright.

She would have clasped me to her glowing frame;
Those warm and odorous lips might soon have
shed
On mine the fragrance and the invisible flame
Which now the cold winds stole; — she would
have laid
Upon my languid heart her dearest head;
I might have heard her voice, tender and sweet;
Her eyes mingling with mine, might soon have fed
My soul with their own joy. — One moment yet
I gazed — we parted then, never again to meet!

Revolt of Islam, Canto xi.

TO F. G.

HER voice did quiver as we parted,
   Yet knew I not that heart was broken
From which it came, and I departed
   Heeding not the words then spoken.
     Misery — O Misery,
   This world is all too wide for thee.

1817.

FIORDISPINA.

THE season was the childhood of sweet June,
Whose sunny hours from morning until noon
Went creeping through the day with silent feet,
Each with its load of pleasure, slow yet sweet;

Like the long years of blest Eternity
Never to be developed.   Joy to thee,
Fiordispina, and thy Cosimo,
For thou the wonders of the depth canst know
Of this unfathomable flood of hours,
Sparkling beneath the heaven which embowers —

      .   .   .   .   .   .

They were two cousins, almost like to twins,
Except that from the catalogue of sins
Nature had rased their love — which could not be
But by dissevering their nativity.
And so they grew together like two flowers
Upon one stem, which the same beams and showers
Lull or awaken in their purple prime,
Which the same hand will gather — the same clime
Shake with decay.   This fair day smiles to see
All those who love — and who e'er loved like thee,
Fiordispina?   Scarcely Cosimo,
Within whose bosom and whose brain now glow
The ardors of a vision which obscure
The very idol of its portraiture.
He faints, dissolved into a sea of love;
But thou art as a planet sphered above;
But thou art Love itself — ruling the motion
Of his subjected spirit: such emotion
Must end in sin or sorrow, if sweet May
Had not brought forth this morn — your wedding-
    day.

                                1820.

TO NIGHT.

SWIFTLY walk over the western wave,
      Spirit of Night!
Out of the misty eastern cave,
Where all the long and lone daylight,
Thou wovest dreams of joy and fear,
Which make thee terrible and dear, —
      Swift be thy flight!

Wrap thy form in a mantle gray,
      Star-inwrought!
Blind with thine hair the eyes of Day;
Kiss her until she be wearied out,
Then wander o'er city, and sea, and land,
Touching all with thine opiate wand —
      Come, long sought!

When I arose and saw the dawn,
      I sighed for thee;
When light rode high, and the dew was gone,
And noon lay heavy on flower and tree,
And the weary Day turned to his rest,
Lingering like an unloved guest,
      I sighed for thee.

Thy brother Death came, and cried,
      Wouldst thou me?
Thy sweet child Sleep, the filmy-eyed,
      Murmured like a noon-tide bee,
Shall I nestle near thy side?
Wouldst thou me? — And I replied,
      No, not thee!

Death will come when thou art dead,
    Soon. too soon —
Sleep will come when thou art fled;
Of neither would I ask the boon
I ask of thee, belovèd Night —
Swift be thine approaching flight,
    Come soon, soon !

           1821.

———•◦•———

A BRIDAL SONG.

THE golden gates of Sleep unbar
  Where Strength and Beauty, met together,
Kindle their image like a star
  In a sea of glassy weather.
Night, with all thy stars look down, —
  Darkness, weep thy holiest dew, —
Never smiled the inconstant moon
    On a pair so true.
Let eyes not see their own delight ; —
Haste, swift Hour, and thy flight
    Oft renew.

Fairies, sprites, and angels keep her !
  Holy stars, permit no wrong !
And return to wake the sleeper,
    Dawn, — ere it be long !
Oh joy ! oh fear ! what will be done
In the absence of the sun !
    Come along !

           1821.

Julian and Maddalo.

A CONVERSATION.

—◦—●◦—

PREFACE.

The meadows with fresh streams, the bees with thyme,
The goats with the green leaves of budding Spring,
Are saturated not — nor Love with tears.

VIRGIL'S GALLUS.

COUNT MADDALO is a Venetian nobleman of ancient family and of great fortune, who, without mixing much in the society of his countrymen, resides chiefly at his magnificent palace in that city. He is a person of the most consummate genius, and capable, if he would direct his energies to such an end, of becoming the redeemer of his degraded country. But it is his weakness to be proud : he derives, from a comparison of his own extraordinary mind with the dwarfish intellects that surround him, an intense apprehension of the nothingness of human life. His passions and his powers are incomparably greater than those of other men ; and, instead of the latter having been employed in curbing the former, they have mutually lent each other strength. His ambition preys upon itself, for want of objects which it can consider worthy of exertion. I say that Maddalo is proud, because I can find no other word to express the concentred and impatient feelings which consume him ; but it is on his own hopes and affections only that he seems to trample, for in social life no human being can be more gentle, patient, and unassuming than Maddalo. He is cheerful, frank, and witty. His more serious conversation is

a sort of intoxication; men are held by it as by a spell. He
has travelled much; and there is an inexpressible charm in his
relation of his adventures in different countries.

Julian is an Englishman of good family, passionately
attached to those philosophical notions which assert the power
of man over his own mind, and the immense improvements of
which, by the extinction of certain moral superstitions, human
society may be yet susceptible. Without concealing the evil
in the world, he is for ever speculating how good may be made
superior. He is a complete infidel, and a scoffer at all things
reputed holy; and Maddalo takes a wicked pleasure in drawing
out his taunts against religion. What Maddalo thinks on these
matters is not exactly known. Julian, in spite of his heterodox
opinions, is conjectured by his friends to possess some good
qualities. How far this is possible the pious reader will deter-
mine. Julian is rather serious.

Of the Maniac I can give no information. He seems, by his
own account, to have been disappointed in love. He was evi-
dently a very cultivated and amiable person when in his right
senses. His story, told at length, might be like many other
stories of the same kind: the unconnected exclamations of his
agony will perhaps be found a sufficient comment for the text
of every heart.

I RODE one evening with Count Maddalo
Upon the bank of land which breaks the flow
Of Adria towards Venice: a bare strand
Of hillocks, heaped from ever-shifting sand,
Matted with thistles and amphibious weeds,
Such as from earth's embrace the salt ooze breeds,
Is this; an uninhabited sea-side,
Which the lone fisher, when his nets are dried,
Abandons; and no other object breaks
The waste, but one dwarf tree and some few stakes
Broken and unrepaired, and the tide makes

A narrow space of level sand thereon,
Where 'twas our wont to ride while day went down.
This ride was my delight.   I love all waste
And solitary places ; where we taste
The pleasure of believing what we see
Is boundless, as we wish our souls to be :
And such was this wide ocean, and this shore
More barren than its billows ; and yet more
Than all, with a remembered friend I love
To ride as then I rode ; — for the winds drove
The living spray along the sunny air
Into our faces ; the blue heavens were bare,
Stripped to their depths by the awakening north ;
And, from the waves, sound like delight broke forth
Harmonizing with solitude, and sent
Into our hearts aërial merriment.
So, as we rode, we talked ; and the swift thought,
Winging itself with laughter, lingered not,
But flew from brain to brain, — such glee was ours,
Charged with light memories of remembered hours,
None slow enough for sadness : till we came
Homeward, which always makes the spirit tame.
This day had been cheerful but cold, and now
The sun was sinking, and the wind also.
Our talk grew somewhat serious, as may be
Talk interrupted with such raillery
As mocks itself, because it cannot scorn
The thoughts it would extinguish : — 'twas forlorn,
Yet pleasing, such as once, so poets tell,
The devils held within the dales of Hell
Concerning God, freewill and destiny :
Of all that earth has been or yet may be,

All that vain men imagine or believe,
Or hope can paint or suffering may achieve,
We descanted, and I (for ever still
Is it not wise to make the best of ill?)
Argued against despondency, but pride
Made my companion take the darker side.
The sense that he was greater than his kind
Had struck, methinks, his eagle spirit blind
By gazing on its own exceeding light.
Meanwhile the sun paused ere it should alight,
Over the horizon of the mountains ; — Oh
How beautiful is sunset, when the glow
Of Heaven descends upon a land like thee,
Thou Paradise of exiles, Italy!
Thy mountains, seas and vineyards and the towers
Of cities they encircle ! — it was ours
To stand on thee, beholding it ; and then,
Just where we had dismounted, the Count's men
Were waiting for us with the gondola. —
As those who pause on some delightful way
Tho' bent on pleasant pilgrimage, we stood
Looking upon the evening and the flood
Which lay between the city and the shore
Paved with the image of the sky . . .   The hoar
And aëry Alps towards the North appeared
Thro' mist, an heaven-sustaining bulwark reared
Between the East and West ; and half the sky
Was roofed with clouds of rich emblazonry
Dark purple at the zenith, which still grew
Down the steep West into a wondrous hue
Brighter than burning gold, even to the rent
Where the swift sun yet paused in his descent

Among the many folded hills : they were
Those famous Euganean hills, which bear
As seen from Lido thro' the harbor piles
The likeness of a clump of peakèd isles —
And then — as if the earth and Sea had been
Dissolved into one lake of fire, were seen
Those mountains towering as from waves of flame
Around the vaporous sun, from which there came
The inmost purple spirit of light, and made
Their very peaks transparent.   "Ere it fade,"
Said my companion, " I will show you soon
A better station " — So, o'er the lagune
We glided, and from that funereal bark
I leaned, and saw the city, and could mark
How from their many isles in evening's gleam
Its temples and its palaces did seem
Like fabrics of enchantment piled to Heaven.
I was about to speak, when — " We are even
Now at the point I meant," said Maddalo,
And bade the gondolieri cease to row.
"Look, Julian, on the West, and listen well
If you hear not a deep and heavy bell."
I looked, and saw between us and the sun
A building on an island ; such a one
As age to age might add, for uses vile,
A windowless, deformed and dreary pile ;
And on the top an open tower, where hung
A bell, which in the radiance swayed and swung ;
We could just hear its hoarse and iron tongue :
The broad sun sank behind it, and it tolled
In strong and black relief — " What we behold
Shall be the madhouse and its belfry tower,"

Said Maddalo, "and ever at this hour
Those who may cross the water, hear that bell
Which calls the maniacs each one from his cell
To vespers."—"As much skill as need to pray
In thanks or hope for their dark lot have they
To their stern Maker," I replied. "O ho!
You talk as in years past," said Maddalo.
"'Tis strange men change not. You were ever still
Among Christ's flock a perilous infidel,
A wolf for the meek lambs — if you can't swim
Beware of Providence." I looked on him,
But the gay smile had faded in his eye,
"And such,"— he cried, "is our mortality,
And this must be the emblem and the sign
Of what should be eternal and divine!—
And like that black and dreary bell, the soul
Hung in a heaven-illumined tower, must toll
Our thoughts and our desires to meet below
Round the rent heart and pray — as madmen do;
For what? they know not, till the night of death
As sunset that strange vision, severeth
Our memory from itself, and us from all
We sought and yet were baffled." I recall
The sense of what he said, altho' I mar
The force of his expressions. The broad star
Of day meanwhile had sunk behind the hill,
And the black bell became invisible,
And the red tower looked gray, and all between
The churches, ships and palaces were seen
Huddled in gloom : — into the purple sea
The orange hues of heaven sunk silently.
We hardly spoke, and soon the gondola
Conveyed me to my lodging by the way.

The following morn was rainy, cold and dim.
Ere Maddalo arose, I called on him,
And whilst I waited, with his child I played ;
A lovelier toy sweet Nature never made,
A serious, subtle, wild, yet gentle being,
Graceful without design and unforeseeing,
With eyes — Oh speak not of her eyes ! — which seem
Twin mirrors of Italian Heaven, yet gleam
With such deep meaning, as we never see
But in the human countenance.   With me
She was a special favorite ; I had nursed
Her fine and feeble limbs when she came first
To this bleak world ; and she yet seemed to know
On second sight her ancient playfellow,
Less changed than she was by six months or so ;
For after her first shyness was worn out
We sate there, rolling billiard balls about,
When the Count entered — salutations past ;
" The words you spoke last night might well have cast
A darkness on my spirit — if man be
The passive thing you say, I should not see
Much harm in the religions and old saws
(Tho' I may never own such leaden laws)
Which break a teachless nature to the yoke :
Mine is another faith " — thus much I spoke
And noting he replied not, added : " See
This lovely child, blithe, innocent and free,
She spends a happy time with little care
While we to such sick thoughts subjected are
As came on you last night — it is our will
That thus enchains us to permitted ill —
We might be otherwise — we might be all

We dream of happy, high, majestical.
Where is the love, beauty and truth we seek
But in our mind ? and if we were not weak
Should we be less in deed than in desire?"
"Aye, if we were not weak — and we aspire
How vainly to be strong!" said Maddalo :
"You talk Utopia." "It remains to know,"
I then rejoined, "and those who try may find
How strong the chains are which our spirit bind;
Brittle perchance as straw . . . We are assured
Much may be conquered, much may be endured
Of what degrades and crushes us. We know
That we have power over ourselves to do
And suffer — what, we know not till we try;
But something nobler than to live and die —
So taught those kings of old philosophy
Who reigned, before Religion made men blind;
And those who suffer with their suffering kind
Yet feel their faith, religion." "My dear friend,"
Said Maddalo, " my judgment will not bend
To your opinion, tho' I think you might
Make such a system refutation-tight
As far as words go. ' I knew one like you
Who to this city came some months ago,
With whom I argued in this sort, and he
Is now gone mad, — and so he answered me, —
Poor fellow ! but if you would like to go
We'll visit him, and his wild talk will show
How vain are such aspiring theories."
"I hope to prove the induction otherwise,
And that a want of that true theory, still,
Which seeks a ' soul of goodness ' in things ill,

Or in himself or others, has thus bowed
His being — there are some by nature proud,
Who patient in all else demand but this :
To love and be beloved with gentleness ;
And being scorned. what wonder if they die
Some living death? this is not destiny
But man's own wilful ill."

                    As thus I spoke
Servants announced the gondola, and we
Through the fast-falling rain and high-wrought sea
Sailed to the island where the madhouse stands.
We disembarked.   The clap of tortured hands,
Fierce yells and howlings and lamentings keen,
And laughter where complaint had merrier been,
Moans, shrieks, and curses, and blaspheming prayers
Accosted us.   We climbed the oozy stairs
Into an old court yard.   I heard on high,
Then, fragments of most touching melody,
But looking up saw not the singer there —
Through the black bars in the tempestuous air
I saw, like weeds on a wrecked palace growing,
Long tangled locks flung wildly forth, and flowing,
Of those who on a sudden were beguiled
Into strange silence, and looked forth and smiled
Hearing sweet sounds. — Then I : " Methinks there
        were
A cure of these with patience and kind care,
If music can thus move . . . but what is he
Whom we seek here? "   " Of his sad history
I know but this," said Maddalo, " he came
To Venice a dejected man, and fame

Said he was wealthy, or he had been so;
Some thought the loss of fortune wrought him woe;
But he was ever talking in such sort
As you do — far more sadly — he seemed hurt,
Even as a man with his peculiar wrong,
To hear but of the oppression of the strong,
Or those absurd deceits (I think with you
In some respects, you know) which carry through
The excellent impostors of this earth
When they outface detection — he had worth,
Poor fellow! but a humorist in his way"—
"Alas, what drove him mad?" "I cannot say;
A lady came with him from France, and when
She left him and returned, he wandered then
About yon lonely isles of desart sand
Till he grew wild — he had no cash or land
Remaining. — the police had brought him here —
Some fancy took him and he would not bear
Removal; so I fitted up for him
Those rooms beside the sea, to please his whim,
And sent him busts and books and urns for flowers
Which had adorned his life in happier hours,
And instruments of music — you may guess
A stranger could do little more or less
For one so gentle and unfortunate,
And those are his sweet strains which charm the
    weight
From madmen's chains, and make this Hell appear
A heaven of sacred silence, hushed to hear."—
" Nay, this was kind of you — he had no claim,
As the world says "— " None — but the very same
Which I on all mankind, were I as he

Fallen to such deep reverse ; — his melody
Is interrupted — now we hear the din
Of madmen, shriek on shriek again begin ;
Let us now visit him ; after this strain
He ever communes with himself again,
And sees nor hears not any." Having said
These words we called the keeper, and he led
To an apartment opening on the sea —
There the poor wretch was sitting mournfully
Near a piano, his pale fingers twined
One with the other, and the ooze and wind
Rushed thro' an open casement, and did sway
His hair, and starred it with the brackish spray ;
His head was leaning on a music book,
And he was muttering, and his lean limbs shook ;
His lips were pressed against a folded leaf
In hue too beautiful for health, and grief
Smiled in their motions as they lay apart —
As one who wrought from his own fervid heart
The eloquence of passion, soon he raised
His sad meek face and eyes lustrous and glazed,
And spoke — sometimes as one who wrote and
    thought
His words might move some heart that heeded not
If sent to distant lands : and then as one
Reproaching deeds never to be undone
With wondering self-compassion ; then his speech
Was lost in grief, and then his words came each
Unmodulated, cold, expressionless ;
But that from one jarred accent you might guess
It was despair made them so uniform :
And all the while the loud and gusty storm

Hissed thro' the window, and we stood behind
Stealing his accents from the envious wind
Unseen.   I yet remember what he said
Distinctly : such impression his words made.

   'Month after month,' he cried, 'to bear this load
And as a jade urged by the whip and goad
To drag life on, which like a heavy chain
Lengthens behind with many a link of pain !—
And not to speak my grief— O not to dare
To give a human voice to my despair,
But live and move, and wretched thing ! smile on
As if I never went aside to groan,
And wear this mask of falsehood even to those
Who are most dear — not for my own repose —
Alas! no scorn or pain or hate could be
So heavy as that falsehood is to me —
But that I cannot bear more altered faces
Than needs must be, more changed and cold embraces,
More misery, disappointment and mistrust
To own me for their father . . .   Would the dust
Were covered in upon my body now !
That the life ceased to toil within my brow !
And then these thoughts would at the least be fled ;
Let us not fear such pain can vex the dead.

  'What Power delights to torture us?   I know
That to myself I do not wholly owe
What now I suffer, tho' in part I may.
Alas! none strewed sweet flowers upon the way
Where wandering heedlessly, I met pale Pain
My shadow, which will leave me not again —
If I have erred, there was no joy in error,

But pain and insult and unrest and terror;
I have not as some do, bought penitence
With pleasure, and a dark yet sweet offence,
For then, — if love and tenderness and truth
Had overlived hope's momentary youth,
My creed should have redeemed me from repenting,
But loathèd scorn and outrage unrelenting
Met love excited by far other seeming
Until the end was gained . . . as one from dreaming
Of sweetest peace, I woke, and found my state
Such as it is. —

       'O Thou, my spirit's mate
Who, for thou art compassionate and wise,
Wouldst pity me from thy most gentle eyes
If this sad writing thou shouldst ever see —
My secret groans must be unheard by thee,
Thou wouldst weep tears bitter as blood to know
Thy lost friend's incommunicable woe.

  'Ye few by whom my nature has been weighed
In friendship, let me not that name degrade
By placing on your hearts the secret load
Which crushes mine to dust.   There is one road
To peace and that is truth, which follow ye!
Love sometimes leads astray to misery.
Yet think not tho' subdued — and I may well
Say that I am subdued — that the full Hell
Within me would infect the untainted breast
Of sacred nature with its own unrest;
As some perverted beings think to find
In scorn or hate a medicine for the mind
Which scorn or hate have wounded — O how vain!

The dagger heals not but may rend again. . . .
Believe that I am ever still the same
In creed as in resolve, and what may tame
My heart, must leave the understanding free,
Or all would sink in this keen agony —
Nor dream that I will join the vulgar cry,
Or with my silence sanction tyranny,
Or seek a moment's shelter from my pain
In any madness which the world calls gain,
Ambition or revenge or thoughts as stern
As those which make me what I am, or turn
To avarice or misanthropy or lust. . . .
Heap on me soon, O grave, thy welcome dust!
Till then the dungeon may demand its prey,
And Poverty and Shame may meet and say —
Halting beside me on the public way —
'That love-devoted youth is ours — let's sit
Beside him — he may live some six months yet.'
Or the red scaffold, as our country bends,
May ask some willing victim, or ye, friends,
May fall under some sorrow which this heart
Or hand may share or vanquish or avert;
I am prepared: in truth with no proud joy
To do or suffer aught, as when a boy
I did devote to justice and to love
My nature, worthless now! . . . .
                                    'I must remove
A veil from my pent mind.   'Tis torn aside!
O, pallid as Death's dedicated bride,
Thou mockery which art sitting by my side,
Am I not wan like thee? at the grave's call
I haste, invited to thy wedding-ball

To greet the ghastly paramour, for whom
Thou hast deserted me . . . and made the tomb
Thy bridal bed . . . but I beside your feet
Will lie and watch ye from my winding sheet —
Thus . . . wide awake tho' dead . . . yet stay O stay !
Go not so soon — I know not what I say —
Hear but my reasons . . . I am mad, I fear,
My fancy is o'erwrought . . . thou art not here . . .
Pale art thou, 'tis most true . . . but thou art gone,
Thy work is finished . . . I am left alone ! —

  . . . . . .

'Nay, was it I who wooed thee to this breast
Which, like a serpent thou envenomest
As in repayment of the warmth it lent ?
Didst thou not seek me for thine own content ?
Did not thy love awaken mine ? I thought
That thou wert she who said ' You kiss me not
Ever, I fear you do not love me now —
In truth I loved even to my overthrow
Her, who would fain forget these words : but they
Cling to her mind, and cannot pass away.

  . . . . . .

'You say that I am proud — that when I speak
My lip is tortured with the wrongs which break
The spirit it expresses. . . . Never one
Humbled himself before, as I have done !
Even the instinctive worm on which we tread
Turns, tho' it wound not — then with prostrate head
Sinks in the dust and writhes like me — and dies ?
No : wears a living death of agonies !
As the slow shadows of the pointed grass

Mark the eternal periods, his pangs pass
Slow, ever-moving, — making moments be
As mine seem — each an immortality !

.   .   .   .   .   .

'That you had never seen me — never heard
My voice, and more than all had ne'er endured
The deep pollution of my loathed embrace —
That your eyes ne'er had lied love in my face —
That, like some maniac monk, I had torn out
The nerves of manhood by their bleeding root
With mine own quivering fingers, so that ne'er
Our hearts had for a moment mingled there
To disunite in horror — these were not
With thee, like some suppressed and hideous thought
Which flits athwart our musings, but can find
No rest within a pure and gentle mind . . .
Thou sealedst them with many a bare broad word
And searedst my memory o'er them, — for I heard
And can forget not . . . they were ministered
One after one, those curses.   Mix them up
Like self-destroying poisons in one cup,
And they will make one blessing which thou ne'er
Didst imprecate for, on me, — death.

.   .   .   .   .   .

'It were
A cruel punishment for one most cruel
If such can love, to make that love the fuel
Of the mind's hell; hate, scorn, remorse, despair:
But *me* — whose heart a stranger's tear might wear
As water-drops the sandy fountain-stone,
Who loved and pitied all things, and could moan

For woes which others hear not, and could see
The absent with the glance of phantasy,
And with the poor and trampled sit and weep,
Following the captive to his dungeon deep;
Me — who am as a nerve o'er which do creep
The else unfelt oppressions of this earth,
And was to thee the flame upon thy hearth,
When all beside was cold — that thou on me
Shouldst rain these plagues of blistering agony —
Such curses are from lips once eloquent
With love's too partial praise — let none relent
Who intend deeds too dreadful for a name
Henceforth, if an example for the same
They seek . . . for thou on me lookedst so, and so —
And didst speak thus . . . and thus . . . I live to show
How much men bear and die not !

.   .   .   .   .   .

'Thou wilt tell
With the grimace of hate how horrible
It was to meet my love when thine grew less;
Thou wilt admire how I could e'er address
Such features to love's work . . . this taunt, tho' true,
(For indeed nature nor in form nor hue
Bestowed on me her choicest workmanship)
Shall not be thy defence . . . for since thy lip
Met mine first, years long past, since thine eye kindled
With soft fire under mine, I have not dwindled
Nor changed in mind or body, or in aught
But as love changes what it loveth not
After long years and many trials.

'How vain
Are words! I thought never to speak again,
Not even in secret, — not to my own heart —
But from my lips the unwilling accents start,
And from my pen the words flow as I write,
Dazzling my eyes with scalding tears . . . my sight
Is dim to see that charactered in vain
On this unfeeling leaf which burns the brain
And eats into it . . . blotting all things fair
And wise and good which time had written there.

'Those who inflict must suffer, for they see
The work of their own hearts and this must be
Our chastisement or recompense — O child!
I would that thine were like to be more mild
For both our wretched sakes . . . for thine the most
Who feelest already all that thou hast lost
Without the power to wish it thine again;
And as slow years pass, a funereal train
Each with the ghost of some lost hope or friend
Following it like its shadow, wilt thou bend
No thought on my dead memory?

    .   .   .   .   .   .

'Alas, love!
Fear me not . . . against thee I would not move
A finger in despite.   Do I not live
That thou mayest have less bitter cause to grieve?
I give thee tears for scorn and love for hate;
And that thy lot may be less desolate
Than his on whom thou tramplest, I refrain
From that sweet sleep which medicines all pain.
Then, when thou speakest of me, never say

He could forgive not.   Here I cast away
All human passions, all revenge, all pride;
I think, speak, act no ill; I do but hide
Under these words like embers, every spark
Of that which has consumed me — quick and dark
The grave is yawning . . . as its roof shall cover
My limbs with dust·and worms under and over
So let Oblivion hide this grief . . . the air
Closes upon my accents, as despair
Upon my heart — let death upon despair ! '

      He ceased, and overcome leant back awhile,
Then rising, with a melancholy smile
Went to a sofa, and lay down, and slept
A heavy sleep, and in his dreams he wept
And muttered some familiar name, and we
Wept without shame in his society.
I think I never was impressed so much;
The man who were not, must have lacked a touch
Of human nature . . . then we lingered not,
Although our argument was quite forgot,
But calling the attendants, went to dine
At Maddalo's; yet neither cheer nor wine
Could give us spirits, for we talked of him
And nothing else, till daylight made stars dim;
And we agreed his was some dreadful ill
Wrought on him boldly, yet unspeakable,
By a dear friend; some deadly change in love
Of one vowed deeply which he dreamed not of;
For whose sake he, it seemed, had fixed a blot
Of falsehood on his mind which flourished not
But in the light of all-beholding truth,

And having stamped this canker on his youth
She had abandoned him — and how much more
Might be his woe, we guessed not — he had store
Of friends and fortune once, as we could guess
From his nice habits and his gentleness ;
These were now lost . . . it were a grief indeed
If he had changed one unsustaining reed
For all that such a man might else adorn
The colors of his mind seemed yet unworn ;
For the wild language of his grief was high,
Such as in measure were called poetry,
And I remember one remark which then
Maddalo made.   He said: " Most wretched men
Are cradled into poetry by wrong,
They learn in suffering what they teach in song."

    If I had been an unconnected man
I, from this moment, should have formed some plan
Never to leave sweet Venice, — for to me
It was delight to ride by the lone sea ;
And then, the town is silent — one may write
Or read in gondolas by day or night,
Having the little brazen lamp alight,
Unseen, uninterrupted ; books are there,
Pictures, and casts from all those statues fair
Which were twin-born with poetry, and all
We seek in towns, with little to recall
Regrets for the green country.   I might sit
In Maddalo's great palace, and his wit
And subtle talk would cheer the winter night
And make me know myself, and the firelight
Would flash upon our faces, till the day

Might dawn and make me wonder at my stay:
But I had friends in London, too: the chief
Attraction here, was that I sought relief
From the deep tenderness that maniac wrought
Within me — 'twas perhaps an idle thought —
But I imagined that if day by day
I watched him, and but seldom went away,
And studied all the beatings of his heart
With zeal, as men study some stubborn art
For their own good, and could by patience find
An entrance to the caverns of his mind,
I might reclaim him from this dark estate:
In friendships I had been most fortunate —
Yet never saw I one whom I would call
More willingly my friend; and this was all
Accomplished not; such dreams of baseless good
Oft come and go in crowds and solitude
And leave no trace — but what I now designed
Made for long years impression on my mind.
The following morning urged by my affairs
I left bright Venice.

After many years
And many changes I returned; the name
Of Venice, and its aspect was the same;
But Maddalo was travelling far away
Among the mountains of Armenia.
His dog was dead. His child had now become
A woman; such as it has been my doom
To meet with few, a wonder of this earth
Where there is little of transcendent worth,
Like one of Shakespeare's women: kindly she,

And with a manner beyond courtesy,
Received her father's friend ; and when I asked
Of the lorn maniac, she her memory tasked
And told as she had heard the mournful tale.
" That the poor sufferer's health began to fail
Two years from my departure, but that then
The lady who had left him, came again.
Her mien had been imperious, but she now
Looked meek — perhaps remorse had brought her low.
Her coming made him better, and they stayed
Together at my father's — for I played
As I remember with the lady's shawl —
I might be six years old — but after all
She left him." . . . " Why, her heart must have been
        tough :
How did it end ? "   " And was not this enough ?
They met — they parted " — " Child, is there no
        more ? "
" Something within that interval which bore
The stamp of *why* they parted, *how* they met :
Yet if thine agèd eyes disdain to wet
Those wrinkled cheeks with youth's remembered
        tears,
Ask me no more, but let the silent years
Be closed and cered over their memory
As yon mute marble where their corpses lie."
I urged and questioned still, she told me how
All happened — but the cold world shall not know.

                                        1818.

Poems of Nature and Man.

MONT BLANC.

LINES WRITTEN IN THE VALE OF CHAMOUNI.

THE everlasting universe of things
Flows through the mind, and rolls its rapid waves,
Now dark — now glittering — now reflecting gloom —
Now lending splendor, where from secret springs
The source of human thought its tribute brings
Of waters, — with a sound but half its own,
Such as a feeble brook will oft assume
In the wild woods, among the mountains lone,
Where waterfalls around it leap for ever,
Where woods and winds contend, and a vast river
Over its rocks ceaslessly bursts and raves.

Thus thou, Ravine of Arve — dark, deep Ravine —
Thou many-colored, many-voicèd vale,
Over whose pines, and crags, and caverns sail
Fast cloud shadows and sunbeams : awful scene,
Where Power in likeness of the Arve comes down
From the ice gulfs that gird his secret throne,
Bursting through these dark mountains like the
        flame
Of lightning thro' the tempest ; — thou dost lie,
Thy giant brood of pines around thee clinging,

Children of elder time, in whose devotion
The chainless winds still come and ever came
To drink their odors, and their mighty swinging
To hear — an old and solemn harmony;
Thine earthly rainbows stretched across the sweep
Of the ethereal waterfall, whose veil
Robes some unsculptured image; the strange sleep
Which when the voices of the desert fail
Wraps all in its own deep eternity; —
Thy caverns echoing to the Arve's commotion,
A loud, lone sound no other sound can tame;
Thou art pervaded with that ceaseless motion,
Thou art the path of that unresting sound —
Dizzy Ravine! and when I gaze on thee
I seem as in a trance sublime and strange
To muse on my own separate phantasy,
My own, my human mind, which passively
Now renders and receives fast influencings,
Holding an unremitting interchange
With the clear universe of things around;
One legion of wild thoughts, whose wandering wings
Now float above thy darkness, and now rest
Where that or thou art no unbidden guest,
In the still cave of the witch Poesy,
Seeking among the shadows that pass by,
Ghosts of all things that are, some shade of thee,
Some phantom, some faint image; till the breast
From which they fled recalls them, thou art there!

Some say that gleams of a remoter world
Visit the soul in sleep, — that death is slumber,
And that its shapes the busy thoughts outnumber
Of those who wake and live. — I look on high;

Has some unknown omnipotence unfurled
The veil of life and death? or do I lie
In dream, and does the mightier world of sleep
Spread far around and inaccessibly
Its circles? For the very spirit fails,
Driven like a homeless cloud from steep to steep
That vanishes among the viewless gales!
Far, far above, piercing the infinite sky,
Mont Blanc appears, — still, snowy, and serene —
Its subject mountains their unearthly forms
Pile around it, ice and rock; broad vales between
Of frozen floods, unfathomable deeps,
Blue as the overhanging heaven, that spread
And wind among the accumulated steeps;
A desert peopled by the storms alone,
Save when the eagle brings some hunter's bone,
And the wolf tracks her there — how hideously
Its shapes are heaped around! rude, bare, and high,
Ghastly, and scarred, and riven. — Is this the scene
Where the old Earthquake-dæmon taught her young
Ruin? Were these their toys? or did a sea
Of fire envelop once this silent snow?
None can reply — all seems eternal now.
The wilderness has a mysterious tongue
Which teaches awful doubt, or faith so mild,
So solemn, so serene, that man may be
But for such faith with nature reconciled;
Thou hast a voice, great Mountain, to repeal
Large codes of fraud and woe; not understood
By all, but which the wise, and great, and good
Interpret, or make felt, or deeply feel.
The fields, the lakes, the forests, and the streams,
Ocean, and all the living things that dwell

Within the dædal earth; lightning, and rain,
Earthquake, and fiery flood, and hurricane,
The torpor of the year when feeble dreams
Visit the hidden buds, or dreamless sleep
Holds every future leaf and flower; — the bound
With which from that detested trance they leap;
The works and ways of man, their death and birth,
And that of him and all that his may be;
All things that move and breathe with toil and sound
Are born and die; revolve, subside and swell.
Power dwells apart in its tranquillity
Remote, serene, and inaccessible:
And *this*, the naked countenance of earth,
On which I gaze, even these primeval mountains
Teach the adverting mind.   The glaciers creep
Like snakes that watch their prey from their far foun-
        tains,
Slow rolling on; there, many a precipice,
Frost and the Sun in scorn of mortal power
Have piled: dome, pyramid, and pinnacle,
A city of death, distinct with many a tower
And wall impregnable of beaming ice.
Yet not a city, but a flood of ruin
Is there, that from the boundaries of the sky
Rolls its perpetual stream; vast pines are strewing
Its destined path, or in the mangled soil
Branchless and shattered stand; the rocks, drawn
        down
From yon remotest waste, have overthrown
The limits of the dead and living world,
Never to be reclaimed.   The dwelling-place
Of insects, beasts, and birds, becomes its spoil;

Their food and their retreat forever gone,
So much of life and joy is lost. The race
Of man flies far in dread : his work and dwelling
Vanish, like smoke before the tempest's stream,
And their place is not known. Below, vast caves
Shine in the rushing torrent's restless gleam,
Which from those secret chasms in tumult welling
Meet in the Vale, and one majestic River,
The breath and blood of distant lands, for ever
Rolls its loud waters to the ocean waves,
Breathes its swift vapors to the circling air.

Mont Blanc yet gleams on high : — the power is
    there,
The still and solemn power of many sights,
And many sounds, and much of life and death.
In the calm darkness of the moonless nights,
In the lone glare of day, the snows descend
Upon that Mountain ; none beholds them there,
Nor when the flakes burn in the sinking sun,
Or the star-beams dart through them : — Winds con·
    tend
Silently there, and heap the snow with breath
Rapid and strong, but silently ! Its home
The voiceless lightning in these solitudes
Keeps innocently, and like vapor broods
Over the snow. The secret strength of things
Which governs thought, and to the infinite dome
Of heaven is as a law, inhabits thee !
And what were thou, and earth, and stars, and sea,
If to the human mind's imaginings
Silence and solitude were vacancy ?

                   1816.

THE ALPS AT DAWN.

BENEATH is a wide plain of billowy mist,
As a lake, paving in the morning sky,
With azure waves which burst in silver light,
Some Indian vale.   Behold it, rolling on
Under the curdling winds, and islanding
The peak whereon we stand, midway, around,
Encinctured by the dark and gloomy forests,
Dim twilight lawns, and stream-illumined caves,
And wind-enchanted shapes of wandering mist;
And far on high the keen sky-cleaving mountains
From icy spires of sunlike radiance fling
The dawn, as lifted Ocean's dazzling spray,
From some Atlantic islet scattered up,
Spangles the wind with lamp-like water-drops.
The vale is girdled with their walls, a howl
Of cataracts from their thaw-cloven ravines
Satiates the listening wind, continuous, vast,
Awful as silence.   Hark ! the rushing snow !
The sun-awakened avalanche ! whose mass,
Thrice sifted by the storm, had gathered there
Flake after flake, in heaven-defying minds
As thought by thought is piled, till some great truth
Is loosened, and the nations echo round,
Shaken to their roots, as do the mountains now.

Prom. Unbound.

LINES WRITTEN AMONG THE
EUGANEAN HILLS.

MANY a green isle needs must be
In the deep wide sea of misery,
Or the mariner, worn and wan,
Never thus could voyage on
Day and night, and night and day,
Drifting on his dreary way,
With the solid darkness black
Closing round his vessel's track;
Whilst above, the sunless sky,
Big with clouds, hangs heavily,
And behind, the tempest fleet
Hurries on with lightning feet,
Riving sail, and cord, and plank,
Till the ship has almost drank
Death from the o'er-brimming deep;
And sinks down, down, like that sleep
When the dreamer seems to be
Weltering through eternity;
And the dim low line before
Of a dark and distant shore
Still recedes, as ever still
Longing with divided will,
But no power to seek or shun,
He is ever drifted on
O'er the unreposing wave
To the haven of the grave.
What, if there no friends will greet;

What, if there no heart will meet
His with love's impatient beat;
Wander wheresoe'er he may,
Can he dream before that day
To find refuge from distress
In friendship's smile, in love's caress?
Then 'twill wreak him little woe
Whether such there be or no:
Senseless is the breast, and cold,
Which relenting love would fold;
Bloodless are the veins and chill
Which the pulse of pain did fill;
Every little living nerve
That from bitter words did swerve
Round the tortured lips and brow,
Are like sapless leaflets now
Frozen upon December's bough.

On the beach of a northern sea
Which tempests shake eternally,
As once the wretch there lay to sleep,
Lies a solitary heap,
One white skull and seven dry bones,
On the margin of the stones,
Where a few gray rushes stand,
Boundaries of the sea and land:
Nor is heard one voice of wail
But the sea-mews, as they sail
O'er the billows of the gale;
Or the whirlwind up and down
Howling, like a slaughtered town,
When a king in glory rides

Through the pomp of fratricides :
Those unburied bones around
There is many a mournful sound ;
There is no lament for him,
Like a sunless vapor, dim,
Who once clothed with life and thought
What now moves nor murmurs not.

Aye, many flowering islands lie
In the waters of wide Agony :
To such a one this morn was led,
My bark by soft winds piloted :
'Mid the mountains Euganean
I stood listening to the pæan,
With which the legioned rooks did hail
The sun's uprise majestical ;
Gathering round with wings all hoar,
Thro' the dewy mist they soar
Like gray shades, till the eastern heaven
Bursts, and then, as clouds of even,
Flecked with fire and azure, lie
In the unfathomable sky,
So their plumes of purple grain,
Starred with drops of golden rain,
Gleam above the sunlit woods,
As in silent multitudes
On the morning's fitful gale
Thro' the broken mist they sail,
And the vapors cloven and gleaming
Follow down the dark steep streaming,
Till all is bright, and clear, and still,
Round the solitary hill.

Beneath is spread like a green sea
The waveless plain of Lombardy,
Bounded by the vaporous air,
Islanded by cities fair;
Underneath day's azure eyes
Ocean's nursling, Venice lies,
A peopled labyrinth of walls,
Amphitrite's destined halls,
Which her hoary sire now paves
With his blue and beaming waves.
Lo! the sun upsprings behind,
Broad, red, radiant, half reclined
On the level quivering line
Of the waters crystalline;
And before that chasm of light,
As within a furnace bright,
Column, tower, and dome, and spire,
Shine like obelisks of fire,
Pointing with inconstant motion
From the altar of dark ocean
To the sapphire-tinted skies;
As the flames of sacrifice
From the marble shrines did rise,
As to pierce the dome of gold
Where Apollo spoke of old.

Sun-girt City, thou hast been
Ocean's child, and then his queen;
Now is come a darker day,
And thou soon must be his prey,
If the power that raised thee here
Hallow so thy watery bier.

A less drear ruin then than now,
With thy conquest-branded brow
Stooping to the slave of slaves
From thy throne, among the waves
Wilt thou be, when the sea-mew
Flies, as once before it flew,
O'er thine isles depopulate,
And all is in its ancient state,
Save where many a palace gate
With green sea-flowers overgrown
Like a rock of ocean's own,
Topples o'er the abandoned sea
As the tides change sullenly.
The fisher on his watery way,
Wandering at the close of day,
Will spread his sail and seize his oar
Till he pass the gloomy shore,
Lest thy dead should, from their sleep
Bursting o'er the starlight deep,
Lead a rapid masque of death
O'er the waters of his path.

Those who alone thy towers behold
Quivering through aërial gold,
As I now behold them here,
Would imagine not they were
Sepulchres, where human forms,
Like pollution-nourished worms
To the corpse of greatness cling,
Murdered, and now mouldering:
But if Freedom should awake
In her omnipotence, and shake

From the Celtic Anarch's hold
All the keys of dungeons cold,
Where a hundred cities lie
Chained like thee, ingloriously,
Thou and all thy sister band
Might adorn this sunny land,
Twining memories of old time
With new virtues more sublime;
If not, perish thou and they,
Clouds which stain truth's rising day
By her sun consumed away,
Earth can spare ye : while like flowers,
In the waste of years and hours,
From your dust new nations spring
With more kindly blossoming.
Perish ! let there only be
Floating o'er thy hearthless sea,
As the garment of thy sky
Clothes the world immortally,
One remembrance, more sublime
Than the tattered pall of Time,
Which scarce hides thy visage wan; —
That a tempest-cleaving Swan
Of the songs of Albion,
Driven from his ancestral streams
By the might of evil dreams,
Found a nest in thee; and Ocean
Welcomed him with such emotion
That its joy grew his, and sprung
From his lips like music flung
O'er a mighty thunder-fit
Chastening terror : — what though yet

Poesy's unfailing river,
Which thro' Albion winds for ever
Lashing with melodious wave
Many a sacred Poet's grave,
Mourn its latest nursling fled !
What though thou with all thy dead
Scarce can for this fame repay
Aught thine own, — oh, rather say
Though thy sins and slaveries foul
Overcloud a sunlike soul !
As the ghost of Homer clings
Round Scamander's wasting springs ;
As divinest Shakespeare's might
Fills Avon and the world with light
Like omniscient power, which he
Imaged 'mid mortality ;
As the love from Petrarch's urn,
Yet amid yon hills doth burn,
A quenchless lamp, by which the heart
Sees things unearthly ; so thou art,
Mighty spirit ; so shall be
The City that did refuge thee.

Lo, the sun floats up the sky
Like thought-wingèd Liberty,
Till the universal light
Seems to level plain and height ;
From the sea a mist has spread,
And the beams of morn lie dead
On the towers of Venice now,
Like its glory long ago.
By the skirts of that gray cloud

Many-domèd Padua proud
Stands, a peopled solitude,
'Mid the harvest shining plain,
Where the peasant heaps his grain
In the garner of his foe,
And the milk-white oxen slow
With the purple vintage strain,
Heaped upon the creaking wain,
That the brutal Celt may swill
Drunken sleep with savage will ;
And the sickle to the sword
Lies unchanged, though many a lord,
Like a weed whose shade is poison,
Overgrows this region's foison,
Sheaves of whom are ripe to come
To destruction's harvest home :
Men must reap the things they sow,
Force from force must ever flow,
Or worse ; but 'tis a bitter woe
That love or reason cannot change
The despot's rage, the slave's revenge.

Padua, thou within whose walls
Those mute guests at festivals,
Son and Mother, Death and Sin,
Played at dice for Ezzelin,
Till Death cried, " I win, I win!"
And Sin cursed to lose the wager,
But Death promised, to assuage her,
That he would petition for
Her to be made Vice-Emperor,
When the destined years were o'er,
Over all between the Po

And the eastern Alpine snow,
Under the mighty Austrian.
Sin smiled so as Sin only can,
And since that time, aye, long before,
Both have ruled from shore to shore,
That incestuous pair, who follow
Tyrants as the sun the swallow,
As Repentance follows Crime,
And as changes follow Time.

In thine halls the lamp of learning,
Padua, now no more is burning;
Like a meteor, whose wild way
Is lost over the grave of day,
It gleams betrayed and to betray:
Once remotest nations came
To adore that sacred flame,
When it lit not many a hearth
On this cold and gloomy earth:
Now new fires from antique light
Spring beneath the wide world's might;
But their spark lies dead in thee,
Trampled out by tyranny.
As the Norway woodman quells,
In the depth of piny dells,
One light frame among the brakes,
While the boundless forest shakes,
And its mighty trunks are torn
By the fire thus lowly born:
The spark beneath his feet is dead,
He starts to see the flames it fed
Howling through the darkened sky
With a myriad tongues victoriously,

And sinks down in fear: so thou,
O Tyranny, beholdest now
Light around thee, and thou hearest
The loud flames ascend, and fearest:
Grovel on the earth: aye, hide
In the dust thy purple pride!
Noon descends around me now:
'Tis the noon of autumn's glow,
When a soft and purple mist
Like a vaporous amethyst,
Or an air-dissolvèd star
Mingling light and fragrance, far
From the curved horizon's bound
To the point of heaven's profound,
Fills the overflowing sky;
And the plains that silent lie
Underneath, the leaves unsodden
Where the infant frost has trodden
With his morning-wingèd feet,
Whose bright print is gleaming yet;
And the red and golden vines,
Piercing with their trellised lines
The rough, dark-skirted wilderness;
The dun and bladed grass no less,
Pointing from this hoary tower
In the windless air; the flower
Glimmering at my feet; the line
Of the olive-sandalled Apennine
In the south dimly islanded;
And the Alps, whose snows are spread
High between the clouds and sun;
And of living things each one;
And my spirit which so long

Darkened this swift stream of song,
Interpenetrated lie
By the glory of the sky:
Be it love, light, harmony,
Odor, or the soul of all
Which from heaven like dew doth fall,
Or the mind which feeds this verse
Peopling the lone universe.

Noon descends, and after noon
Autumn's evening meets me soon,
Leading the infantine moon,
And that one star, which to her
Almost seems to minister
Half the crimson light she brings
From the sunset's radiant springs:
And the soft dreams of the morn,
(Which like wingèd winds had borne
To that silent isle, which lies
'Mid remembered agonies,
The frail bark of this lone being,)
Pass, to other sufferers fleeing,
And its antient pilot, Pain,
Sits beside the helm again.

Other flowering isles must be
In the sea of life and agony:
Other spirits float and flee
O'er that gulf: even now, perhaps,
On some rock the wild wave wraps,
With folded wings they waiting sit
For my bark, to pilot it
To some calm and blooming cove,

Where for me, and those I love,
May a windless bower be built,
Far from passion, pain, and guilt,
In a dell 'mid lawny hills,
Which the wild sea-murmur fills,
And soft sunshine, and the sound
Of old forests echoing round,
And the light and smell divine
Of all flowers that breathe and shine :
We may live so happy there,
That the spirits of the air,
Envying us, may even entice
To our healing paradise
The polluting multitude ;
But their rage would be subdued
By that clime divine and calm,
And the winds whose wings rain balm
On the uplifted soul, and leaves
Under which the bright sea heaves ;
While each breathless interval
In their whisperings musical
The inspirèd soul supplies
With its own deep melodies,
And the love which heals all strife
Circling, like the breath of life,
All things in that sweet abode
With its own mild brotherhood :
They, not it would change ; and soon
Every sprite beneath the moon
Would repent its envy vain,
And the earth grow young again.

October 1818.

THE WORLD'S WANDERERS.

TELL me, thou star, whose wings of light
Speed thee in thy fiery flight,
In what cavern of the night
    Will thy pinions close now?

Tell me, moon, thou pale and gray
Pilgrim of heaven's homeless way,
In what depth of night or day
    Seekest thou repose now?

Weary wind, who wanderest
Like the world's rejected guest,
Hast thou still some secret nest
    On the tree or billow?

                  1820.

TO THE MOON.

ART thou pale for weariness
Of climbing heaven and gazing on the earth,
    Wandering companionless
Among the stars that have a different birth, —
And ever changing, like a joyless eye
That finds no object worth its constancy?

                  1820.

STANZAS.

WRITTEN IN DEJECTION, NEAR NAPLES.

THE sun is warm, the sky is clear,
  The waves are dancing fast and bright,
Blue isles and snowy mountains wear
  The purple noon's transparent might,
  The breath of the moist earth is light,
Around its unexpanded buds ;
  Like many a voice of one delight,
The winds, the birds, the ocean floods,
The City's voice itself is soft like Solitude's.

I see the Deep's untrampled floor
  With green and purple seaweeds strown ;
I see the waves upon the shore,
  Like light dissolved in star-showers, thrown :
  I sit upon the sands alone,
The lightning of the noon-tide ocean
  Is flashing round me, and a tone
Arises from its measured motion,
How sweet! did any heart now share in my emotion.

Alas! I have nor hope nor health,
  Nor peace within nor calm around,
Nor that content surpassing wealth
  The sage in meditation found,
  And walked with inward glory crowned —
Nor fame, nor power, nor love, nor leisure.
  Others I see whom these surround —

Smiling they live and call life pleasure ; —
To me that cup has been dealt in another measure.

Yet now despair itself is mild,
　　Even as the winds and waters are ;
I could lie down like a tired child,
　　And weep away the life of care
　　Which I have borne and yet must bear,
Till death like sleep might steal on me,
　　And I might feel in the warm air
My cheek grow cold, and hear the sea
Breathe o'er my dying brain its last monotony.

Some might lament that I were cold,
　　As I, when this sweet day is gone,
Which my lost heart, too soon grown old,
　　Insults with this untimely moan ;
　　They might lament — for I am one
Whom men love not, — and yet regret,
　　Unlike this day, which, when the sun
Shall on its stainless glory set,
Will linger, though enjoyed, like joy in memory yet.
　　　　　　　　　　　　　　　　　1818.

A FRAGMENT.

YE gentle visitations of calm thought —
　　Moods like the memories of happier earth,
　　Which come arrayed in thoughts of little worth,
Like stars in clouds by the weak winds enwrought,
　　But that the clouds depart and stars remain,
　　While they remain, and ye, alas, depart!

THE FOREST AT EVENING.

IN silence then they took the way
Beneath the forest's solitude.
It was a vast and antique wood,
Thro' which they took their way;
And the gray shades of evening
O'er that green wilderness did fling
Still deeper solitude.
Pursuing still the path that wound
The vast and knotted trees around
Thro' which slow shades were wandering,
To a deep lawny dell they came,
To a stone seat beside a spring.
O'er which the columned wood did frame
A roofless temple, like the fane
Where, ere new creeds could faith obtain,
Man's early race once knelt beneath
The overhanging deity.
O'er this fair fountain hung the sky,
Now spangled with rare stars.   The snake,
The pale snake, that with eager breath
Creeps here his noontide thirst to slake,
Is beaming with many a mingled hue,
Shed from yon dome's eternal blue,
When he floats on that dark and lucid flood
In the light of his own loveliness;
And the birds that in the fountain dip
Their plumes, with fearless fellowship
Above and round him wheel and hover.
The fitful wind is heard to stir

One solitary leaf on high ;
The chirping of the grasshopper
Fills every pause.   There is emotion
In all that dwells at noontide here :
Then, thro' the intricate wild wood,
A maze of life and light and motion
Is woven.   But there is stillness now :
Gloom, and the trance of Nature now :
The snake is in his cave asleep ;
The birds are on the branches dreaming :
Only the shadows creep :
Only the glow-worm is gleaming :
Only the owls and the nightingales
Wake in this dell when daylight fails,
And gray shades gather in the woods :
And the owls have all fled far away
In a merrier glen to hoot and play,
For the moon is veiled and sleeping now.
The accustomed nightingale still broods
On her accustomed bough,
But she is mute ; for her false mate
Has fled and left her desolate.

Rosalind and Helen.

ITALY AND SORROW.

ALAS ! Italian winds are mild,
But my bosom is cold — wintry cold —
When the warm air weaves, among the fresh leaves,
Soft music, my poor brain is wild,
And I am weak like a nursling child
Though my soul with grief is gray and old.

THE ZUCCA.

I SAW two little dark-green leaves
Lifting the light mould at their birth, and then
I half-remembered my forgotten dream.
And day by day, green as a gourd in June,
The plant grew fresh and thick, yet no one knew
What plant it was; its stem and tendrils seemed
Like emerald snakes, mottled and diamonded
With azure mail and streaks of woven silver;
And all the sheaths that folded the dark buds
Rose like the crest of cobra-di-capel,
Until the golden eye of the bright flower
Through the dark lashes of those veinèd lids,
Disencumbered of their silent sleep,
Gazed like a star into the morning light.
Its leaves were delicate, you almost saw
The pulses
With which the purple velvet flower was fed
To overflow, and like a poet's heart
Changing bright fancy to sweet sentiment,
Changed half the light to fragrance.   It soon fell,
And to a green and dewy embryo-fruit
Left all its treasured beauty.   Day by day
I nursed the plant, and on the double flute
Played to it on the sunny winter days
Soft melodies, as sweet as April rain
On silent leaves, and sang those words in which
Passion makes Echo taunt the sleeping strings;
And I would send tales of forgotten love
Late into the lone night, and sing wild songs

Of maids deserted in the olden time,
And weep like a soft cloud in April's bosom
Upon the sleeping eyelids of the plant,
So that perhaps it dreamed that Spring was come,
And crept abroad into the moonlight air,
And loosened all its limbs, as, noon by noon,
The sun averted less his oblique beam.

INDIAN.

And the plant died not in the frost?

LADY.
                              It grew;
And went out of the lattice which I left
Half open for it, trailing its quaint spires
Along the garden and across the lawn,
And down the slope of moss and through the tufts
Of wild-flower roots, and stumps of trees o'ergrown
With simple lichens, and old hoary stones,
On to the margin of the glassy pool,
Even to a nook of unblown violets
And lilies-of-the-valley yet unborn,
Under a pine with ivy overgrown.
And there its fruit lay like a sleeping lizard
Under the shadows; but when Spring indeed
Came to unswathe her infants, and the lilies
Peeped from their bright green marks to wonder at
This shape of autumn couched in their recess,
Then it dilated, and it grew until
One half lay floating on the fountain wave,
Whose pulse, elapsed in unlike sympathies,

Kept time
Among the snowy water-lily buds.
Its shape was such as summer melody
Of the south wind in spicy vales might give
To some light cloud bound from the golden dawn
To fairy isles of evening, and it seemed
In hue and form that it had been a mirror
Of all the hues and forms around it and
Upon it pictured by the sunny beams
Which, from the bright vibrations of the pool,
Were thrown upon the rafters and the roof
Of boughs and leaves, and on the pillared stems
Of the dark sylvan temple, and reflections
Of every infant flower and star of moss
And veined leaf in the azure odorous air.
And thus it lay in the Elysian calm
Of its own beauty, floating on the line
Which, like a film in purest space, divided
The heaven beneath the water from the heaven
Above the clouds; and every day I went
Watching its growth and wondering;
And as the day grew hot, methought I saw
A glassy vapor dancing on the pool,
And on it little quaint and filmy shapes,
With dizzy motion, wheel and rise and fall,
Like clouds of gnats with perfect lineaments.

                    An Unfinished Drama.   1822.

TO A SKYLARK.

HAIL to thee, blithe spirit !
Bird thou never wert,
That from heaven, or near it,
Pourest thy full heart
In profuse strains of unpremeditated art.

Higher still and higher
From the earth thou springest
Like a cloud of fire ;
The blue deep thou wingest,
And singing still dost soar, and soaring ever singest.

In the golden lightning
Of the sunken sun,
O'er which clouds are brightning,
Thou dost float and run ;
Like an unbodied joy whose race is just begun.

The pale purple even
Melts around thy flight ;
Like a star of heaven,
In the broad day-light
Thou art unseen, but yet I hear thy shrill delight,

Keen as are the arrows
Of that silver sphere,
Whose intense lamp narrows
In the white dawn clear,
Until we hardly see, we feel that it is there.

All the earth and air
   With thy voice is loud,
As, when night is bare,
   From one lonely cloud
The moon rains out her beams, and heaven is over-
    flowed.

What thou art we know not;
   What is most like thee?
From rainbow clouds there flow not
   Drops so bright to see,
As from thy presence showers a rain of melody.

Like a poet hidden
   In the light of thought,
Singing hymns unbidden,
   Till the world is wrought
To sympathy with hopes and fears it heeded not:

Like a high-born maiden
   In a palace tower,
Soothing her love-laden
   Soul in secret hour
With music sweet as love, which overflows her bower:

Like a glow-worm golden
   In a dell of dew,
Scattering unbeholden
   Its aërial hue
Among the flowers and grass, which screen it from
    the view:

Like a rose embowered
In its own green leaves,
By warm winds deflowered,
Till the scent it gives
Makes faint with too much sweet these heavy-wingèd
thieves :

Sound of vernal showers
On the twinkling grass,
Rain-awakened flowers,
All that ever was
Joyous, and clear, and fresh, thy music doth surpass :

Teach us, sprite or bird,
What sweet thoughts are thine :
I have never heard
Praise of love or wine
That panted forth a flood of rapture so divine.

Chorus Hymenæal,
Or triumphal chaunt,
Matched with thine would be all
But an empty vaunt,
A thing wherein we feel there is some hidden want.

What objects are the fountains
Of thy happy strain?
What fields, or waves, or mountains?
What shapes of sky or plain?
What love of thine own kind? what ignorance of
pain?

With thy clear keen joyance
    Languor cannot be :
Shadow of annoyance
    Never came near thee :
Thou lovest ; but ne'er knew love's sad satiety.

Waking or asleep,
    Thou of death must deem
Things more true and deep
    Than we mortals dream,
Or how could thy notes flow in such a crystal stream?

We look before and after,
    And pine for what is not :
Our sincerest laughter
    With some pain is fraught ;
Our sweetest songs are those that tell of saddest
        thought.

Yet if we could scorn
    Hate, and pride, and fear ;
If we were things born
    Not to shed a tear,
I know not how thy joy we ever should come near.

Better than all measures
    Of delightful sound,
Better than all treasures
    That in books are found,
Thy skill to poet were, thou scorner of the ground !

Teach me half the gladness
That thy brain must know,
Such harmonious madness
From my lips would flow,
The world should listen then, as I am listening now.

1820.

————◦•◦————

THE NIGHTINGALE.

DAYLIGHT on its last purple cloud
Was lingering gray, and soon her strain
The Nightingale began ; now loud,
Climbing in circles the windless sky,
Now dying music ; suddenly
'Tis scattered in a thousand notes,
And now to the hushed ear it floats
Like field smells known in infancy,
Then failing, soothes the air again.

Rosalind and Helen.

————◦•◦————

THE WOODMAN AND THE NIGHTINGALE.

A WOODMAN whose rough heart was out of tune
(I think such hearts yet never came to good)
Hated to hear, under the stars or moon,

One nightingale in an interfluous wood
Satiate the hungry dark with melody ; —
And as a vale is watered by a flood,

Or as the moonlight fills the open sky
Struggling with darkness — as a tuberose
Peoples some Indian dell with scents which lie

Like clouds above the flower from which they rose,
The singing of that happy nightingale
In this sweet forest, from the golden close

Of evening, till the star of dawn may fail,
Was interfused upon the silentness ;
The folded roses and the violets pale

Heard her within their slumbers, the abyss
Of heaven with all its planets ; the dull ear
Of the night-cradled earth ; the loneliness

Of the circumfluous waters, — every sphere
And every flower and beam and cloud and wave,
And every wind of the mute atmosphere,

And every beast stretched in its rugged cave,
And every bird lulled on its mossy bough,
And every silver moth fresh from the grave,

Which is its cradle — ever from below
Aspiring like one who loves too fair, too far,
To be consumed within the purest glow

Of one serene and unapproachèd star,
As if it were a lamp of earthly light,
Unconscious, as some human lovers are,

Itself how low, how high beyond all height
The heaven where it would perish ! — and every form
That worshipped in the temple of the night

Was awed into delight, and by the charm
Girt as with an interminable zone,
Whilst that sweet bird, whose music was a storm

Of sound, shook forth the dull oblivion
Out of their dreams; harmony became love
In every soul but one.

. . . . . .

And so this man returned with axe and saw
At evening close from killing the tall treen,
The soul of whom by nature's gentle law

Was each a wood-nymph, and kept ever green
The pavement and the roof of the wild copse,
Chequering the sunlight of the blue serene

With jaggèd leaves, — and from the forest tops
Singing the winds to sleep — or weeping oft
Fast showers of aërial water drops

Into their mother's bosom, sweet and soft,
Nature's pure tears which have no bitterness; —
Around the cradles of the birds aloft

They spread themselves into the loveliness
Of fan-like leaves, and over pallid flowers
Hang like moist clouds:— or, where high branches
    kiss,

Make a green space among the silent bowers,
Like a vast fane in a metropolis,
Surrounded by the columns and the towers

All overwrought with branch-like traceries
In which there is religion — and the mute
Persuasion of unkindled melodies,

Odors and gleams and murmurs, which the lute
Of the blind pilot-spirit of the blast
Stirs as it sails, now grave and now acute,

Wakening the leaves and waves, ere it has past
To such brief unison as on the brain
One tone, which never can recur, has cast,

One accent never to return again.

    .   .   .   .   .   .

The world is full of Woodmen who expel
Love's gentle Dryads from the haunts of life,
And vex the nightingales in every dell.

                                 1818.

THE TOWER OF FAMINE.

AMID the desolation of a city,
Which was the cradle, and is now the grave
Of an extinguished people; so that pity

Weeps o'er the shipwrecks of oblivion's wave,
There stands the Tower of Famine.   It is built
Upon some prison homes, whose dwellers rave

For bread, and gold, and blood: pain, linked to guilt,
Agitates the light flame of their hours,
Until its vital oil is spent or spilt:

There stands the pile, a tower amid the towers
And sacred domes; each marble-ribbèd roof,
The brazen-gated temples, and the bowers

Of solitary wealth ; the tempest-proof
Pavilions of the dark Italian air,
Are by its presence dimmed — they stand aloof,

And are withdrawn — so that the world is bare,
As if a spectre wrapt in shapeless terror
Amid a company of ladies fair

Should glide and glow, till it became a mirror
Of all their beauty, and their hair and hue,
The life of their sweet eyes, with all its error,
Should be absorbed, till they to marble grew.

1820.

———◆◆◆———

EVENING.

PONTE A MARE, PISA.

THE sun is set ; the swallows are asleep ;
  The bats are flitting fast in the gray air ;
The slow soft toads out of damp corners creep,
  And evening's breath, wandering here and there
Over the quivering surface of the stream,
Wakes not one ripple from its summer dream.

There is no dew on the dry grass to-night,
  Nor damp within the shadow of the trees ;
The wind is intermitting, dry, and light ;
  And in the inconstant motion of the breeze
The dust and straws are driven up and down,
And whirled about the pavement of the town.

Within the surface of the fleeting river
  The wrinkled image of the city lay,
Immovably unquiet, and for ever
  It trembles, but it never fades away;
Go to the . . .
You, being changed, will find it then as now.

The chasm in which the sun has sunk is shut
  By darkest barriers of cinereous cloud,
Like mountain over mountain huddled — but
  Growing and moving upwards in a crowd,
And over it a space of watery blue,
Which the keen evening star is shining through.

                                        1821.

AND, like a dying lady, lean and pale,
Who totters forth, wrapt in a gauzy veil,
Out of her chamber, led by the insane
And feeble wanderings of her fading brain,
The moon arose up in the murky east,
A white and shapeless mass.

                                        1820.

WHEN soft winds and sunny skies
With the green earth harmonize,
And the young and dewy dawn,
Bold as an unhunted fawn,
Up the windless heaven is gone,—
Laugh — for ambushed in the day,
Clouds and whirlwinds watch their prey.

                                        1821.

Poems of Pure Nature.

PASSAGE OF THE APENNINES.

Listen, listen, Mary mine,
To the whisper of the Apennine,
It bursts on the roof like the thunder's roar,
Or like the sea on a northern shore,
Heard in its raging ebb and flow
By the captives pent in the cave below.
The Apennine in the light of day
Is a mighty mountain dim and gray,
Which between the earth and sky doth lay;
But when night comes, a chaos dread
On the dim starlight then is spread,
And the Apennine walks abroad with the storm.

1818.

THE CLOUD.

I bring fresh showers for the thirsting flowers,
    From the seas and the streams;
I bear light shade for the leaves when laid
    In their noon-day dreams.
From my wings are shaken the dews that waken
    The sweet buds every one,

When rocked to rest on their mother's breast,
    As she dances about the sun.
I wield the flail of the lashing hail,
    And whiten the green plains under,
And then again I dissolve it in rain,
    And laugh as I pass in thunder.

I sift the snow on the mountains below,
    And their great pines groan aghast;
And all the night 'tis my pillow white,
    While I sleep in the arms of the blast.
Sublime on the towers of my skiey bowers,
    Lightning my pilot sits,
In a cavern under is fettered the thunder,
    It struggles and howls at fits;
Over earth and ocean, with gentle motion,
    This pilot is guiding me,
Lured by the love of the genii that move
    In the depths of the purple sea;
Over the rills, and the crags, and the hills,
    Over the lakes and the plains,
Wherever he dream, under mountain or stream,
    The Spirit he loves remains;
And I all the while bask in heaven's blue smile,
    Whilst he is dissolving in rains.

The sanguine sunrise, with his meteor eyes,
    And his burning plumes outspread,
Leaps on the back of my sailing rack,
    When the morning star shines dead,
As on the jag of a mountain crag,
    Which an earthquake rocks and swings,

An eagle alit one moment may sit
    In the light of its golden wings.
And when Sunset may breathe, from the lit sea
    beneath,
    Its ardors of rest and of love,
And the crimson pall of eve may fall
    From the depth of heaven above,
With wings folded I rest, on mine airy nest,
    As still as a brooding dove.

That orbèd maiden with white fire laden,
    Whom mortals call the moon,
Glides glimmering o'er my fleece-like floor,
    By the midnight breezes strewn;
And wherever the beat of her unseen feet,
    Which only the angels hear,
May have broken the woof of my tent's thin roof,
    The stars peep behind her and peer;
And I laugh to see them whirl and flee,
    Like a swarm of golden bees,
When I widen the rent in my wind-built tent,
    Till the calm rivers, lakes, and seas,
Like strips of the sky fallen through me on high,
    Are each paved with the moon and these.

I bind the sun's throne with a burning zone,
    And the moon's with a girdle of pearl;
The volcanos are dim, and the stars reel and swim,
    When the whirlwinds my banner unfurl.
From cape to cape, with a bridge-like shape,
    Over a torrent sea,
Sunbeam-proof, I hang like a roof,
    The mountains its columns be.

The triumphal arch through which I march
    With hurricane, fire and snow,
When the powers of the air are chained to my chair,
    Is the million-colored bow;
The sphere-fire above its soft colors wove,
    While the moist earth was laughing below.

I am the daughter of earth and water,
    And the nursling of the sky;
I pass through the pores of the ocean and shores;
    I change, but I cannot die.
For after the rain when with never a stain,
    The pavilion of heaven is bare,
And the winds and sunbeams with their convex
    gleams,
    Build up the blue dome of air,
I silently laugh at my own cenotaph,
    And out of the caverns of rain,
Like a child from the womb, like a ghost from the
    tomb,
    I arise and unbuild it again.

                    1820.

THE DAWN.

The pale stars are gone!
For the sun, their swift shepherd,
To their folds them compelling.
In the depths of the dawn,
Hastes, in meteor-eclipsing array, and they flee
    Beyond his blue dwelling,
    As fawns flee the leopard.
               Prom. Unbound.

DAWN AND DESIRE.

My coursers are fed with the lightning,
　They drink of the whirlwind's stream,
And when the red morning is bright'ning
　They bathe in the fresh sunbeam ;
　They have strength for their swiftness I deem.

I desire : and their speed makes night kindle ;
　I fear : they outstrip the Typhoon ;
Ere the cloud piled on Atlas can dwindle　.
　We encircle the earth and the moon :
　We shall rest from long labors at noon.

' On the brink of the night and the morning
　My coursers are wont to respire ;
But the Earth has just whispered a warning
　That their flight must be swifter than fire :
　They shall drink the hot speed of desire !
　　　　　　　　　　Prom. Unbound.

TWILIGHT AND DESIRE.

The young moon has fed
　Her exhausted horn
　　With the sunset's fire :
The weak day is dead,
　But the night is not born ;
And, like loveliness panting with wild desire
　While it trembles with fear and delight,

Hesperus flies from awakening night,
And pants in its beauty and speed with light
    Fast-flashing, soft, and bright.
Thou beacon of love! thou lamp of the free!
    Guide us far, far away,
To climes where now veiled by the ardor of day
    Thou art hidden
    From waves on which weary noon,
    Faints in her summer swoon,
Between Kingless continents sinless as Eden,
Around mountains and islands inviolably
    Prankt on the sapphire sea.
                  Hellas.

ALL SUSTAINING LOVE.

THOU art the wine whose drunkenness is all
We can desire, O Love! and happy souls,
Ere from thy vine the leaves of autumn fall,

Catch thee, and feed from their o'erflowing bowls
Thousands who thirst for thy ambrosial dew; —
Thou art the radiance which where ocean rolls

Investest it; and when the heavens are blue
Thou fillest them; and when the earth is fair
The shadow of thy moving wings imbue

Its deserts and its mountains, till they wear
Beauty like some bright robe; — thou ever soarest
Among the towers of men, and as soft air

In spring, which moves the unawakened forest,
Clothing with leaves its branches bare and bleak,
Thou floatest among men; and aye implorest

That which from thee they should implore : — the weak
Alone kneel to thee, offering up the hearts
The strong have broken — yet where shall any seek

A garment whom thou clothest not?
Prince Athanase.   1817.

————●◇●————

SONG OF SPIRITS.

" Where there is one pervading, one alone."

To the deep, to the deep,
            Down, down !
Through the shade of sleep,
Through the cloudy strife
Of Death and of Life ;
Through the veil and the bar
Of things which seem and are
Even to the steps of the remotest throne,
            Down, down !

While the sound whirls around,
            Down, down !
As the fawn draws the hound,
As the lightning the vapor,
As a weak moth the taper ;
Death, despair ; love, sorrow ;
Time both ; to-day, to-morrow ;
As steel obeys the spirit of the stone,
            Down, down !

Through the gray, void abysm,
                    Down, down !
Where the air is no prism,
And the moon and stars are not,
And the cavern-crags wear not
The radiance of Heaven,
Nor the gloom to Earth given,
Where there is one pervading, one alone,
                    Down, down !

In the depth of the deep
                    Down, down !
Like veiled lightning asleep,
Like the spark nursed in embers,
The last look Love remembers,
Like a diamond, which shines
On the dark wealth of mines,
A spell is treasured but for thee alone.
                    Down, down !
                              Prom. Unbound.

—•◦•—

HYMN TO ASIA.

That light whose smile kindles the Universe,
That Beauty in which all things work and move.
                              ADONAIS, LIV.

LIFE of Life ! thy lips enkindle
   With their love the breath between them ;
And thy smiles before they dwindle
   Make the cold air fire ; then screen them
In those looks, where whoso gazes
Faints, entangled in their mazes.

Child of Light ! thy limbs are burning
  Thro' the vest which seems to hide them ;
As the radiant lines of morning
  Thro' the clouds ere they divide them ;
And this atmosphere divinest
Shrouds thee wheresoe'er thou shinest.

Fair are others ; none beholds thee,
  But thy voice sounds low and tender
Like the fairest, for it folds thee
  From the sight, that liquid splendor,
And all feel, yet see thee never,
As I feel now, lost for ever !

Lamp of Earth ! where'er thou movest
  Its dim shapes are clad with brightness,
And the souls of whom thou lovest
  Walk upon the winds with lightness,
Till they fail, as I am failing,
Dizzy, lost, yet unbewailing !

ASIA ANSWERS.

My soul is an enchanted boat,
  Which, like a sleeping swan, doth float
Upon the silver waves of thy sweet singing ;
  And thine doth like an angel sit
  Beside a helm conducting it,
Whilst all the winds with melody are ringing.
  It seems to float ever, forever,
  Upon that many-winding river,
  Between mountains, woods, abysses,
  A paradise of wildernesses !

Till, like one in slumber bound,
Borne to the ocean, I float down, around,
Into a sea profound, of ever-spreading sound.

———•◦•———

ECHO SONG TO ASIA.

ECHOES (*unseen*).

ECHOES we: listen!
  We cannot stay:
As dew-stars glisten
  Then fade away —
    Child of Ocean!

O, follow, follow!
  As our voice recedeth
Thro' the caverns hollow,
  Where the forest spreadeth;

(*More distant.*)

  O, follow, follow!
Thro' the caverns hollow,
As the song floats thou pursue,
Where the wild bee never flew,
Thro' the noon-tide darkness deep,
By the odor-breathing sleep
Of faint night-flowers, and the waves
At the fountain-lighted caves,
While our music, wild and sweet,
Mocks thy gently falling feet,
    Child of Ocean!

Prom. Unbound.

THE SPIRITS OF THE EARTH AND
THE MOON.

IONE.

> EVEN whilst we speak
New notes arise. What is that awful sound?

PANTHEA.

'Tis the deep music of the rolling world
Kindling within the strings of the waved air,
Æolian modulations.

IONE.

> Listen too,
How every pause is filled with under-notes,
Clear, silver, icy, keen, awakening tones,
Which pierce the sense, and live within the soul,
As the sharp stars pierce winter's crystal air
And gaze upon themselves within the sea.

PANTHEA.

But see where through two openings in the forest
Which hanging branches overcanopy,
And where two runnels of a rivulet,
Between the close moss violet-inwoven,
Have made their path of melody, like sisters
Who part with sighs that they may meet in smiles,
Turning their dear disunion to an isle
Of lovely grief, a wood of sweet sad thoughts ;

Two visions of strange radiance float upon
The ocean-like enchantment of strong sound,
Which flows intenser, keener, deeper yet
Under the ground and through the windless air.

IONE.

I see a chariot like that thinnest boat,
In which the mother of the months is borne
By ebbing night into her western cave,
When she upsprings from interlunar dreams,
O'er which is curved an orblike canopy
Of gentle darkness, and the hills and woods
Distinctly seen through that dusk airy veil,
Regard like shapes in an enchanter's glass ;
Its wheels are solid clouds, azure and gold,
Such as the genii of the thunder-storm
Pile on the floor of the illumined sea
When the sun rushes under it ; they roll
And move and grow as with an inward wind ;
Within it sits a wingèd infant, white
Its countenance, like the whiteness of bright snow,
Its plumes are as feathers of sunny frost,
Its limbs gleam white, through the wind-flowing folds
Of its white robe, woof of etherial pearl.
Its hair is white, the brightness of white light
Scattered in strings ; yet its two eyes are heavens
Of liquid darkness, which the Deity
Within seems pouring, as a storm is poured
From jaggèd clouds, out of their arrowy lashes,
Tempering the cold and radiant air around,
With fire that is not brightness ; in its hand

It sways a quivering moon-beam, from whose point
A guiding power directs the chariot's prow
Over its wheelèd clouds, which as they roll
Over the grass, and flowers, and waves, wake sounds,
Sweet as a singing rain of silver dew.

PANTHEA.

And from the other opening in the wood
Rushes, with loud and whirlwind harmony,
A sphere, which is as many thousand spheres,
Solid as crystal, yet through all its mass
Flow, as through empty space, music and light:
Ten thousand orbs involving and involved,
Purple and azure, white, and green, and golden,
Sphere within sphere; and every space between
Peopled with unimaginable shapes,
Such as ghosts dream dwell in the lampless deep,
Yet each inter-transpicuous, and they whirl
Over each other with a thousand motions,
Upon a thousand sightless axles spinning,
And with the force of self-destroying swiftness,
Intensely, slowly, solemnly roll on,
Kindling with mingled sounds, and many tones,
Intelligible words and music wild.
With mighty whirl the multitudinous orb
Grinds the bright brook into an azure mist
Of elemental subtlety, like light;
And the wild odor of the forest flowers,
The music of the living grass and air,
The emerald light of leaf-entangled beams
Round its intense yet self-conflicting speed,

Seem kneaded into one aërial mass
Which drowns the sense.   Within the orb itself,
Pillowed upon its alabaster arms,
Like to a child o'erwearied with sweet toil,
On its own folded wings, and wavy hair,
The Spirit of the Earth is laid asleep,
And you can see its little lips are moving,
Amid the changing light of their own smiles,
Like one who talks of what he loves in dream.

IONE.

'Tis only mocking the orb's harmony.

PANTHEA.

And from a star upon its forehead, shoot,
Like swords of azure fire, or golden spears
With tyrant-quelling myrtle overtwined,
Embleming heaven and earth united now,
Vast beams like spokes of some invisible wheel
Which whirl as the orb whirls, swifter than thought
Filling the abyss with sun-like lightnings,
And perpendicular now, and now transverse,
Pierce the dark soil, and as they pierce and pass,
Make bare the secrets of the earth's deep heart;
Infinite mine of adamant and gold,
Valueless stones, and unimagined gems,
And caverns on crystalline columns poised
With vegetable silver overspread;
Wells of unfathomed fire, and water, springs
Whence the great sea, even as a child is fed,
Whose vapors clothe earth's monarch mountain-tops
With kingly, ermine snow.   The beams flash on

And make appear the melancholy ruins
Of cancelled cycles ; anchors, beaks of ships ;
Planks turned to marble ; quivers, helms, and spears,
And gorgon-headed targes, and the wheels
Of scythèd chariots, and the emblazonry
Of trophies, standards, and armorial beasts,
Round which death laughed, sepulchred emblems
Of dead destruction, ruin within ruin !
The wrecks beside of many a city vast,
Whose population which the earth grew over
Was mortal, but not human ; see, they lie,
Their monstrous works, and uncouth skeletons,
Their statues, homes and fanes ; prodigious shapes
Huddled in gray annihilation, split,
Jammed in the hard, black deep ; and over these,
The anatomies of unknown wingèd things,
And fishes which were isles of living scale,
And serpents, bony chains, twisted around
The iron crags, or within heaps of dust
To which the tortuous strength of their last pangs
Had crushed the iron crags ; and over these
The jaggèd alligator, and the might
Of earth-convulsing behemoth, which once
Were monarch beasts, and on the slimy shores,
And weed-overgrown continents of earth,
Increased and multiplied like summer worms
On an abandoned corpse, till the blue globe
Wrapt deluge round it like a cloke, and they
Yelled, gasped, and were abolished ; or some God
Whose throne was in a comet, past, and cried,
Be not ! And like my words they were no more.

Prom. Unbound.

THE MOON AND THE EARTH.

THE MOON.

BROTHER mine, calm wanderer,
Happy globe of land and air,
Some Spirit is darted like a beam from thee,
    Which penetrates my frozen frame,
    And passes with the warmth of flame
With love, and odor, and deep melody
    Through me, through me !

.   .   .   .   .   .

The snow upon my lifeless mountains
Is loosened into living fountains,
My solid oceans flow, and sing, and shine:
    A spirit from my heart bursts forth,
    It clothes with unexpected birth
My cold bare bosom: Oh! it must be thine
        On mine, on mine !

Gazing on thee I feel, I know
Green stalks burst forth, and bright flowers grow,
And living shapes upon my bosom move:
    Music is in the sea and air,
    Wingèd clouds soar here and there,
Dark with the rain new buds are dreaming of:
        'Tis Love, all Love!

THE EARTH.

It interpenetrates my granite mass,
Through tangled roots and trodden clay doth
    pass

Into the utmost leaves and delicatest flowers;
   Upon the winds, among the clouds 'tis spread,
   It wakes a life in the forgotten dead,
They breathe a spirit up from their obscurest bowers.

   .   .   .   .   .   .

THE MOON.

   The shadow of white death has past
   From my path in heaven at last,
A clinging shroud of solid frost and sleep;
   And through my newly-woven bowers,
   Wander happy paramours,
Less mighty, but as mild as those who keep
   Thy vales more deep.

THE EARTH.

   As the dissolving warmth of dawn may fold
   A half unfrozen dew-globe, green, and gold,
And crystalline, till it becomes a wingèd mist,
   And wanders up the vault of the blue day,
   Outlives the noon, and on the sun's last ray
Hangs o'er the sea, a fleece of fire and amethyst —

THE MOON.

   Thou art folded, thou art lying
   In the light which is undying
Of thine own joy, and heaven's smile divine;
   All suns and constellations shower
   On thee a light, a life, a power
Which doth array thy sphere; thou pourest thine
   On mine, on mine!

THE EARTH.

I spin beneath my pyramid of night,
Which points into the heavens dreaming delight,
Murmuring victorious joy in my enchanted sleep;
    As a youth lulled in love-dreams faintly sighing,
    Under the shadow of his beauty lying,
Which round his rest a watch of light and warmth
        doth keep.

THE MOON.

As in the soft and sweet eclipse,
When soul meets soul on lovers' lips,
High hearts are calm, and brightest eyes are dull;
    So when thy shadow falls on me,
    Then am I mute and still, by thee
Covered; of thy love, Orb most beautiful,
        Full, oh, too full!

Thou art speeding round the sun
Brightest world of many a one;
Green and azure sphere which shinest
With a light which is divinest
Among all the lamps of Heaven
To whom life and light is given;
I, thy crystal paramour
Borne beside thee by a power
Like the polar Paradise,
Magnet-like of lovers' eyes;
I, a most enamoured maiden
Whose weak brain is overladen
With the pleasure of her love,

Maniac-like around thee move
Gazing, an insatiate bride,
On thy form from every side
Like a Mænad, round the cup
Which Agave lifted up
In the weird Cadmæan forest.
Brother, wheresoe'er thou soarest
I must hurry, whirl and follow
Through the heavens wide and hollow,
Sheltered by the warm embrace
Of thy soul from hungry space,
Drinking from thy sense and sight
Beauty, majesty, and might,
As a lover or cameleon
Grows like what it looks upon,
As a violet's gentle eye
Gazes on the azure sky
Until its hue grows like what it beholds,
As a gray and watery mist
Glows like solid amethyst
Athwart the western mountain it enfolds,
When the sunset sleeps
Upon its snow —

THE EARTH.

And the weak day weeps
That it should be so.
Oh, gentle Moon, the voice of thy delight
Falls on me like thy clear and tender light
Soothing the seaman, borne the summer night,
Through isles for ever calm.

Prom. Unbound.

THE MUSIC OF THE WOODS.

SEMICHORUS I. OF SPIRITS.

THE path thro' which that lovely twain
    Have past, by cedar, pine, and yew,
    And each dark tree that ever grew,
    Is curtained out from Heaven's wide blue,
Nor sun, nor moon, nor wind, nor rain,
      Can pierce its interwoven bowers,
    Nor aught, save where some cloud of dew,
Drifted along the earth-creeping breeze,
Between the trunks of the hoar trees,
      Hangs each a pearl in the pale flowers
Of the green laurel, blown anew;
And bends, and then fades silently,
One frail and fair anemone:
Or when some star of many a one
• That climbs and wanders thro' steep night,
Has found the cleft thro' which alone
Beams fall from high those depths upon
Ere it is borne away, away,
By the swift Heavens that cannot stay,
It scatters drops of golden light,
Like lines of rain that ne'er unite:
And the gloom divine is all around;
And underneath is the mossy ground.

SEMICHORUS II.

There the voluptuous nightingales,
    Are awake thro' all the broad noon-day.
When one with bliss or sadness fails.

And thro' the windless ivy-boughs,
  Sick with sweet love, droops dying away
On its mate's music-panting bosom;
Another from the swinging blossom,
  Watching to catch the languid close
Of the last strain, then lifts on high
The wings of the weak melody,
'Till some new strain of feeling bear
  The song, and all the woods are mute;
When there is heard thro' the dim air
The rush of wings, and rising there
  Like many a lake-surrounded flute,
Sounds overflow the listener's brain
So sweet, that joy is almost pain.

SEMICHORUS I.

There those enchanted eddies play
  Of echoes, music-tongued, which draw,
  By Demogorgon's mighty law,
  With melting rapture, or sweet awe,
All spirits on that secret way;
  As inland boats are driven to Ocean
Down streams made strong with mountain-thaw:
  And first there comes a gentle sound
  To those in talk or slumber bound,
  And wakes the destined. Soft emotion
Attracts, impels them: those who saw
  Say from the breathing earth behind
  There steams a plume-uplifting wind
Which drives them on their path, while they
  Believe their own swift wings and feet

The sweet desires within obey:
And so they float upon their way,
Until, still sweet, but loud and strong,
The storm of sound is driven along,
    Sucked up and hurrying: as they fleet
    Behind, its gathering billows meet
And to the fatal mountain bear
Like clouds amid the yielding air.

First Faun.

Canst thou imagine where those spirits live
Which make such delicate music in the woods?
We haunt within the least frequented caves
And closest coverts, and we know these wilds,
Yet never meet them, tho' we hear them oft:
Where may they hide themselves?

Second Faun.

                'Tis hard to tell:
I have heard those more skilled in spirits say,
The bubbles, which the enchantment of the sun
Sucks from the pale faint water-flowers that pave
The oozy bottom of clear lakes and pools.
Are the pavilions where such dwell and float
Under the green and golden atmosphere
Which noontide kindles thro' the woven leaves;
And when these burst, and the thin fiery air,
The which they breathed within those lucent domes,
Ascends to flow like meteors thro' the night,
They ride on them, and rein their headlong speed,

And bow their burning crests, and glide in fire
Under the waters of the earth again.

FIRST FAUN.

If such live thus, have others other lives,
Under pink blossoms or within the bells
Of meadow flowers, or folded violets deep,
Or on their dying odors, when they die,
Or in the sunlight of the spherèd dew?

SECOND FAUN.

Aye, many more which we may well divine.
But, should we stay to speak, noontide would come,
And thwart Silenus find his goats undrawn,
And grudge to sing those wise and lovely songs
Of fate, and chance, and God, and Chaos old,
And Love, and the chained Titan's woful doom,
And how he shall be loosed, and make the earth
One brotherhood: delightful strains which cheer
Our solitary twilights, and which charm
To silence the unenvying nightingales.

Prom. Unbound. 1819.

Classic Poems of Nature.

HYMN OF APOLLO.

THE sleepless Hours who watch me as I lie,
   Curtained with star-inwoven tapestries,
From the broad moonlight of the sky,
   Fanning the busy dreams from my dim eyes, —
Waken me when their Mother, the gray Dawn,
Tells them that dreams and that the moon is gone.

Then I arise, and climbing Heaven's blue dome,
   I walk over the mountains and the waves,
Leaving my robe upon the ocean foam;
   My footsteps pave the clouds with fire; the caves
Are filled with my bright presence, and the air
Leaves the green earth to my embraces bare.

The sunbeams are my shafts, with which I kill
   Deceit, that loves the night and fears the day;
All men who do or even imagine ill
   Fly me, and from the glory of my ray
Good minds and open actions take new might,
Until diminished by the reign of night.

I feed the clouds, the rainbows and the flowers
  With their etherial colors; the Moon's globe
And the pure stars in their eternal bowers
  Are cinctured with my power as with a robe:
Whatever lamps on Earth or Heaven may shine,
Are portions of one power, which is mine.

I stand at noon upon the peak of Heaven,
  Then with unwilling steps I wander down
Into the clouds of the Atlantic even;
  For grief that I depart they weep and frown:
What look is more delightful than the smile
With which I soothe them from the western isle?

I am the eye with which the Universe
  Beholds itself and knows itself divine;
All harmony of instrument or verse,
  All prophecy, all medicine are mine,
All light of art or nature; — to my song,
Victory and praise in their own right belong.

                      1820.

———◦•◦———

HYMN OF PAN.

  FROM the forests and highlands
    We come, we come;
  From the river-girt islands,
    Where loud waves are dumb
      Listening to my sweet pipings.
  The wind in the reeds and the rushes,
    The bees on the bells of thyme,

The birds on the myrtle bushes,
    The cicale above in the lime,
And the lizards below in the grass,
Were as silent as ever old Tmolus was,
        Listening to my sweet pipings.

Liquid Peneus was flowing,
    And all dark Tempe lay
In Pelion's shadow, outgrowing
    The light of the dying day,
        Speeded by my sweet pipings.
The Sileni, and Sylvans, and Fauns,
    And the Nymphs of the woods and waves,
To the edge of the moist river-lawns,
    And the brink of the dewy caves,
And all that did then attend and follow
Were silent with love, as you now, Apollo,
        With envy of my sweet pipings.

'   I sang of the dancing stars,
        I sang of the dædal Earth,
And of Heaven — and the giant wars,
    . And Love, and Death, and Birth, —
        And then I changed my pipings, —
Singing how down the vale of Mænalus
    I pursued a maiden and clasped a reed :
Gods and men, we are all deluded thus !
    It breaks in our bosom and then we bleed :
All wept, as I think both ye now would.
If envy or age had not frozen your blood,
        At the sorrow of my sweet pipings.
                                    1820.

THE BIRTH OF PLEASURE.

AT the creation of the Earth
Pleasure, that divinest birth,
From the soil of Heaven did rise,
Wrapt in sweet wild melodies —
Like an exhalation wreathing
To the sound of air low-breathing
Through Æolian pines, which make
A shade and shelter to the lake
Whence it rises soft and slow;
Her life breathing [limbs] did flow
In the harmony divine
Of an ever-lengthening line
Which enwrapt her perfect form
With a beauty clear and warm.

1819.

ARETHUSA.

ARETHUSA arose
From her couch of snows
In the Acroceraunian mountains, —
From cloud and from crag,
With many a jag,
Shepherding her bright fountains.
She leapt down the rocks,
With her rainbow locks
Streaming among the streams; —

Her steps paved with green
The downward ravine
Which slopes to the western gleams:
And gliding and springing
She went, ever singing,
In murmurs as soft as sleep;
The Earth seemed to love her,
And Heaven smiled above her,
As she lingered towards the deep.

Then Alpheus bold,
On his glacier cold,
With his trident the mountains strook.;
And opened a chasm
In the rocks; — with the spasm
All Erymanthus shook.
And the black south wind
It concealed behind
The urns of the silent snow,
And earthquake and thunder
Did rend in sunder
The bars of the springs below:
The beard and the hair
Of the River-god were
Seen through the torrent's sweep,
As he followed the light
Of the fleet nymph's flight
To the brink of the Dorian deep.

"Oh, save me! Oh, guide me!
And bid the deep hide me,
For he grasps me now by the hair!"

The loud Ocean heard,
To its blue depth stirred,
And divided at her prayer;
And under the water
The Earth's white daughter
Fled like a sunny beam;
Behind her descended
Her billows, unblended
With the brackish Dorian stream: —
Like a gloomy stain
On the emerald main
Alpheus rushed behind, —
As an eagle pursuing
A dove to its ruin
Down the streams of the cloudy wind.

Under the bowers
Where the Ocean Powers
Sit on their pearlèd thrones,
Through the coral woods
Of the weltering floods,
Over heaps of unvalued stones;
Through the dim beams
Which amid the streams
Weave a network of colored light;
And under the caves,
Where the shadowy waves
Are as green as the forest's night: —
Outspeeding the shark,
And the sword-fish dark,
Under the ocean foam,
And up through the rifts

Of the mountain clifts
They past to their Dorian home.

And now from their fountains
In Enna's mountains,
Down one vale where the morning basks,
Like friends once parted
Grown single-hearted,
They ply their watery tasks.
At sunrise they leap
From their cradles steep
In the cave of the shelving hill;
At noon-tide they flow
Through the woods below
And the meadows of Asphodel;
And at night they sleep
In the rocking deep
Beneath the Ortygian shore;—
Like spirits that lie
In the azure sky
When they love but live no more.

1820.

———◦◦◦———

SONG OF PROSERPINE.

WHILE GATHERING FLOWERS ON THE PLAIN OF ENNA.

SACRED Goddess, Mother Earth,
Thou from whose immortal bosom,
Gods, and men, and beasts have birth,
Leaf and blade, and bud and blossom,

Breathe thine influence most divine
On thine own child, Proserpine.

If with mists of evening dew
   Thou dost nourish these young flowers
Till they grow. in scent and hue,
   Fairest children of the hours,
Breathe thine influence most divine
On thine own child, Proserpine.

                    1820.

Poems of Home Life.

TO MARY SHELLEY.

O Mary dear, that you were here
With your brown eyes bright and clear,
And your sweet voice, like a bird
Singing love to its lone mate
In the ivy bower disconsolate;
Voice the sweetest ever heard!
And your brow more . . .
Than the   sky
Of this azure Italy.
Mary dear, come to me soon,
I am not well whilst thou art far;
As sunset to the spherèd moon,
As twilight to the western star,
Thou, belovèd, art to me.

O Mary dear, that you were here;
The Castle echo whispers "Here!"

1818.

TO WILLIAM SHELLEY.

(With what truth I may say —
Roma! Roma! Roma!
Non è più come era prima!)

My lost William, thou in whom
   Some bright spirit lived, and did

That decaying robe consume
  Which its lustre faintly hid,
Here its ashes find a tomb,
  But beneath this pyramid
Thou art not — if a thing divine
Like thee can die, thy funeral shrine
Is thy mother's grief and mine.

Where art thou, my gentle child?
  Let me think thy spirit feeds,
With its life intense and mild,
  The love of living leaves and weeds,
Among these tombs and ruins wild ; —
  Let me think that through low seeds
Of the sweet flowers and sunny grass,
Into their hues and scents may pass
A portion ———

                                1819.

TO WILLIAM SHELLEY.

THY little footsteps on the sands
  Of a remote and lonely shore ;
The twinkling of thine infant hands,
  Where now the worm will feed no more :
Thy mingled look of love and glee
When we returned to gaze on thee.

LETTER TO MARIA GISBORNE.

LEGHORN, *July* 1, 1820.

THE spider spreads her webs, whether she be
In poet's tower, cellar, or barn, or tree ;
The silkworm in the dark green mulberry leaves
His winding sheet and cradle ever weaves ;
So I, a thing whom moralists call worm,
Sit spinning still round this decaying form,
From the fine threads of rare and subtle thought —
No net of words in garish colors wrought
To catch the idle buzzers of the day —
But a soft cell, where when that fades away,
Memory may clothe in wings my living name
And feed it with the asphodels of fame,
Which in those hearts which must remember me
Grow, making love an immortality.

Whoever should behold me now, I wist,
Would think I were a mighty mechanist,
Bent with sublime Archimedean art
To breathe a soul into the iron heart
Of some machine portentous, or strange gin,
Which by the force of figured spells might win
Its way over the sea, and sport therein ;
For round the walls are hung dread engines, such
As Vulcan never wrought for Jove to clutch
Ixion or the Titan ; — or the quick
Wit of that man of God, St. Dominic,
To convince Atheist, Turk, or Heretic,
Or those in philanthropic council met,

Who thought to pay some interest for the debt
They owed to Jesus Christ for their salvation,
By giving a faint foretaste of damnation
To Shakespeare, Sidney, Spenser and the rest
Who made our land an island of the blest,
When lamp-like Spain, who now relumes her fire
On Freedom's hearth, grew dim with Empire : —
With thumbscrews, wheels, with tooth and spike and
    jag,
Which fishers found under the utmost crag
Of Cornwall and the storm-encompassed isles,
Where to the sky the rude sea rarely smiles
Unless in treacherous wrath, as on the morn
When the exulting elements in scorn
Satiated with destroyed destruction, lay
Sleeping in beauty on their mangled prey,
As panthers sleep ; — and other strange and dread
Magical forms the brick floor overspread ——
Proteus transformed to metal did not make
More figures, or more strange ; nor did he take
Such shapes of unintelligible brass,
Or heap himself in such a horrid mass
Of tin and iron not to be understood ;
And forms of unimaginable wood,
To puzzle Tubal Cain and all his brood :
Great screws, and cones, and wheels, and groovèd
    blocks,
The elements of what will stand the shocks
Of wave and wind and time. — Upon the table
More knacks and quips there be than I am able
To catalogize in this verse of mine : —
A pretty bowl of wood — not full of wine,

But quicksilver; that dew which the gnomes drink
When at their subterranean toil they swink,
Pledging the demons of the earthquake, who
Reply to them in lava — cry halloo !
And call out to the cities o'er their head, —
Roofs, towers and shrines, the dying and the dead,
Crash through the chinks of earth — and then all
    quaff
Another rouse, and hold their sides and laugh.
This quicksilver no gnome has drunk — within
The walnut bowl it lies, veinèd and thin,
In color like the wake of light that stains
The Tuscan deep, when from the moist moon rains
The inmost shower of its white fire — the breeze
Is still — blue heaven smiles over the pale seas.
And in this bowl of quicksilver — for I
Yield to the impulse of an infancy
Outlasting manhood — I have made to float
A rude idealism of a paper boat : —
A hollow screw with cogs — Henry will know
The thing I mean and laugh at me, — if so
He fears not I should do more mischief. — Next
Lie bills and calculations much perplext,
With steam-boats, frigates, and machinery quaint
Traced over them in blue and yellow paint.
Then comes a range of mathematical
Instruments, for plans nautical and statical ;
A heap of rosin, a queer broken glass
With ink in it ; — a china cup that was
What it will never be again, I think,
A thing from which sweet lips were wont to drink
The liquor doctors rail at — and which I

Will quaff in spite of them — and when we die
We'll toss up who died first of drinking tea,
And cry out, — "heads or tails?" where'er we be.
Near that a dusty paint box, some odd hooks,
A half-burnt match, an ivory block, three books,
Where conic sections, spherics, logarithms,
To great Laplace, from Saunderson and Sims,
Lie heaped in their harmonious disarray
Of figures, — disentangle them who may.
Baron de Tott's Memoirs beside them lie,
And some odd volumes of old chemistry.
Near those a most inexplicable thing,
With lead in the middle — I'm conjecturing
How to make Henry understand ; but no —
I'll leave, as Spenser says, with many mo,
This secret in the pregnant womb of time,
Too vast a matter for so weak a rhyme.

And here like some weird Archimage sit I,
Plotting dark spells, and devilish enginery,
The self-impelling steam-wheels of the mind
Which pump up oaths from clergymen, and grind
The gentle spirit of our meek reviews
Into a powdery foam of salt abuse,
Ruffling the ocean of their self-content ; —
I sit — and smile or sigh as is my bent,
But not for them — Libeccio rushes round
With an inconstant and an idle sound,
I heed him more than them — the thunder-smoke
Is gathering on the mountains, like a cloak
Folded athwart their shoulders broad and bare ;
The ripe corn under the undulating air

Undulates like an ocean : — and the vines
Are trembling wide in all their trellised lines —
The murmur of the awakening sea doth fill
The empty pauses of the blast ; — the hill
Looks hoary through the white electric rain,
And from the glens beyond, in sullen strain,
The interrupted thunder howls ; above
One chasm of heaven smiles, like the eye of Love
On the unquiet world ; — while such things are.
How could one worth your friendship heed the war
Of worms ? the shriek of the world's carrion jays,
Their censure, or their wonder, or their praise ?

You are not here ! the quaint witch Memory sees
In vacant chairs, your absent images,
And points where once you sat, and now should be
But are not. — I demand if ever we
Shall meet as then we met ; — and she replies,
Veiling in awe her second-sighted eyes ;
" I know the past alone — but summon home
My sister Hope, — she speaks of all to come."
But I, an old diviner, who knew well
Every false verse of that sweet oracle,
Turned to the sad enchantress once again,
And sought a respite from my gentle pain,
In citing every passage o'er and o'er
Of our communion — how on the sea shore
We watched the ocean and the sky together,
Under the roof of blue Italian weather ;
How I ran home through last year's thunder-storm,
And felt the transverse lightning linger warm
Upon my cheek — and how we often made

Feasts for each other, where good will outweighed
The frugal luxury of our country cheer,
As well it might, were it less firm and clear
Than ours must ever be ; — and how we spun
A shroud of talk to hide us from the sun
Of this familiar life, which seems to be
But is not, — or is but quaint mockery
Of all we would believe, and sadly blame
The jarring and inexplicable frame
Of this wrong world : — and then anatomize
The purposes and thoughts of men whose eyes
Were closed in distant years ; — or widely guess
The issue of the earth's great business,
When we shall be as we no longer are —
Like babbling gossips safe, who hear the war
Of winds, and sigh, but tremble not ; — or how
You listened to some interrupted flow
Of visionary rhyme, — in joy and pain
Struck from the inmost fountains of my brain,
With little skill perhaps ; — or how we sought
Those deepest wells of passion or of thought
Wrought by wise poets in the waste of years,
Staining their sacred waters with our tears ;
Quenching a thirst ever to be renewed !
Or how I, wisest lady ! then indued
The language of a land which now is free,
And winged with thoughts of truth and majesty,
Flits round the tyrant's sceptre like a cloud,
And bursts the peopled prisons, and cries aloud,
" My name is Legion ! " that majestic tongue
Which Calderon over the desert flung
Of ages and of nations ; and which found

An echo in our hearts, and with the sound
Startled oblivion ; — thou wert then to me
As is a nurse — when inarticulately
A child would talk as its grown parents do.
If living winds the rapid clouds pursue,
If hawks chase doves through the etherial way,
Huntsmen the innocent deer, and beasts their prey,
Why should not we rouse with the spirit's blast
Out of the forest of the pathless past
These recollected pleasures?

                  You are now
In London, that great sea, whose ebb and flow
At once is deaf and loud. and on the shore
Vomits its wrecks, and still howls on for more.
Yet in its depth what treasures !   You will see
That which was Godwin, — greater none than he
Though fallen — and fallen on evil times — to stand
Among the spirits of our age and land,
Before the dread tribunal of *to come*
The   foremost, — while Rebuke cowers pale and
    dumb.
You will see Coleridge — he who sits obscure
In the exceeding lustre, and the pure
Intense irradiation of a mind,
Which, with its own internal lightning blind,
Flags wearily through darkness and despair —
A cloud-encircled meteor of the air,
A hooded eagle among blinking owls. —
You will see Hunt — one of those happy souls
Which are the salt of the earth, and without whom
This world would smell like what it is — a tomb ;

Who is what others seem; his room no doubt
Is still adorned by many a cast from Shout,
With graceful flowers tastefully placed about;
And coronals of bay from ribbons hung,
And brighter wreaths in neat disorder flung;
The gifts of the most learn'd among some dozens
Of female friends, sisters-in-law and cousins.
And there is he with his eternal puns,.
Which beat the dullest brain for smiles, like duns
Thundering for money at a poet's door;
Alas! it is no use to say, " I'm poor! "
Or oft in graver mood, when he will look
Things wiser than were ever read in book,
Except in Shakespeare's wisest tenderness. —
You will see Hogg, — and I cannot express
His virtues, — though I know that they are great,
Because he locks, then barricades the gate
Within which they inhabit; — of his wit
And wisdom, you'll cry out when you are bit.
He is a pearl within an oyster shell,
One of the richest of the deep; — and there
Is English Peacock with his mountain fair
Turned into a Flamingo; — that shy bird
That gleams i' the Indian air — have you not heard
When a man marries, dies, or turns Hindoo,
His best friends hear no more of him? — but you
Will see him, and will like him too, I hope,
With the milk-white Snowdonian Antelope
Matched with this camelopard — his fine wit
Makes such a wound, the knife is lost in it;
A strain too learnèd for a shallow age,
Too wise for selfish bigots; let his page

Which charms the chosen spirits of the time,
Fold itself up for the serener clime
Of years to come, and find its recompense
In that just expectation. — Wit and sense,
Virtue and human knowledge ; all that might
Make this dull world a business of delight,
Are all combined in Horace Smith. — And these,
With some exceptions, which I need not teaze
Your patience by descanting on, — are all
You and I know in London.

              I recall
My thoughts, and bid you look upon the night.
As water does a sponge, so the moonlight
Fills the void, hollow, universal air —
What see you ? — unpavilioned heaven is fair
Whether the moon, into her chamber gone,
Leaves midnight to the golden stars, or wan
Climbs with diminished beams the azure steep ;
Or whether clouds sail o'er the inverse deep,
Piloted by the many-wandering blast,
And the rare stars rush through them dim and
    fast : —
All this is beautiful in every land. —
But what see you beside ? — a shabby stand
Of Hackney coaches — a brick house or wall
Fencing some lonely court, white with the scrawl
Of our unhappy politics ; — or worse —
A wretched woman reeling by, whose curse
Mixed with the watchman's, partner of her trade,
You must accept in place of serenade —
Or yellow-haired Pollonia murmuring

To Henry, some unutterable thing.
I see a chaos of green leaves and fruit
Built round dark caverns, even to the root
Of the living stems that feed them — in whose bowers
There sleep in their dark dew the folded flowers;
Beyond, the surface of the unsickled corn
Trembles not in the slumbering air, and borne
In circles quaint, and ever changing dance,
Like wingèd stars the fire-flies flash and glance,
Pale in the open moonshine, but each one
Under the dark trees seems a little sun,
A meteor tamed; a fixed star gone astray
From the silver regions of the milky way; —
Afar the Contadino's song is heard,
Rude, but made sweet by distance — and a bird
Which cannot be the Nightingale, and yet
I know none else that sings so sweet as it
At this late hour; — and then all is still —
Now Italy or London, which you will!

Next winter you must pass with me; I'll have
My house by that time turned into a grave
Of dead despondence and low-thoughted care,
And all the dreams which our tormentors are;
Oh! that Hunt, Hogg, Peacock and Smith were there
With every thing belonging to them fair! —
We will have books, Spanish, Italian, Greek;
And ask one week to make another week
As like his father, as I'm unlike mine,
Which is not his fault, as you may divine.
Though we eat little flesh and drink no wine,
Yet let's be merry: we'll have tea and toast;

Custards for supper, and an endless host
Of syllabubs and jellies and mince-pies,
And other such lady-like luxuries, —
Feasting on which we will philosophize!
And we'll have fires out of the Grand Duke's wood,
To thaw the six weeks' winter in our blood.
And then we'll talk ; — what shall we talk about?
Oh! there are themes enough for many a bout
Of thought-entangled descant ; — as to nerves —
With cones and parallelograms and curves
I've sworn to strangle them if once they dare
To bother me — when you are with me there.
And they shall never more sip laudanum,
From Helicon or Himeros ; — well, come,
And in despite of God and of the devil,
We'll make our friendly philosophic revel
Outlast the leafless time ; till buds and flowers
Warn the obscure inevitable hours,
Sweet meeting by sad parting to renew ; —
" To-morrow to fresh woods and pastures new."

1820.

THE AZIOLA.

" Do you not hear the Aziola cry?
    Methinks she must be nigh,"
      Said Mary, as we sate
In dusk, ere stars were lit, or candles brought;
      And I, who thought
   This Aziola was some tedious woman,
    Asked, " Who is Aziola ? "   How elate

I felt to know that it was nothing human,
    No mockery of myself to fear or hate:
        And Mary saw my soul,
And laughed, and said, " Disquiet yourself not;
        'Tis nothing but a little downy owl."

Sad Aziola ! many an eventide
    Thy music I had heard
By wood and stream, meadow and mountain-side,
    And fields and marshes wide,
Such as nor voice, nor lute, nor wind, nor bird,
    The soul ever stirred ;
Unlike and far sweeter than them all.
Sad Aziola ! from that moment I
    Loved thee and thy sad cry.

                                    1821.

THE BOAT ON THE SERCHIO.

OUR boat is asleep on Serchio's stream,
Its sails are folded like thoughts in a dream,
The helm sways idly, hither and thither ;
    Dominic, the boatman, has brought the mast
    And the oars and the sails ; but 'tis sleeping fast,
Like a beast, unconscious of its tether.

The stars burnt out in the pale blue air,
And the thin white moon lay withering there,
To tower, and cavern, and rift and tree,
The owl and the bat fled drowsily.
Day had kindled the dewy woods,
    And the rocks above and the stream below,

And the vapors in their multitudes,
  And the Apennine's shroud of summer snow,
And clothed with light of aëry gold
The mists in their eastern caves uprolled.

Day had awakened all things that be,
The lark and the thrush and the swallow free,
  And the milkmaid's song and the mower's scythe,
And the matin-bell and the mountain bee:
Fire-flies were quenched on the dewy corn,
  Glow-worms went out on the river's brim,
  Like lamps which a student forgets to trim:
The beetle forgot to wind his horn,
  The crickets were still in the meadow and hill:
Like a flock of rooks at a farmer's gun
Night's dreams and terrors, every one,
Fled from the brains which are their prey
From the lamp's death to the morning ray.

All rose to do the task He set to each,
  Who shaped us to his ends and not our own;
The million rose to learn, and one to teach
  What none yet ever knew or can be known.
    And many rose
  Whose woe was such that fear became desire; —
Melchior and Lionel were not among those;
They from the throng of men had stepped aside,
And made their home under the green hill side.
It was that hill, whose intervening brow
  Screens Lucca from the Pisan's envious eye,
Which the circumfluous plain waving below,
  Like a wide lake of green fertility,

With streams and fields and marshes bare,
    Divides from the far Apennines — which lie
Islanded in the immeasurable air.

"What think you, as she lies in her green cove,
Our little sleeping boat is dreaming of ?"
"If morning dreams are true, why I should guess
That she was dreaming of our idleness,
And of the miles of watery way
We should have led her by this time of day." —

    "Never mind," said Lionel,
    "Give care to the winds, they can bear it well
    About yon poplar tops ; and see!
    The white clouds are driving merrily,
    And the stars we miss this morn will light
    More willingly our return to-night. —
    How it whistles, Dominic's long black hair !
    List, my dear fellow ; the breeze blows fair :
    Hear how it sings into the air."

  . . . . . .

The chain is loosed, the sails are spread,
    The living breath is fresh behind,
As with dews and sunrise fed,
    Comes the laughing morning wind ; —
The sails are full, the boat makes head
Against the Serchio's torrent fierce,
Then flags with intermitting course,
    And hangs upon the wave, and stems
    The tempest of the . . . .
Which fervid from its mountain source

Shallow, smooth and strong doth come, —
Swift as fire, tempestuously
It sweeps into the affrighted sea;
In morning's smile its eddies coil,
Its billows sparkle, toss and boil,
Torturing all its quiet light
Into columns fierce and bright.

The Serchio, twisting forth
Between the marble barriers which it clove
At Ripafratta, leads through the dead chasm
The wave that died the death which lovers love,
Living in what it sought; as if this spasm
Had not yet past, the toppling mountains cling,
But the clear stream in full enthusiasm
Pours itself on the plain, then wandering
Down one clear path of effluence crystalline,
Sends its superfluous waves, that they may fling
At Arno's feet tribute of corn and wine,
Then, through the pestilential deserts wild
Of tangled marsh and woods of stunted pine,
It rushes to the Ocean.

1821.

THE WITCH OF ATLAS.

TO MARY.

How, my dear Mary, are you critic-bitten
    (For vipers kill, though dead), by some review,
That you condemn these verses I have written,
    Because they tell no story, false or true !
What, though no mice are caught by a young kitten,
    May it not leap and play as grown cats do,
Till its claws come ?   Prithee, for this one time,
Content thee with a visionary rhyme.

What hand would crush the silken-wingèd fly,
    The youngest of inconstant April's minions,
Because it cannot climb the purest sky,
    Where the swan sings, amid the sun's dominions?
Not thine.   Thou knowest 'tis its doom to die,
    When day shall hide within her twilight pinions,
The lucent eyes, and the eternal smile,
Serene as thine, which lent it life awhile.

To thy fair feet a wingèd Vision came,
    Whose date should have been longer than a day,
And o'er thy head did beat its wings for fame,
    And in thy sight its fading plumes display;
The watery bow burned in the evening flame,
    But the shower fell, the swift sun went his way —

And that is dead. —— O, let me not believe
That any thing of mine is fit to live!

Wordsworth informs us he was nineteen years
    Considering and retouching Peter Bell;
Watering his laurels with the killing tears
    Of slow, dull care, so that their roots to hell
Might pierce, and their wide branches blot the
        spheres
    Of heaven, with dewy leaves and flowers; this
        well
May be, for Heaven and Earth conspire to foil
The over-busy gardener's blundering toil.

My Witch indeed is not so sweet a creature
    As Ruth or Lucy, whom his graceful praise
Clothes for our grandsons — but she matches Peter,
    Though he took nineteen years, and she three
        days
In dressing.   Light the vest of flowing metre
    She wears; he, proud as dandy with his stays,
Has hung upon his wiry limbs a dress
Like King Lear's "looped and windowed ragged-
    ness."

If you strip Peter, you will see a fellow,
    Scorched by Hell's hyperequatorial climate
Into a kind of a sulphureous yellow:
    A lean mark, hardly fit to fling a rhyme at;
In shape a Scaramouch, in hue Othello.
    If you unveil my Witch, no priest nor primate
Can shrive you of that sin, — if sin there be
In love, when it becomes idolatry.

The Witch of Atlas.

BEFORE those cruel Twins, whom at one birth
 Incestuous Change bore to her father Time,
Error and Truth, had hunted from the Earth
 All those bright natures which adorned its prime,
And left us nothing to believe in, worth
 The pains of putting into learnèd rhyme,
A lady-witch there lived on Atlas' mountain
Within a cavern, by a secret fountain.

Her mother was one of the Atlantides :
 The all-beholding Sun had ne'er beholden
In his wide voyage o'er continents and seas
 So fair a creature, as she lay enfolden
In the warm shadow of her loveliness ; —
 He kissed her with his beams, and made all golden
The chamber of gray rock in which she lay —
She, in that dream of joy, dissolved away.

'Tis said, she first was changed into a vapor,
 And then into a cloud, such clouds as flit,
Like splendor-wingèd moths about a taper,
 Round the red west when the sun dies in it :
And then into a meteor, such as caper
 On hill-tops when the moon is in a fit :
Then, into one of those mysterious stars
Which hide themselves between the Earth and Mars.

197

Ten times the Mother of the Months had bent
  Her bow beside the folding-star, and bidden
With that bright sign the billows to indent
  The sea-deserted sand — like children chidden,
At her command they ever came and went —
  Since in that cave a dewy splendor hidden
Took shape and motion: with the living form
Of this embodied Power, the cave grew warm.

A lovely lady garmented in light
  From her own beauty — deep her eyes, as are
Two openings of unfathomable night
  Seen through a tempest's cloven roof — her hair
Dark — the dim brain whirls dizzy with delight,
  Picturing her form; her soft smiles shone afar,
And her low voice was heard like love, and drew
All living things towards this wonder new.

And first the spotted camelopard came,
  And then the wise and fearless elephant;
Then the sly serpent, in the golden flame
  Of his own volumes intervolved; — all gaunt
And sanguine beasts her gentle looks made tame.
  They drank before her at her sacred fount;
And every beast of beating heart grew bold,
Such gentleness and power even to behold.

The brinded lioness led forth her young,
  That she might teach them how they should
      forego
Their inborn thirst of death; the pard unstrung
  His sinews at her feet, and sought to know,

With looks whose motions spoke without a tongue,
  How he might be as gentle as the doe.
The magic circle of her voice and eyes
All savage natures did imparadise.

And old Silenus, shaking a green stick
  Of lilies, and the wood-gods in a crew
Came, blithe, as in the olive copses thick
  Cicadæ are, drunk with the noonday dew:
And Dryope and Faunus followed quick,
  Teazing the God to sing them something new;
Till in this cave they found the lady lone,
Sitting upon a seat of emerald stone.

And universal Pan, 'tis said, was there,
  And though none saw him, — through the adamant
Of the deep mountains, through the trackless air,
  And through those living spirits, like a want
He passed out of his everlasting lair
  Where the quick heart of the great world doth pant,
And felt that wondrous lady all alone, —
And she felt him, upon her emerald throne.

And every nymph of stream and spreading tree,
  And every shepherdess of Ocean's flocks,
Who drives her white waves over the green sea,
  And Ocean with the brine on his gray locks,
And quaint Priapus with his company,
  All came, much wondering how the enwombèd
    rocks
Could have brought forth so beautiful a birth; —
Her love subdued their wonder and their mirth.

The herdsmen and the mountain maidens came,
   And the rude kings of pastoral Garamant —
Their spirits shook within them, as a flame
   Stirred by the air under a cavern gaunt :
Pigmies, and Polyphemes, by many a name,
   Centaurs and Satyrs, and such shapes as haunt
Wet clefts, — and lumps neither alive nor dead,
Dog-headed, bosom-eyed, and bird-footed.

For she was beautiful — her beauty made
   The bright world dim, and every thing beside
Seemed like the fleeting image of a shade :
   No thought of living spirit could abide,
Which to her looks had ever been betrayed,
   On any object in the world so wide,
On any hope within the circling skies,
But on her form, and in her inmost eyes.

Which when the lady knew, she took her spindle
   And twined three threads of fleecy mist, and three
Long lines of light, such as the dawn may kindle
   The clouds and waves and mountains with ; and
     she
As many star-beams, ere their lamps could dwindle
   In the belated moon, wound skilfully ;
And with these threads a subtle veil she wove —
A shadow for the splendor of her love.

The deep recesses of her odorous dwelling
   Were stored with magic treasures — sounds of air,
Which had the power all spirits of compelling,
   Folded in cells of crystal silence there ;

Such as we hear in youth, and think the feeling
  Will never die — yet ere we are aware,
The feeling and the sound are fled and gone,
And the regret they leave remains alone.

And there lay Visions swift, and sweet, and quaint,
  Each in its thin sheath, like a chrysalis,
Some eager to burst forth, some weak and faint
  With the soft burden of intensest bliss ;
It was its work to bear to many a saint
  Whose heart adores the shrine which holiest is,
Even Love's : — and others white, green, gray and
      black,
And of all shapes — and each was at her beck.

And odors in a kind of aviary
  Of ever-blooming Eden-trees she kept,
Clipt in a floating net, a love-sick Fairy
  Had woven from dew-beams while the moon yet
      slept ;
As bats at the wired window of a dairy,
  They beat their vans ; and each was an adept,
When loosed and missioned, making wings of winds,
To stir sweet thoughts or sad, in destined minds.

And liquors clear and sweet. whose healthful might
  Could medicine the sick soul to happy sleep,
And change eternal death into a night
  Of glorious dreams — or if eyes needs must weep,
Could make their tears all wonder and delight,
  She in her crystal vials did closely keep :
If men could drink of those clear vials, 'tis said
The living were not envied of the dead.

Her cave was stored with scrolls of strange device,
  The works of some Saturnian Archimage,
Which taught the expiations at whose price
  Men from the Gods might win that happy age
Too lightly lost, redeeming native vice;
  And which might quench the earth-consuming
    rage
Of gold and blood — till men should live and move
Harmonious as the sacred stars above.

And how all things that seem untamable,
  Not to be checked and not to be confined,
Obey the spells of wisdom's wizard skill;
  Time, Earth and Fire — the Ocean and the Wind
And all their shapes — and man's imperial will;
  And other scrolls whose writings did unbind
The inmost lore of Love — let the profane
Tremble to ask what secrets they contain.

And wondrous works of substances unknown,
  To which the enchantment of her father's power
Had changed those ragged blocks of savage stone,
  Were heaped in the recesses of her bower;
Carved lamps and chalices, and vials which shone
  In their own golden beams — each like a flower,
Out of whose depth a fire-fly shakes his light
Under a cypress in a starless night.

At first she lived alone in this wild home,
  And her own thoughts were each a minister,
Clothing themselves, or with the ocean foam,
  Or with the wind, or with the speed of fire,

To work whatever purposes might come
  Into her mind; such power her mighty Sire
Had girt them with, whether to fly or run,
Through all the regions which he shines upon.

The Ocean-nymphs and Hamadryades,
  Oreads and Naiads, with long weedy locks,
Offered to do her bidding through the seas,
  Under the earth, and in the hollow rocks,
And far beneath the matted roots of trees,
  And in the gnarlèd heart of stubborn oaks,
So they might live for ever in the light
Of her sweet presence — each a satellite.

"This may not be," the wizard maid replied:
  "The fountains where the Naiades bedew
Their shining hair, at length are drained and dried;
  The solid oaks forget their strength, and strew
Their latest leaf upon the mountains wide;
  The boundless ocean like a drop of dew
Will be consumed — the stubborn centre must
Be scattered, like a cloud of summer dust.

"And ye with them will perish, one by one; —
  If I must sigh to think that this shall be,
If I must weep when the surviving Sun
  Shall smile on your decay — Oh, ask not me
To love you till your little race is run;
  I cannot die as ye must — over me
Your leaves shall glance — the streams in which ye
      dwell
Shall be my paths henceforth, and so — farewell!"

She spoke and wept : — the dark and azure well
　　Sparkled beneath the shower of her bright tears,
And every little circlet where they fell
　　Flung to the cavern-roof inconstant spheres
And intertangled lines of light ; — a knell
　　Of sobbing voices came upon her ears
From those departing Forms, o'er the serene
Of the white streams and of the forest green.

All day the wizard lady sate aloof,
　　Spelling out scrolls of dread antiquity,
Under the cavern's fountain-lighted roof;
　　Or broidering the pictured poesy
Of some high tale upon her growing woof,
　　Which the sweet splendor of her smiles could dye
In hues outshining Heaven — and ever she
Added some grace to the wrought poesy.

While on her hearth lay blazing many a piece
　　Of sandal wood, rare gums and cinnamon ;
Men scarcely know how beautiful fire is —
　　Each flame of it is as a precious stone
Dissolved in ever-moving light, and this
　　Belongs to each and all who gaze upon.
The Witch beheld it not, for in her hand
She held a woof that dimmed the burning brand.

This lady never slept, but lay in trance
　　All night within the fountain — as in sleep.
Its emerald crags glowed in her beauty's glance;
　　Through the green splendor of the water deep

She saw the constellations reel and dance
   Like fire-flies — and withal did ever keep
The tenor of her contemplations calm,
With open eyes, closed feet and folded palm.

And when the whirlwinds and the clouds descended
   From the white pinnacles of that cold hill,
She past at dewfall to a space extended,
   Where in a lawn of flowering asphodel
Amid a wood of pines and cedars blended,
   There yawned an inextinguishable well
Of crimson fire — full even to the brim,
And overflowing all the margin trim.

Within the which she lay when the fierce war
   Of wintry winds shook that innocuous liquor
In many a mimic moon and bearded star
   O'er woods and lawns; — the serpent heard it
     flicker,
In sleep, and dreaming still, he crept afar —
   And when the windless snow descended thicker
Than autumn leaves, she watched it as it came
Melt on the surface of the level flame.

She had a Boat, which some say Vulcan wrought
   For Venus, as the chariot of her star;
But it was found too feeble to be fraught
   With all the ardors in that sphere which are,
And so she sold it, and Apollo bought
   And gave it to this daughter: from a car
Changed to the fairest and the lightest boat
Which ever upon mortal stream did float.

And others say, that, when but three hours old,
   The first-born Love out of his cradle leapt,
And clove dun Chaos with his wings of gold,
   And like a horticultural adept,
Stole a strange seed, and wrapt it up in mould,
   And sowed it in his mother's star, and kept
Watering it all the summer with sweet dew,
And with his wings fanning it as it grew.

The plant grew strong and green, the snowy flower
   Fell, and the long and gourd-like fruit began
To turn the light and dew by inward power
   To its own substance; woven tracery ran
Of light firm texture, ribbed and branching, o'er
   The solid rind, like a leaf's veinèd fan —
Of which Love scooped this boat — and with soft
     motion
Piloted it round the circumfluous ocean.

This boat she moored upon her fount, and lit
   A living spirit within all its frame,
Breathing the soul of swiftness into it.
   Couched on the fountain like a panther tame,
One of the twain at Evan's feet that sit —
   Or as on Vesta's sceptre a swift flame —
Or on blind Homer's heart a wingèd thought, —
In joyous expectation lay the boat.

Then by strange art she kneaded fire and snow
   Together, tempering the repugnant mass
With liquid love — all things together grow
   Through which the harmony of love can pass;

And a fair Shape out of her hands did flow —
　A living Image, which did far surpass
In beauty that bright shape of vital stone
Which drew the heart out of Pygmalion.

A sexless thing it was, and in its growth
　It seemed to have developed no defect
Of either sex, yet all the grace of both, —
　In gentleness and strength its limbs were decked;
The bosom lightly swelled with its full youth,
　The countenance was such as might select
Some artist that his skill should never die,
Imaging forth such perfect purity.

From its smooth shoulders hung two rapid wings,
　Fit to have borne it to the seventh sphere,
Tipt with the speed of liquid lightnings,
　Dyed in the ardors of the atmosphere:
She led her creature to the boiling springs
　Where the light boat was moored, and said, "Sit
　　here!"
And pointed to the prow, and took her seat
Beside the rudder, with opposing feet.

And down the streams which clove those mountains
　　vast,
　Around their inland islets, and amid
The panther-peopled forests, whose shade cast
　Darkness and odors, and a pleasure hid
In melancholy gloom, the pinnace past;
　By many a star-surrounded pyramid

Of icy crag cleaving the purple sky,
And caverns yawning round unfathomably.

The silver noon into that winding dell,
 With slanted gleam athwart the forest tops,
Tempered like golden evening, feebly fell :
 A green and glowing light, like that which drops
From folded lilies in which glow-worms dwell,
 When earth over her face night's mantle wraps ;
Between the severed mountains lay on high
Over the stream, a narrow rift of sky.

And ever as she went, the Image lay
 With folded wings and unawakened eyes ;
And o'er its gentle countenance did play
 The busy dreams, as thick as summer flies,
Chasing the rapid smiles that would not stay,
 And drinking the warm tears, and the sweet sighs
Inhaling, which, with busy murmur vain,
They had aroused from that full heart and brain.

And ever down the prone vale, like a cloud
 Upon a stream of wind, the pinnace went :
Now lingering on the pools, in which abode
 The calm and darkness of the deep content
In which they paused ; now o'er the shallow road
 Of white and dancing waters, all besprent
With sand and polished pebbles : — mortal boat
In such a shallow rapid could not float.

And down the earthquaking cataracts which shiver
 Their snow-like waters into golden air,

Or under chasms unfathomable ever
  Sepulchre them, till in their rage they tear
A subterranean portal for the river,
  It fled — the circling sunbows did upbear
Its fall down the hoar precipice of spray,
Lighting it far upon its lampless way.

And when the wizard lady would ascend
  The labyrinths of some many-winding vale,
Which to the inmost mountain upward tend —
  She called " Hermaphroditus! " — and the pale
And heavy hue which slumber could extend
  Over its lips and eyes, as on the gale
A rapid shadow from a slope of grass,
Into the darkness of the stream did pass.

And it unfurled its heaven-colored pinions,
  With stars of fire spotting the stream below ;
And from above into the Sun's dominions
  Flinging a glory, like the golden glow
In which spring clothes her emerald-wingèd minions,
  All interwoven with fine feathery snow
And moonlight splendor of intensest rime,
With which frost paints the pines in winter time.

And then it winnowed the Elysian air
  Which ever hung about that lady bright,
With its ethereal vans — and speeding there,
  Like a star up the torrent of the night,
Or a swift eagle in the morning glare
  Breasting the whirlwind with impetuous flight,
The pinnace, oared by those enchanted wings,
Clove the fierce streams towards their upper springs.

The water flashed like sunlight by the prow
　Of a noon-wandering meteor flung to Heaven;
The still air seemed as if the waves did flow
　In tempest down the mountains; loosely driven
The lady's radiant hair streamed to and fro:
　Beneath, the billows having vainly striven
Indignant and impetuous, roared to feel
The swift and steady motion of the keel.

Or, when the weary moon was in the wane,
　Or in the noon of interlunar night,
The lady-witch in visions could not chain
　Her spirit; but sailed forth under the light
Of shooting stars, and bade extend amain
　Its storm-outspeeding wings, the Hermaphrodite;
She to the Austral waters took her way,
Beyond the fabulous Thamondocana,

Where, like a meadow which no scythe has shaven,
　Which rain could never bend, or whirl-blast shake,
With the Antarctic constellations paven,
　Canopus and his crew, lay the Austral lake —
There she would build herself a windless haven
　Out of the clouds whose moving turrets make .
The bastions of the storm, when through the sky
The spirits of the tempest thundered by.

A haven beneath whose translucent floor
　The tremulous stars sparkled unfathomably,
And around which the solid vapors hoar,
　Based on the level waters, to the sky

Lifted their dreadful crags, and like a shore
  Of wintry mountains, inaccessibly
Hemmed in with rifts and precipices gray,
And hanging crags, many a cove and bay.

And whilst the outer lake beneath the lash
  Of the wind's scourge, foamed like a wounded
    thing ;
And the incessant hail with stony clash
  Ploughed up the waters, and the flagging wing
Of the roused cormorant in the lightning flash
  Looked like the wreck of some wind-wandering
Fragment of inky thunder-smoke — this haven
Was as a gem to copy Heaven engraven.

On which that lady played her many pranks,
  Circling the image of a shooting star,
Even as a tiger on Hydaspes' banks
  Outspeeds the antelopes which speediest are,
In her light boat ; and many quips and cranks
  She played upon the water, till the car
Of the late moon, like a sick matron wan,
To journey from the misty east began.

And then she called out of the hollow turrets
  Of those high clouds, white, golden and vermilion,
The armies of her ministering spirits —
  In mighty legions, million after million,
They came, each troop emblazoning its merits
  On meteor flags ; and many a proud pavilion
Of the intertexture of the atmosphere
They pitched upon the plain of the calm mere.

They framed the imperial tent of their great Queen
   Of woven exhalations, underlaid
With lambent lightning fire, as may be seen
   A dome of thin and open ivory inlaid
With crimson silk — cressets from the serene
   Hung there, and on the water for her tread
A tapestry of fleece-like mist was strewn,
Dyed in the beams of the ascending moon.

And on a throne o'erlaid with starlight, caught
   Upon those wandering isles of aëry dew,
Which highest shoals of mountain shipwreck not,
   She sate, and heard all that had happened new
Between the earth and moon, since they had brought
   The last intelligence — and now she grew
Pale as that moon, lost in the watery night —
And now she wept, and now she laughed outright.

These were tame pleasures ; she would often climb
   The steepest ladder of the crudded rack
Up to some beakèd cape of cloud sublime,
   And like Arion on the dolphin's back
Ride singing through the shoreless air ; — oft-time
   Following the serpent lightning's winding track,
She ran upon the platforms of the wind,
And laughed to hear the fire-balls roar behind.

And sometimes to those streams of upper air
   Which whirl the earth in its diurnal round,
She would ascend, and win the spirits there
   To let her join their chorus.   Mortals found

That on those days the sky was calm and fair,
  And mystic snatches of harmonious sound
Wandered upon the earth where'er she past,
  And happy thoughts of hope, too sweet to last.

But her choice sport was, in the hours of sleep,
  To glide adown old Nilus, where he threads
Egypt and Æthiopia, from the steep
  Of utmost Axumè, until he spreads,
Like a calm flock of silver-fleecèd sheep,
  His waters on the plain: and crested heads
Of cities and proud temples gleam amid,
And many a vapor-belted pyramid.

By Mœris and the Mareotid lakes,
  Strewn with faint blooms like bridal chamber floors,
Where naked boys bridling tame water-snakes,
  Or charioteering ghastly alligators,
Had left on the sweet waters mighty wakes
  Of those huge forms — within the brazen doors
Of the great Labyrinth slept both boy and beast,
Tired with the pomp of their Osirian feast.

And where within the surface of the river
  The shadows of the massy temples lie,
And never are erased — but tremble ever
  Like things which every cloud can doom to die,
Through lotus-paven canals, and wheresoever
  The works of man pierced that serenest sky
With tombs, and towers, and fanes. 'twas her delight
To wander in the shadow of the night.

With motion like the spirit of that wind
   Whose soft step deepens slumber, her light feet·
Past through the peopled haunts of human kind,
   Scattering sweet visions from her presence sweet,
Through fane, and palace-court, and labyrinth mined
   With many a dark and subterranean street
Under the Nile; through chambers high and deep
She past, observing mortals in their sleep.

A pleasure sweet doubtless it was to see
   Mortals subdued in all the shapes of sleep.
Here lay two sister twins in infancy;
   There, a lone youth who in his dreams did weep;
Within, two lovers linkèd innocently
   In their loose locks which over both did creep
Like ivy from one stem; — and there lay calm
Old age with snow-bright hair and folded palm.

But other troubled forms of sleep she saw,
   Not to be mirrored in a holy song —
Distortions foul of supernatural awe,
   And pale imaginings of visioned wrong;
And all the code of custom's lawless law
   Written upon the brows of old and young:
"This," said the wizard maiden, " is the strife
Which stirs the liquid surface of man's life."

And little did the sight disturb her soul. —
   We, the weak mariners of that wide lake
Where'er its shores extend or billows roll,
   Our course unpiloted and starless make

O'er its wild surface to an unknown goal : —
   But she in the calm depths her way could take,
Where in bright bowers immortal forms abide
Beneath the weltering of the restless tide.

And she saw princes couched under the glow
   Of sunlike gems ; and round each temple-court
In dormitories ranged, row after row,
   She saw the priests asleep — all of one sort —
For all were educated to be so. —
   The peasants in their huts, and in the port
The sailors she saw cradled on the waves,
And the dead lulled within their dreamless graves.

And all the forms in which those spirits lay
   Were to her sight like the diaphanous
Veils, in which those sweet ladies oft array
   Their delicate limbs, who would conceal from us
Only their scorn of all concealment: they
   Move in the light of their own beauty thus.
But these and all now lay with sleep upon them,
And little thought a Witch was looking on them.

She, all those human figures breathing there,
   Beheld as living spirits — to her eyes
The naked beauty of the soul lay bare,
   And often through a rude and worn disguise
She saw the inner form most bright and fair —
   And then she had a charm of strange device,
Which, murmured on mute lips with tender tone,
Could make that spirit mingle with her own.

Alas! Aurora, what wouldst thou have given
 For such a charm when Tithon became gray?
Or how much, Venus, of thy silver Heaven
 Wouldst thou have yielded, ere Proserpina
Had half (oh! why not all?) the debt forgiven
 Which dear Adonis had been doomed to pay,
To any witch who would have taught you it?
The Heliad doth not know its value yet.

'Tis said in after times her spirit free
 Knew what love was, and felt itself alone —
But holy Dian could not chaster be
 Before she stooped to kiss Endymion,
Than now this lady — like a sexless bee
 Tasting all blossoms, and confined to none,
Among those mortal forms, the wizard-maiden
Past with an eye serene and heart unladen.

To those she saw most beautiful, she gave
 Strange panacea in a crystal bowl : —
They drank in their deep sleep of that sweet wave,
 And lived thenceforward as if some control,
Mightier than life, were in them ; and the grave
 Of such, when death oppressed the weary soul,
Was as a green and overarching bower
Lit by the gems of many a starry flower.

For on the night when they were buried, she
 Restored the embalmer's ruining, and shook
The light out of the funeral lamps, to be
 A mimic day within that deathy nook ;

And she unwound the woven imagery
  Of second childhood's swaddling bands, and took
The coffin, its last cradle, from its niche,   .
And threw it with contempt into a ditch.

And there the body lay, age after age,
  Mute, breathing, beating, warm and undecaying,
Like one asleep in a green hermitage,
  With gentle smiles about its eyelids playing,
And living in its dreams beyond the rage
  Of death or life ; while they were still arraying
In liveries ever new, the rapid, blind
And fleeting generations of mankind.   .

And she would write strange dreams upon the brain
  Of those who were less beautiful, and make
All harsh and crooked purposes more vain
  Than in the desert is the serpent's wake
Which the sand covers, — all his evil gain
  The miser in such dreams would rise and shake
Into a beggar's lap ; — the lying scribe
Would his own lies betray without a bribe.

The priests would write an explanation full,
  Translating hieroglyphics into Greek,
How the god Apis really was a bull,
  And nothing more ; and bid the herald stick
The same against the temple doors, and pull
  The old cant down ; they licensed all to speak
Whate'er they thought of hawks, and cats, and geese
By pastoral letters to each diocese.

The king would dress an ape up in his crown
   And robes, and seat him on his glorious seat,
And on the right hand of the sunlike throne
   Would place a gaudy mock-bird to repeat
The chatterings of the monkey. — Every one
   Of the prone courtiers crawled to kiss the feet
Of their great Emperor, when the morning came,
And kissed — alas, how many kiss the same !

The soldiers dreamed that they were blacksmiths, and
   Walked out of quarters in somnambulism ;
Round the red anvils you might see them stand
   Like Cyclopses in Vulcan's sooty abysm,
Beating their swords to ploughshares ; — in a band
   The gaolers sent those of the liberal schism
Free through the streets of Memphis, much, I wis
To the annoyance of king Amasis.

And timid lovers who had been so coy,
   They hardly knew whether they loved or not,
Would rise out of their rest, and take sweet joy,
   To the fulfilment of their inmost thought ;
And when next day the maiden and the boy
   Met one another, both, like sinners caught,
Blushed at the thing which each believed was done
Only in fancy — till the tenth moon shone ;

And then the Witch would let them take no ill :
   Of many thousand schemes which lovers find,
The Witch found one, — and so they took their fill
   Of happiness in marriage warm and kind.

Friends who, by practice of some envious skill,
    Were torn apart, a wide wound, mind from mind !
She did unite again with visions clear
Of deep affection and of truth sincere.

These were the pranks she played among the cities
    Of mortal men, and what she did to sprites
And Gods, entangling them in her sweet ditties
    To do her will, and show their subtle slights,
I will declare another time ; for it is
    A tale more fit for the weird winter nights,
Than for these garish summer days, when we
Scarcely believe much more than we can see.

                                            1820.

—•■•—

THE QUESTION.

I DREAMED that, as I wandered by the way,
  Bare winter suddenly was changed to spring,
And gentle odors led my steps astray,
  Mixed with a sound of waters murmuring
Along a shelving bank of turf, which lay
  Under a copse, and hardly dared to fling
Its green arms round the bosom of the stream,
But kissed it and then fled, as thou mightest in dream

There grew pied wind-flowers and violets,
  Daisies, those pearled Arcturi of the earth,
The constellated flower that never sets;
  Faint oxlips; tender bluebells, at whose birth
The sod scarce heaved; and that tall flower that
    wets —
  Like a child, half in tenderness and mirth —
Its mother's face with heaven-collected tears,
When the low wind, its playmate's voice, it hears.

And in the warm hedge grew lush eglantine,
  Green cow-bind and the moonlight-colored May,

220

And cherry blossoms, and white cups, whose wine
  Was the bright dew yet drained not by the day;
And wild roses, and ivy serpentine,
  With its dark buds and leaves, wandering astray;
And flowers azure, black, and streaked with gold,
Fairer than any wakened eyes behold.

And nearer to the river's trembling edge
  There grew broad flag-flowers, purple prankt with
    white,
And starry river buds among the sedge,
  And floating water-lilies, broad and bright,
Which lit the oak that overhung the hedge
  With moonlight beams of their own watery light;
And bulrushes, and reeds of such deep green
As soothed the dazzled eye with sober sheen.

Methought that of these visionary flowers
  I made a nosegay, bound in such a way
That the same hues, which in their natural bowers
  Were mingled or opposed, the like array
Kept these imprisoned children of the Hours
  Within my hand, — and then, elate and gay,
I hastened to the spot whence I had come,
That I might there present it ! — Oh ! to whom?

                                        1820.

TO EMILIA VIVIANI.

MADONNA, wherefore hast thou sent to me
  Sweet basil and mignonette?
Embleming love and health, which never yet
In the same wreath might be.
  Alas, and they are wet!
Is it with thy kisses or thy tears?
    For never rain or dew
    Such fragrance drew
From plant or flower — the very doubt endears
    My sadness ever new,
The sighs I breathe, the tears I shed for thee.

1821.

Epipsychidion.

VERSES ADDRESSED TO THE NOBLE AND UNFORTUNATE
LADY EMILIA VIVIANI, NOW IMPRISONED IN THE
CONVENT OF ST. ANNE, PISA.

L'anima amante si slancia fuori del creato, e si crea nell' infinito un
Mondo tutto per essa, diverso assai da questo oscuro e pauroso baratro.
— *Her own words.*

MY Song, I fear that thou wilt find but few
Who fitly shall conceive thy reasoning,
Of such hard matter dost thou entertain;
Whence, if by misadventure, chance should bring
Thee to base company (as chance may do),
Quite unaware of what thou dost contain,
I prithee, comfort thy sweet self again,
My last delight! tell them that they are dull,
And bid them own that thou art beautiful.

ADVERTISEMENT.

[BY SHELLEY.]

THE writer of the following lines died at Florence, as he was
preparing for a voyage to one of the wildest of the Sporades,
which he had bought, and where he had fitted up the ruins
of an old building, and where it was his hope to have realized
a scheme of life, suited perhaps to that happier and better
world of which he is now an inhabitant, but hardly practicable
in this. His life was singular; less on account of the romantic

223

vicissitudes which diversified it, than the ideal tinge which it received from his own character and feelings. The present Poem, like the Vita Nuova of Dante, is sufficiently intelligible to a certain class of readers without a matter-of-fact history of the circumstances to which it relates; and to a certain other class it must ever remain incomprehensible, from a defect of a common organ of perception for the ideas of which it treats. Not but that, *gran vergogna sarebbe a colui, che rimasse cosa sotto veste di figura, o .di colore rettorico: e domandato non sapesse denudare le sue parole da cotal veste, in guisa che avessero verace intendimento.*

The present poem appears to have been intended by the writer as the dedication to some longer one. The stanza on the opposite page is almost a literal translation from Dante's famous Canzone

Voi, ch' intendendo, il terzo ciel movete, etc.

The presumptuous application of the concluding lines to his own composition will raise a smile at the expense of my unfortunate friend: be it a smile not of contempt, but pity.

EPIPSYCHIDION.

SWEET Spirit! Sister of that orphan one,
Whose empire is the name thou weepest on,
In my heart's temple I suspend to thee
These votive wreaths of withered memory.

Poor captive bird! who, from thy narrow cage,
Pourest such music, that it might assuage
The rugged hearts of those who prisoned thee,
Were they not deaf to all sweet melody;
This song shall be thy rose: its petals pale
Are dead, indeed, my adored Nightingale!

But soft and fragrant is the faded blossom,
And it has no thorn left to wound thy bosom.

High, spirit-wingèd Heart ! who dost for ever
Beat thine unfeeling bars with vain endeavor,
Till those bright plumes of thought, in which arrayed
It over-soared this low and worldly shade,
Lie shattered ; and thy panting, wounded breast
Stains with dear blood its unmaternal nest !
I weep vain tears : blood would less bitter be,
Yet poured forth gladlier, could it profit thee.

Seraph of Heaven ! too gentle to be human,
Veiling beneath that radiant form of Woman
All that is insupportable in thee
Of light, and love, and immortality !
Sweet Benediction in the eternal Curse !
Veiled Glory of this lampless Universe !
Thou Moon beyond the clouds ! Thou living Form
Among the Dead ! Thou Star above the Storm !
Thou Wonder, and thou Beauty, and thou Terror !
Thou Harmony of Nature's art ! Thou Mirror
In whom, as in the splendor of the Sun,
All shapes look glorious which thou gazest on !
Aye, even the dim words which obscure thee now
Flash, lightning-like, with unaccustomed glow ;
I pray thee that thou blot from this sad song
All of its much mortality and wrong,
With those clear drops, which start like sacred dew
From the twin lights thy sweet soul darkens through,
Weeping, till sorrow becomes ecstasy :
Then smile on it, so that it may not die.

I never thought before my death to see
Youth's vision thus made perfect.   Emily,
I love thee ; though the world by no thin name
Will hide that love from its unvalued shame.
Would we two had been twins of the same mother!
Or, that the name my heart lent to another
Could be a sister's bond for her and thee,
Blending two beams of one eternity !
Yet were one lawful and the other true,
These names, though dear, could paint not, as is due,
How beyond refuge I am thine.   Ah me !
I am not thine : I am a part of *thee*.

Sweet Lamp ! my moth-like Muse has burnt its
     wings ;
Or, like a dying swan who soars and sings,
Young Love should teach Time, in his own gray
     style,
All that thou art.   Art thou not void of guile,
A lovely soul formed to be blest and bless ?
A well of sealed and secret happiness,
Whose waters like blithe light and music are,
Vanquishing dissonance and gloom ?   A Star
Which moves not in the moving Heavens, alone ?
A smile amid dark frowns ? a gentle tone
Amid rude voices ? a belovèd light ?
A Solitude, a Refuge, a Delight ?
A Lute, which those whom love has taught to play
Make music on, to soothe the roughest day
And lull fond grief asleep ? a buried treasure ?
A cradle of young thoughts of wingless pleasure ?
A violet-shrouded grave of Woe ? — I measure

The world of fancies, seeking one like thee,
And find — alas ! mine own infirmity.

She met me, Stranger, upon life's rough way,
And lured me towards sweet Death ; as Night by Day,
Winter by Spring, or Sorrow by swift Hope,
Led into light, life, peace.   An antelope,
In the suspended impulse of its lightness,
Were less ethereally light : the brightness
Of her divinest presence trembles through
Her limbs, as underneath a cloud of dew
Embodied in the windless Heaven of June
Amid the splendor-wingèd stars, the Moon
Burns, inextinguishably beautiful :
And from her lips, as from a hyacinth full
Of honey-dew, a liquid murmur drops,
Killing the sense with passion ; sweet as stops
Of planetary music heard in trance.
In her mild lights the starry spirits dance,
The sun-beams of those wells which ever leap
Under the lightnings of the soul — too deep
For the brief fathom-line of thought or sense.
The glory of her being, issuing thence,
Stains the dead, blank, cold air with a warm shade
Of unentangled intermixture, made
By Love, of light and motion : one intense
Diffusion, one serene Omnipresence,
Whose flowing outlines mingle in their flowing
Around her cheeks and utmost fingers glowing
With the unintermitted blood, which there
Quivers, (as in a fleece of snow-like air
The crimson pulse of living morning quiver,)

Continuously prolonged, and ending never,
Till they are lost, and in that Beauty furled
Which penetrates and clasps and fills the world;
Scarce visible from extreme loveliness.

Warm fragrance seems to fall from her light dress
And her loose hair; and where some heavy tress
The air of her own speed has disentwined,
The sweetness seems to satiate the faint wind;
And in the soul a wild odor is felt,
Beyond the sense, like fiery dews that melt
Into the bosom of a frozen bud. ——
See where she stands! a mortal shape indued
With love and life and light and deity,
And motion which may change but cannot die;
An image of some bright Eternity;
A shadow of some golden dream; a Splendor
Leaving the third sphere pilotless; a tender
Reflection of the eternal Moon of Love
Under whose motions life's dull billows move;
A Metaphor of Spring and Youth and Morning;
A Vision like incarnate April, warning,
With smiles and tears, Frost the Anatomy
Into his summer grave.

　　　　　　Ah, woe is me!
What have I dared? where am I lifted? how
Shall I descend, and perish not? I know
That Love makes all things equal: I have heard
By mine own heart this joyous truth averred:
The spirit of the worm beneath the sod
In love and worship, blends itself with God.

Spouse! Sister! Angel! Pilot of the Fate
Whose course has been so starless! O too late
Belovèd! O too soon adored, by me!
For in the fields of immortality
My spirit should at first have worshipped thine,
A divine presence in a place divine;
Or should have moved beside it on this earth,
A shadow of that substance, from its birth;
But not as now: — I love thee; yes, I feel
That on the fountain of my heart a seal
Is set, to keep its waters pure and bright
For thee, since in those *tears* thou hast delight.
We — are we not formed, as notes of music are,
For one another, though dissimilar;
Such difference without discord, as can make
Those sweetest sounds, in which all spirits shake
As trembling leaves in a continuous air?

Thy wisdom speaks in me, and bids me dare
Beacon the rocks on which high hearts are wreckt.
I never was attached to that great sect,
Whose doctrine is, that each one should select
Out of the crowd a mistress or a friend,
And all the rest, though fair and wise, commend
To cold oblivion, though it is in the code
Of modern morals, and the beaten road
Which those poor slaves with weary footsteps
        tread,
Who travel to their home among the dead
By the broad highway of the world, and so
With one chained friend, perhaps a jealous foe,
The dreariest and the longest journey go.

True Love in this differs from gold and clay
That to divide is not to take away.
Love is like understanding that grows bright
Gazing on many truths; 'tis like thy light,
Imagination ! which from earth and sky,
And from the depths of human phantasy,
As from a thousand prisms and mirrors, fills
The Universe with glorious beams, and kills
Error, the worm, with many a sun-like arrow
Of its reverberated lightning.   Narrow
The heart that loves, the brain that contemplates,
The life that wears, the spirit that creates
One object, and one form, and builds thereby
A sepulchre for its eternity.

Mind from its object differs most in this:
Evil from good ; misery from happiness ;
The baser from the nobler ; the impure
And frail, from what is clear and must endure.
If you divide suffering and dross, you may
Diminish till it is consumed away ;
If you divide pleasure and love and thought,
Each part exceeds the whole ; and we know not
How much, while any yet remains unshared,
Of pleasure may be gained, of sorrow spared :
This truth is that deep well, whence sages draw
The unenvied light of hope ; the eternal law
By which those live, to whom this world of life
Is as a garden ravaged, and whose strife
Tills for the promise of a later birth
The wilderness of this Elysian earth.

There was a Being whom my spirit oft
Met on its visioned wanderings, far aloft,
In the clear golden prime of my youth's dawn,
Upon the fairy isles of sunny lawn,
Amid the enchanted mountains, and the caves
Of divine sleep, and on the air-like waves
Of wonder-level dream, whose tremulous floor
Paved her light steps ; — on an imagined shore,
Under the gray beak of some promontory
She met me, robed in such exceeding glory,
That I beheld her not.   In solitudes
Her voice came to me through the whispering woods,
And from the fountains, and the odors deep
Of flowers, which, like lips murmuring in their sleep
Of the sweet kisses which had lulled them there,
Breathed but of *her* to the enamoured air ;
And from the breezes whether low or loud,
And from the rain of every passing cloud,
And from the singing of the summer-birds,
And from all sounds, all silence.   In the words
Of antique verse and high romance, — in form,
Sound, color — in whatever checks that Storm
Which with the shattered present chokes the past ;
And in that best philosophy, whose taste
Makes this cold common hell, our life, a doom
As glorious as a fiery martyrdom ;
Her Spirit was the harmony of truth. —

Then, from the caverns of my dreamy youth
I sprang, as one sandalled with plumes of fire,
And towards the loadstar of my one desire,
I flitted, like a dizzy moth, whose flight

Is as a dead leaf's in the owlet light,
When it would seek in Hesper's setting sphere
A radiant death, a fiery sepulchre,
As if it were a lamp of earthly flame. —
But She, whom prayers or tears then could not tame,
Past, like a God throned on a wingèd planet,
Whose burning plumes to tenfold swiftness fan it,
Into the dreary cone of our life's shade ;
And as a man with mighty loss dismayed,
I would have followed, though the grave between
Yawned like a gulf whose spectres are unseen :
When a voice said : — " O Thou of hearts the weakest,
The phantom is beside thee whom thou seekest."
Then I — " where? " the world's echo answered
      " where ! "
And in that silence, and in my despair,
I questioned every tongueless wind that flew
Over my tower of mourning, if it knew
Whither 'twas fled, this soul out of my soul ;
And murmured names and spells which have control
Over the sightless tyrants of our fate ;
But neither prayer nor verse could dissipate
The night which closed on her ; nor uncreate
That world within this Chaos, mine and me,
Of which she was the veiled Divinity,
The world I say of thoughts that worshipped her :
And therefore I went forth, with hope and fear
And every gentle passion sick to death,
Feeding my course with expectation's breath,
Into the wintry forest of our life ;
And struggling through its error with vain strife,
And stumbling in my weakness and my haste, .

And half bewildered by new forms, I past
Seeking among those untaught foresters
If I could find one form resembling hers,
In which she might have masked herself from me.
There, — One, whose voice was venomed melody
Sate by a well, under blue night-shade bowers;
The breath of her false mouth was like faint flowers,
Her touch was as electric poison, — flame
Out of her looks into my vitals came,
And from her living cheeks and bosom flew
A killing air, which pierced like honey-dew
Into the core of my green heart, and lay
Upon its leaves; until, as hair grown gray
O'er a young brow, they hid its unblown prime
With ruins of unseasonable time.

In many mortal forms I rashly sought
The shadow of that idol of my thought.
And some were fair — but beauty dies away:
Others were wise — but honeyed words betray:
And One was true — oh ! why not true to me?
Then, as a hunted deer that could not flee,
I turned upon my thoughts, and stood at bay,
Wounded and weak and panting; the cold day
Trembled, for pity of my strife and pain.
When, like a noon-day dawn, there shone again
Deliverance. One stood on my path who seemed
As like the glorious shape which I had dreamed,
As is the Moon, whose changes ever run
Into themselves, to the eternal Sun ;
The cold chaste Moon, the Queen of Heaven's bright
     isles,

Who makes all beautiful on which she smiles,
That wandering shrine of soft yet icy flame
Which ever is transformed, yet still the same,
And warms not but illumines. Young and fair
As the descended Spirit of that sphere.
She hid me, as the Moon may hide the night
From its own darkness, until all was bright
Between the Heaven and Earth of my calm mind,
And, as a cloud charioted by the wind.
She led me to a cave in that wild place,
And sate beside me, with her downward face
Illumining my slumbers, like the Moon
Waxing and waning o'er Endymion.
And I was laid asleep, spirit and limb,
And all my being became bright or dim
As the Moon's image in a summer sea,
According as she smiled or frowned on me;
And there I lay, within a chaste cold bed:
Alas, I then was nor alive nor dead: —
For at her silver voice came Death and Life,
Unmindful each of their accustomed strife,
Masked like twin babes, a sister and a brother,
The wandering hopes of one abandoned mother,
And through the cavern without wings they flew,
And cried " Away, he is not of our crew."
I wept, and though it be a dream, I weep.

What storms then shook the ocean of my sleep,
Blotting that Moon, whose pale and waning lips
Then shrank as in the sickness of eclipse; —
And how my soul was as a lampless sea,
And who was then its Tempest; and when She.

The Planet of that hour, was quenched, what frost
Crept o'er those waters, till from coast to coast
The moving billows of my being fell
Into a death of ice, immovable; —
And then — what earthquakes made it gape and
     split,
The white Moon smiling all the while on it,
These words conceal : — If not, each word would be
The key of stanchless tears. Weep not for me !

At length, into the obscure Forest came
The Vision I had sought through grief and shame.
Athwart that wintry wilderness of thorns
Flashed from her motion splendor like the Morn's,
And from her presence life was radiated
Through the gray earth and branches bare and dead ;
So that her way was paved, and roofed above
With flowers as soft as thoughts of budding love ;
And music from her respiration spread
Like light, — all other sounds were penetrated
By the small, still, sweet spirit of that sound,
So that the savage winds hung mute around ;
And odors warm and fresh fell from her hair
Dissolving the dull cold in the frore air :
Soft as an Incarnation of the Sun,
When light is changed to love, this glorious One
Floated into the cavern where I lay,
And called my Spirit, and the dreaming clay
Was lifted by the thing that dreamed below
As smoke by fire, and in her beauty's glow
I stood, and felt the dawn of my long night
Was penetrating me with living light ;

I knew it was the Vision veiled from me
So many years — that it was Emily.

   Twin Spheres of light who rule this passive Earth,
This world of love, this *me*; and into birth
Awaken all its fruits and flowers, and dart
Magnetic might into its central heart;
And lift its billows and its mists, and guide
By everlasting laws, each wind and tide
To its fit cloud, and its appointed cave;
And lull its storms, each in the craggy grave
Which was its cradle, luring to faint bowers
The armies of the rain-bow-wingèd showers;
And, as those married lights, which from the towers
Of Heaven look forth and fold the wandering globe
In liquid sleep and splendor, as a robe;
And all their many-mingled influence blend,
If equal, yet unlike, to one sweet end; —
So ye, bright regents, with alternate sway
Govern my sphere of being, night and day!
Thou, not disdaining even a borrowed might;
Thou, not eclipsing a remoter light;
And, through the shadow of the seasons three,
From Spring to Autumn's sere maturity,
Light it into the Winter of the tomb,
Where it may ripen to a brighter bloom.
Thou too, O Comet beautiful and fierce,
Who drew the heart of this frail Universe
Towards thine own; till, wreckt in that convulsion,
Alternating attraction and repulsion,
Thine went astray and that was rent in twain;
Oh, float into our azure heaven again!

Be there love's folding-star at thy return;
The living Sun will feed thee from its urn
Of golden fire; the Moon will veil her horn
In thy last smiles; adoring Even and Morn
Will worship thee with incense of calm breath
And lights and shadows; as the star of Death
And Birth is worshipped by those sisters wild
Called Hope and Fear — upon the heart are piled
Their offerings, — of this sacrifice divine
A World shall be the altar.
                                        Lady mine,
Scorn not these flowers of thought, the fading birth
Which from its heart of hearts that plant puts forth
Whose fruit, made perfect by thy sunny eyes,
Will be as of the trees of Paradise.

    The day is come, and thou wilt fly with me.
To whatsoe'er of dull mortality
Is mine, remain a vestal sister still;
To the intense, the deep, the imperishable,
Not mine but me, henceforth be thou united
Even as a bride, delighting and delighted.
The hour is come: — the destined Star has risen
Which shall descend upon a vacant prison.
The walls are high, the gates are strong, thick set
The sentinels — but true love never yet
Was thus constrained: it overleaps all fence:
Like lightning, with invisible violence
Piercing its continents; like Heaven's free breath,
Which he who grasps can hold not; liker Death,
Who rides upon a thought, and makes his way
Through temple, tower, and palace, and the array

Of arms; more strength has Love than he or they;
For it can burst his charnel, and make free
The limbs in chains, the heart in agony,
The soul in dust and chaos.
                              Emily,
A ship is floating in the harbor now,
A wind is hovering o'er the mountain's brow;
There is a path on the sea's azure floor,
No keel has ever ploughed that path before;
The halcyons brood around the foamless isles;
The treacherous Ocean has forsworn its wiles;
The merry mariners are bold and free:
Say, my heart's sister, wilt thou sail with me?
Our bark is as an albatross, whose nest
Is a far Eden of the purple East;
And we between her wings will sit, while Night
And Day, and Storm, and Calm, pursue their flight,
Our ministers, along the boundless Sea,
Treading each other's heels, unheededly.
It is an isle under Ionian skies,
Beautiful as a wreck of Paradise,
And, for the harbors are not safe and good,
This land would have remained a solitude
But for some pastoral people native there,
Who from the Elysian, clear, and golden air
Draw the last spirit of the age of gold,
Simple and spirited; innocent and bold.
The blue Ægean girds this chosen home,
With ever-changing sound and light and foam,
Kissing the sifted sands, and caverns hoar;
And all the winds wandering along the shore
Undulate with the undulating tide:

There are thick woods where sylvan forms abide;
And many a fountain, rivulet, and pond,
As clear as elemental diamond,
Or serene morning air; and far beyond,
The mossy tracks made by the goats and deer
(Which the rough shepherd treads but once a year,)
Pierce into glades, caverns, and bowers, and halls
Built round with ivy, which the waterfalls
Illumining, with sound that never fails
Accompany the noon-day nightingales;
And all the place is peopled with sweet airs;
The light clear element which the isle wears
Is heavy with the scent of lemon-flowers,
Which floats like mist laden with unseen showers,
And falls upon the eye-lids like faint sleep;
And from the moss violets and jonquils peep,
And dart their arrowy odor through the brain
Till you might faint with that delicious pain.
And every motion, odor, beam, and tone,
With that deep music is in unison:
Which is a soul within the soul — they seem
Like echoes of an antenatal dream. —
It is an isle 'twixt Heaven, Air, Earth, and Sea,
Cradled, and hung in clear tranquillity;
Bright as that wandering Eden Lucifer,
Washed by the soft blue Oceans of young air
It is a favored place. Famine or Blight,
Pestilence, War and Earthquake, never light
Upon its mountain-peaks; blind vultures, they
Sail onward far upon their fatal way:
The wingèd storms, chaunting their thunder-psalm
To other lands, leave azure chasms of calm

Over this isle, or weep themselves in dew,
From which its fields and woods ever renew
Their green and golden immortality.
And from the sea there rise, and from the sky
There fall, clear exhalations, soft and bright,
Veil after veil, each hiding some delight,
Which Sun or Moon or zephyr draw aside,
Till the isle's beauty, like a naked bride
Glowing at once with love and loveliness,
Blushes and trembles at its own excess:
Yet, like a buried lamp, a Soul no less
Burns in the heart of this delicious isle,
An atom of th' Eternal, whose own smile
Unfolds itself, and may be felt, not seen
O'er the gray rocks, blue waves, and forests green,
Filling their bare and void interstices. —
But the chief marvel of the wilderness
Is a lone dwelling, built by whom or how
None of the rustic island-people know:
'Tis not a tower of strength, though with its height
It overtops the woods; but, for delight,
Some wise and tender Ocean-King, ere crime
Had been invented, in the world's young prime,
Reared it, a wonder of that simple time,
An envy of the isles, a pleasure-house
Made sacred to his sister and his spouse.
It scarce seems now a wreck of human art,
But, as it were Titanic; in the heart
Of Earth having assumed its form, then grown
Out of the mountains, from the living stone,
Lifting itself in caverns light and high:
For all the antique and learnèd imagery

Has been erased, and in the place of it
The ivy and the wild-vine interknit
The volumes of their many-twining stems ;
Parasite flowers illume with dewy gems
The lampless halls, and when they fade, the sky
Peeps through their winter-woof of tracery
With Moon-light patches, or star atoms keen,
Or fragments of the day's intense serene ; —
Working mosaic on their Parian floors.
And, day and night, aloof, from the high towers
And terraces, the Earth and Ocean seem
To sleep in one another's arms, and dream
Of waves, flowers, clouds, woods, rocks, and all that
     we
Read in their smiles, and call reality.

  This isle and house are mine, and I have vowed
Thee to be lady of the solitude. —
And I have fitted up some chambers there
Looking towards the golden Eastern air,
And level with the living winds, which flow
Like waves above the living waves below. —
I have sent books and music there, and all
Those instruments with which high spirits call
The future from its cradle, and the past
Out of its grave, and make the present last
In thoughts and joys which sleep, but cannot die,
Folded within their own eternity.
Our simple life wants little, and true taste
Hires not the pale drudge Luxury, to waste
The scene it would adorn, and therefore still,
Nature, with all her children, haunts the hill.

The ring-dove, in the embowering ivy, yet
Keeps up her love-lament, and the owls flit
Round the evening tower, and the young stars
    glance
Between the quick bats in their twilight dance;
The spotted deer bask in the fresh moon-light
Before our gate, and the slow, silent night
Is measured by the pants of their calm sleep.
Be this our home in life, and when years heap
Their withered hours, like leaves, on our decay,
Let us become the over-hanging day,
The living soul of this Elysian isle,
Conscious, inseparable, one.   Meanwhile
We two will rise, and sit, and walk together,
Under the roof of blue Ionian weather,
And wander in the meadows, or ascend
The mossy mountains, where the blue heavens bend
With lightest winds, to touch their paramour;
Or linger, where the pebble-paven shore,
Under the quick, faint kisses of the sea
Trembles and sparkles as with ecstasy,—
Possessing and possest by all that is
Within that calm circumference of bliss,
And by each other, till to love and live
Be one:—or, at the noontide hour, arrive
Where some old cavern hoar seems yet to keep
The moonlight of the expired night asleep,
Through which the awakened day can never peep;
A veil for our seclusion, close as Night's,
Where secure sleep may kill thine innocent lights;
Sleep, the fresh dew of languid love, the rain
Whose drops quench kisses till they burn again.

And we will talk, until thought's melody
Become too sweet for utterance, and it die
In words, to live again in looks, which dart
With thrilling tone into the voiceless heart,
Harmonizing silence without a sound.
Our breath shall intermix, our bosoms bound,
And our veins beat together; and our lips
With other eloquence than words, eclipse
The soul that burns between them, and the wells
Which boil under our being's inmost cells,
The fountains of our deepest life, shall be
Confused in passion's golden purity,
As mountain-springs under the morning Sun.
We.shall become the same, we shall be one
Spirit within two frames, oh ! wherefore two?
One passion in twin-hearts, which grows and grew
Till like two meteors of expanding flame,
Those spheres instinct with it become the same,
Touch, mingle, are transfigured; ever still
Burning, yet ever inconsumable :
In one another's substance finding food,
Like flames too pure and light and unimbued
To nourish their bright lives with baser prey,
Which point to Heaven and cannot pass away :
One hope within two wills, one will beneath
Two overshadowing minds, one life, one death,
One Heaven, one Hell, one immortality,
And one annihilation.   Woe is me !
The wingèd words on which my soul would pierce
Into the height of love's rare Universe,
Are chains of lead around its flight of fire. —
I pant, I sink, I tremble, I expire !

Weak Verses, go, kneel at your Sovereign's feet,
And say : — "We are the masters of thy slave ;
What wouldest thou with us and ours and thine?"
Then call your sisters from Oblivion's cave,
All singing loud : "Love's very pain is sweet,
But its reward is in the world divine
Which, if not here, it builds beyond the grave."
So shall ye live when I am there. Then haste
Over the hearts of men, until ye meet
Marina, Vanna, Primus, and the rest,
And bid them love each other and be blest :
And leave the troop which errs, and which reproves,
And come and be my guest, — for I am Love's.

1820.

FRAGMENT.

Is it that in some brighter sphere
We part from friends we meet with here?
Or do we see the Future pass
Over the Present's dusky glass?
Or what is that that makes us seem
To patch up fragments of a dream,
Part of which comes true, and part
Beats and trembles in the heart?

1819.

Poems to Liberty, Greece, and Italy.

— ◦ ■ ◦ —

ODE TO NAPLES.

EPODE I. *a.*

I STOOD within the city disinterred;
  And heard the autumnal leaves like light footfalls
Of spirits passing through the streets; and heard
    The Mountain's slumberous voice at intervals
      Thrill through those roofless halls;
The oracular thunder penetrating shook
    The listening soul in my suspended blood;
I felt that Earth out of her deep heart spoke —
    I felt, but heard not: — through white columns
      glowed
      The isle-sustaining Ocean-flood,
A plane of light between two Heavens of azure:
  Around me gleamed many a bright sepulchre
Of whose pure beauty, Time, as if his pleasure
Were to spare Death, had never made erasure;
    But every living lineament was clear
    As in the sculptor's thought; and there
The wreaths of stony myrtle, ivy and pine,
    Like winter leaves o'ergrown by moulded snow,
    Seemed only not to move and grow

Because the crystal silence of the air
  Weighed on their life; even as the Power divine
  Which then lulled all things, brooded upon mine.

EPODE II. a.

    Then gentle winds arose
    With many a mingled close
Of wild Æolian sound and mountain-odor keen;
    And where the Baian ocean
    Welters with airlike motion,
Within, above, around its bowers of starry green,
  Moving the sea-flowers in those purple caves
    Even as the ever stormless atmosphere
      Floats o'er the Elysian realm,
  It bore me like an Angel, o'er the waves
    Of sunlight, whose swift pinnace of dewy air
      No storm can overwhelm;
      I sailed, where ever flows
      Under the calm Serene
      A spirit of deep emotion
      From the unknown graves
      Of the dead kings of Melody.
Shadowy Aornos darkened o'er the helm
The horizontal æther; heaven stript bare
Its depths over Elysium, where the prow
Made the invisible water white as snow; .
From that Typhæan mount, Inarime
  There streamed a sunlight vapor, like the
    standard
      Of some ætherial host;
      Whilst from all the coast,

Louder and louder, gathering round, there
    wandered
Over the oracular woods and divine sea
Prophesyings which grew articulate —
They seize me — I must speak them — be they fate !

STROPHE *a*. 1.

Naples ! thou Heart of men which ever pantest
   Naked, beneath the lidless eye of heaven !
Elysian city which to calm inchantest
   The mutinous air and sea : they round thee, even
   As sleep round Love, are driven !
Metropolis of a ruined Paradise
   Long lost, late won, and yet but half regained !
Bright Altar of the bloodless sacrifice,
   Which armèd Victory offers up unstained
   To Love, the flower-enchained !
Thou which wert once, and then didst cease to be,
Now art, and henceforth ever shalt be, free,
   If Hope and Truth and Justice can avail,
      Hail, hail, all hail !

STROPHE *β*. 2.

. Thou youngest giant birth
   Which from the groaning earth
Leap'st, clothed in armor of impenetrable scale !
   Last of the Intercessors !
   Who 'gainst the Crowned Transgressors
Pleadest before God's love ! Arrayed in Wisdom's
     mail,
   Wave thy lightning lance in mirth

Nor let thy high heart fail,
Though from their hundred gates the leagued
 Oppressors,
With hurried legions move !
Hail, hail, all hail !

ANTISTROPHE α. I.

What though Cimmerian Anarchs dare blaspheme
 Freedom and thee ? thy shield is as a mirror
To make their blind slaves see, and with fierce gleam
 To turn his hungry sword upon the wearer;
  A new Actæon's error
Shall theirs have been — devoured by their own
 hounds !
 Be thou like the imperial Basilisk
Killing thy foe with unapparent wounds !
 Gaze on oppression, till at that dread risk
 Aghast she pass from the Earth's disk :
Fear not, but gaze — for freemen mightier grow,
And slaves more feeble, gazing on their foe ;
 If Hope and Truth and Justice may avail,
 Thou shalt be great. — All hail !

ANTISTROPHE β. 2.

From Freedom's form divine,
From Nature's inmost shrine,
Strip every impious gaud, rend Error veil by veil :
 O'er Ruin desolate,
 O'er Falsehood's fallen state,
Sit thou sublime, unawed ; be the Destroyer pale !
 And equal laws be thine,

And wingèd words let sail,
Freighted with truth even from the throne of God :
That wealth, surviving fate,
Be thine. — All hail !

ANTISTROPHE *a. γ.*

Didst thou not start to hear Spain's thrilling. pæan
From land to land re-echoed solemnly,
Till silence became music ?   From the Ææan
To the cold Alps, eternal Italy
Starts to hear thine !   The Sea
Which paves the desert streets of Venice laughs
In light and music ; widowed Genoa wan
By moonlight spells ancestral epitaphs,
Murmuring, where is Doria ? fair Milan,
Within whose veins long ran
The viper's palsying venom, lifts her heel
To bruise his head.   The signal and the seal
(If Hope and Truth and Justice can avail)
Art Thou of all these hopes. — O hail !

ANTISTROPHE *β. γ.*

Florence ! beneath the sun,
Of cities fairest one,
Blushes within her bower for Freedom's expectation :
From eyes of quenchless hope
Rome tears the priestly cope,
As ruling once by power, so now by admiration,
As athlete stript to run
From a remoter station
For the high prize lost on Philippi's shore : —

As then Hope, Truth, and Justice did avail,
So now may Fraud and Wrong! O hail!

EPODE I. β.

Hear ye the march as of the Earth-born Forms
   Arrayed against the ever-living Gods?
The crash and darkness of a thousand storms
   Bursting their inaccessible abodes
      Of crags and thunder clouds?
See ye the banners blazoned to the day,
   Inwrought with emblems of barbaric pride?
Dissonant threats kill Silence far away,
   The serene Heaven which wraps our Eden wide
      With iron light is dyed,
The Anarchs of the North lead forth their legions
     Like Chaos o'er creation, uncreating;
An hundred tribes nourished on strange religions
And lawless slaveries, — down the aërial regions
     Of the white Alps, desolating,
     Famished wolves that bide no waiting,
Blotting the glowing footsteps of old glory,
Trampling our columned cities into dust,
     Their dull and savage lust
     On Beauty's corse to sickness satiating —
They come! The fields they tread look black and
     hoary
With fire — from their red feet the streams run gory!

EPODE II. β.

Great Spirit, deepest Love!
Which rulest and dost move

All things which live and are, within the Italian shore;
'Who spreadest heaven around it,
Whose woods, rocks, waves, surround it;
Who sittest in thy star, o'er Ocean's western floor,
Spirit of beauty! at whose soft command
The sunbeams and the showers distil its foison
From the Earth's bosom chill:
O bid those beams be each a blinding brand
Of lightning! bid those showers be dews of poison!
Bid the Earth's plenty kill!
Bid thy bright Heaven above,
Whilst light and darkness bound it,
Be their tomb who planned
To make it ours and thine!
Or, with thine harmonizing ardors fill
And raise thy sons, as o'er the prone horizon
Thy lamp feeds every twilight wave with fire —
Be man's high hope and unextinct desire,
The instrument to work thy will divine!
Then clouds from sunbeams, antelopes from
leopards,
And frowns and fears from Thee,
Would not more swiftly flee
Than Celtic wolves from the Ausonian shepherds. —
Whatever, Spirit, from thy starry shrine
Thou yieldest or withholdest, Oh let be
This city of thy worship ever free!

August 25, 1820.

GREECE TO SLAVERY.

LET there be light! said Liberty,
And like sunrise from the sea,
Athens arose! — Around her born,
Shone like mountains in the morn
Glorious states; — and are they now
Ashes, wrecks, oblivion?   Go,
Where Thermæ and Asopus swallowed
Persia, as the sand does foam.
Deluge upon deluge followed,
Discord, Macedon, and Rome :
And lastly thou !   Temples and towers,
Citadels and marts, and they
Who live and die there, have been ours,
And may be thine, and must decay;
But Greece and her foundations are
Built below the tide of war,
Based on the crystalline sea
Of thought and its eternity ;
Her citizens, imperial spirits,
Rule the present from the past,
On all this world of men inherits
Their seal is set.

Hellas.

———◦◦◦———

CHORUS.

IN the great morning of the world,
The spirit of God with might unfurl'd
The flag of Freedom over Chaos,

And all its banded anarchs fled,
Like vultures frightened from Imaus,
  Before an earthquake's tread. —
So from Time's tempestuous dawn
Freedom's splendor burst and shone : —
Thermopylæ and Marathon
Caught, like mountains beacon-lighted,
  The springing Fire. — The wingèd glory
On Philippi half alighted,
  Like an eagle on a promontory.
Its unwearied wings could fan
The quenchless ashes of Milan.
From age to age, from man to man,
  It lived ; and lit from land to land,
  Florence, Albion, Switzerland.
Then night fell ; and, as from night,
Re-assuming fiery flight,
From the West swift Freedom came,
  Against the course of Heaven and doom,
A second sun arrayed in flame,
  To burn, to kindle, to illume.
From far Atlantis its young beams
Chased the shadows and the dreams.
France, with all her sanguine steams,
  Hid, but quench'd it not ; again
  Through clouds its shafts of glory rain
  From utmost Germany to Spain.   .
As an eagle fed with morning
Scorns the embattled tempest's warning,
When she seeks her aerie hanging
  In the mountain-cedar's hair,
And her brood expect the clanging

Of her wings through the wild air,
Sick with famine : — Freedom, so
To what of Greece remaineth now
Returns ; her hoary ruins glow
Like orient mountains lost in day ;
   Beneath the safety of her wings
Her renovated nurslings prey,
   And in the naked lightnings
Of truth they purge their dazzled eyes.
Let Freedom leave — where'er she flies,
A Desert, or a Paradise :
   Let the beautiful and the brave
   Share her glory, or a grave.

Hellas.

CHORUS.

WORLDS on worlds are rolling ever
   From creation to decay,
Like the bubbles on a river
   Sparkling, bursting, borne away.
But they are still immortal
Who, through birth's orient portal
And death's dark chasm hurrying to and fro,
   Clothe their unceasing flight
   In the brief dust and light
Gather'd around their chariots as they go ;
   New shapes they still may weave,
   New gods, new laws receive,
Bright or dim are they as the robes they last
   On Death's bare ribs had cast.

A power from the unknown God,
  A Promethean conqueror came ;
Like a triumphal path he trod
    The thorns of death and shame.
    A mortal shape to him
    Was like the vapor dim
Which the orient planet animates with light ;
    Hell, Sin, and Slavery came,
    Like blood-hounds mild and tame,
Nor preyed, until their Lord had taken flight ;
    The moon of Mahomet
    Arose, and it shall set :
While blazoned as on heaven's immortal noon
    The cross leads generations on.

Swift as the radiant shapes of sleep
    From one whose dreams are Paradise
Fly, when the fond wretch wakes to weep,
    And day peers forth with her blank eyes ;
    So fleet, so faint, so fair,
    The Powers of earth and air
Fled from the folding star of Bethlehem :
    Apollo, Pan, and Love,
    And even Olympian Jove
Grew weak, for killing Truth had glared on them ;
    Our hills and seas and streams
    Dispeopled of their dreams,
Their waters turned to blood, their dew to tears,
    Wailed for the golden years.
                                        Hellas.

CHORUS.

THE world's great age begins anew,
   The golden years return,
The earth doth like a snake renew
   Her winter weeds outworn :
Heaven smiles, and faiths and empires gleam,
Like wrecks of a dissolving dream.

A brighter Hellas rears its mountains
   From waves serener far ;
A new Peneus rolls his fountains
   Against the morning-star.
Where fairer Tempes bloom, there sleep
Young Cyclads on a sunnier deep.

A loftier Argo cleaves the main,
   Fraught with a later prize ;
Another Orpheus sings again,
   And loves, and weeps, and dies.
A new Ulysses leaves once more
Calypso for his native shore.

O, write no more the tale of Troy,
   If earth Death's scroll must be !
Nor mix with Laian rage the joy
   Which dawns upon the free :
Although a subtler Sphinx renew
Riddles of death Thebes never knew.

Another Athens shall arise,
   And to remoter time

Bequeath, like sunset to the skies,
  The splendor of its prime ;
And leave, if nought so bright may live,
All earth can take or Heaven can give.

Saturn and Love their long repose
  Shall burst, more bright and good
Than all who fell, than One who rose,
  Than many unsubdued :
Not gold, not blood, their altar dowers,
But votive tears and symbol flowers.

O cease ! must hate and death return ?
  Cease ! must men kill and die ?
Cease ! drain not to its dregs the urn
  Of bitter prophecy.
The world is weary of the past,
O might it die or rest at last !

                                        Hellas.

———◦◇◦———

THE NEW WORLD.

DEMOGORGON.

THOU, Earth, calm empire of a happy soul,
  Sphere of divinest shapes and harmonies,
Beautiful orb ! gathering as thou dost roll
  The love which paves thy path along the skies :

THE EARTH.

I hear : I am as a drop of dew that dies.

DEMOGORGON.

Thou, Moon, which gazest on the nightly Earth
  With wonder, as it gazes upon thee;
Whilst each to men, and beasts, and the swift birth
  Of birds, is beauty, love, calm, harmony;

THE MOON.

I hear: I am a leaf shaken by thee!

DEMOGORGON.

Ye kings of suns and stars, Dæmons and Gods,
  Etherial Dominations, who possess
Elysian, windless, fortunate abodes
  Beyond Heaven's constellated wilderness:

A VOICE FROM ABOVE.

Our great Republic hears, we are blest, and bless.

DEMOGORGON.

Ye happy dead, whom beams of brightest verse
  Are clouds to hide, not colors to portray,
Whether your nature is that universe
  Which once ye saw and suffered —

A VOICE FROM BENEATH.

                    Or as they
Whom we have left, we change and pass away.

DEMOGORGON.

Ye elemental Genii, who have homes
From man's high mind even to the central stone
Of sullen lead ; from Heaven's star-fretted domes
To the dull weed some sea-worm battens on :

A CONFUSED VOICE.

We hear : thy words waken Oblivion.

DEMOGORGON.

Spirits, whose homes are flesh : ye beasts and birds.
Ye worms, and fish ; ye living leaves and buds ;
Lightning and wind ; and ye untamable herds,
Meteors and mists, which throng air's solitudes :

A VOICE.

Thy voice to us is wind among still woods.

DEMOGORGON.

Man, who wert once a despot and a slave ;
A dupe and a deceiver ; a decay ;
A traveller from the cradle to the grave
Through the dim night of this immortal day :

ALL.

Speak : thy strong words may never pass away.

DEMOGORGON.

This is the day, which down the void abysm
At the Earth-born's spell yawns for Heaven's despot-
    ism,
   And Conquest is dragged captive through the deep:
Love, from its awful throne of patient power
In the wise heart, from the last giddy hour
   Of dead endurance, from the slippery, steep,
And narrow verge of crag-like agony, springs
And folds over the world its healing wings.

Gentleness, Virtue, Wisdom, and Endurance,   -
These are the seals of that most firm assurance,
   Which bars the pit over Destruction's strength;
And if, with infirm hand, Eternity,
Mother of many acts and hours, should free
   The serpent that would clasp her with his length;
These are the spells by which to re-assume
An empire o'er the disentangled doom.

To suffer woes which Hope thinks infinite;
To forgive wrongs darker than death or night;
   To defy Power, which seems omnipotent;
To love, and bear; to hope till Hope creates
From its own wreck the thing it contemplates;
   Neither to change, nor falter, nor repent;
This, like thy glory, Titan, is to be
Good, great and joyous, beautiful and free;
This is alone Life, Joy, Empire, and Victory.

Prom. Unbound. 1820.

LIFE may change, but it may fly not;
Hope may vanish, but can die not;
Truth be veil'd, but still it burneth;
Love repulsed, — but it returneth!

Yet were Life a charnel where
Hope lay coffin'd with Despair;
Yet were truth a sacred lie,
Love were lust — if Liberty

Lent not life its soul of light,
Hope its iris of delight,
Truth its prophet's robe to wear,
Love its power to give and bear.

Hellas.

The Sensitive Plant.

PART FIRST

A SENSITIVE Plant in a garden grew,
And the young winds fed it with silver dew,
And it opened its fan-like leaves to the light,
And closed them beneath the kisses of night.

And the Spring arose on the garden fair,
Like the Spirit of Love felt everywhere;
And each flower and herb on Earth's dark breast
Rose from the dreams of its wintry rest.

But none ever trembled and panted with bliss
In the garden, the field, or the wilderness,
Like a doe in the noon-tide with love's sweet want,
As the companionless Sensitive Plant.

The snow-drop, and then the violet,
Arose from the ground with warm rain wet,
And their breath was mixed with fresh odor, sent
From the turf, like the voice and the instrument.

Then the pied wind-flowers and the tulip tall,
And narcissi, the fairest among them all,
Who gaze on their eyes in the stream's recess,
Till they die of their own dear loveliness;

262

And the Naiad-like lily of the vale,
Whom youth makes so fair and passion so pale,
That the light of its tremulous bells is seen
Through their pavilions of tender green ;

And the hyacinth purple, and white, and blue,
Which flung from its bells a sweet peal anew
Of music so delicate, soft, and intense,
It was felt like an odor within the sense ;

And the rose like a nymph to the bath addrest,
Which unveiled the depth of her glowing breast,
Till, fold after fold, to the fainting air
The soul of her beauty and love lay bare :

And the wand-like lily, which lifted up,
As a Mænad, its moonlight-colored cup,
Till the fiery star, which is its eye,
Gazed through clear dew on the tender sky ;

And the jessamine faint, and the sweet tuberose,
The sweetest flower for scent that blows ;
And all rare blossoms from every clime
Grew in that garden in perfect prime.

And on the stream whose inconstant bosom
Was prankt under boughs of embowering blossom,
With golden and green light, slanting through
Their heaven of many a tangled hue,

Broad water-lilies lay tremulously,
And starry river-buds glimmered by,
And around them the soft stream did glide and dance
With a motion of sweet sound and radiance.

And the sinuous paths of lawn and of moss,
Which led through the garden along and across,
Some open at once to the sun and the breeze,
Some lost among bowers of blossoming trees,

Were all paved with daisies and delicate bells
As fair as the fabulous asphodels,
And flowrets which drooping as day drooped too
Fell into pavilions, white, purple, and blue,
To roof the glow-worm from the evening dew.

And from this undefiled Paradise
The flowers (as an infant's awakening eyes
Smile on its mother, whose singing sweet
Can first lull, and at last must awaken it,)

When Heaven's blithe winds had unfolded them,
As mine-lamps enkindle a hidden gem,
Shone smiling to Heaven, and every one
Shared joy in the light of the gentle sun;

For each one was interpenetrated
With the light and the odor its neighbor shed,
Like young lovers whom youth and love make dear
Wrapped and filled by their mutual atmosphere.

But the Sensitive Plant which could give small fruit
Of the love which it felt from the leaf to the root,
Received more than all, it loved more than ever,
Where none wanted but it, could belong to the giver,

For the Sensitive Plant has no bright flower;
Radiance and odor are not its dower;
It loves, even like Love, its deep heart is full,
It desires what it has not, the beautiful!

The light winds which from unsustaining wings
Shed the music of many murmurings ;
The beams which dart from many a star
Of the flowers whose hues they bear afar ;

The plumèd insects swift and free,
Like golden boats on a sunny sea,
Laden with light and odor, which pass
Over the gleam of the living grass ;

The unseen clouds of the dew, which lie
Like fire in the flowers till the sun rides high,
Then wander like spirits among the spheres,
Each cloud faint with the fragrance it bears ;

The quivering vapors of dim noontide,
Which like a sea o'er the warm earth glide,
In which every sound, and odor, and beam,
Move, as reeds in a single stream ;

Each and all like ministering angels were
For the Sensitive Plant sweet joy to bear,
Whilst the lagging hours of the day went by
Like windless clouds o'er a tender sky.

And when evening descended from heaven above,
And the Earth was all rest, and the air was all love,
And delight, tho' less bright, was far more deep,
And the day's veil fell from the world of sleep,

And the beasts, and the birds, and the insects were
    drowned
In an ocean of dreams without a sound ;
Whose waves never mark, tho' they ever impress
The light sand which paves it, consciousness ;

(Only over head the sweet nightingale
Ever sang more sweet as the day might fail,
And snatches of its Elysian chant
Were mixed with the dreams of the Sensitive Plant).

The Sensitive Plant was the earliest
Up-gathered into the bosom of rest;
A sweet child weary of its delight;
The feeblest and yet the favorite,
Cradled within the embrace of night.

PART SECOND.

There was a Power in this sweet place,
An Eve in this Eden; a ruling grace
Which to the flowers did they waken or dream,
Was as God is to the starry scheme.

A Lady, the wonder of her kind,
Whose form was upborne by a lovely mind
Which, dilating, had moulded her mien and motion
Like a sea-flower unfolded beneath the ocean,

Tended the garden from morn to even:
And the meteors of that sublunar heaven,
Like the lamps of the air when night walks forth,
Laughed round her footsteps up from the Earth!

She had no companion of mortal race,
But her tremulous breath and her flushing face
Told, whilst the morn kissed the sleep from her eyes
That her dreams were less slumber than Paradise:

As if some bright Spirit for her sweet sake
Had deserted heaven while the stars were awake,
As if yet around her he lingering were,
Tho' the veil of daylight concealed him from her.

Her step seemed to pity the grass it prest;
You might hear by the heaving of her breast,
That the coming and going of the wind
Brought pleasure there and left passion behind.

And wherever her airy footstep trod,
Her trailing hair from the grassy sod
Erased its light vestige, with shadowy sweep,
Like a sunny storm o'er the dark green deep.

I doubt not the flowers of that garden sweet
Rejoiced in the sound of her gentle feet;
I doubt not they felt the spirit that came
From her glowing fingers thro' all their frame.

She sprinkled bright water from the stream
On those that were faint with the sunny beam;
And out of the cups of the heavy flowers
She emptied the rain of the thunder showers.

She lifted their heads with her tender hands,
And sustained them with rods and with osier-bands;
If the flowers had been her own infants she
Could never have nursed them more tenderly.

And all killing insects and gnawing worms,
And things of obscene and unlovely forms
She bore in a basket of Indian woof,
Into the rough woods far aloof,

In a basket, of grasses and wild flowers full,
The freshest her gentle hands could pull
For the poor banished insects, whose intent,
Although they did ill, was innocent.

But the bee and the beamlike ephemeris
Whose path is the lightning's, and soft moths that
    kiss
The sweet lips of the flowers, and harm not, did she
Make her attendant angels be.

And many an antenatal tomb,
Where butterflies dream of the life to come,
She left clinging round the smooth and dark
Edge of the odorous cedar bark.

This fairest creature from earliest spring
Thus moved through the garden ministering
All the sweet season of summer tide,
And ere the first leaf looked brown — she died !

PART THIRD.

Three days the flowers of the garden fair,
Like stars when the moon is awakened, were,
Or the waves of Baiæ, ere luminous
She floats up through the smoke of Vesuvius.

And on the fourth, the Sensitive Plant
Felt the sound of the funeral chaunt,
And the steps of the bearers, heavy and slow,
And the sobs of the mourners deep and low ;

The weary sound and the heavy breath,
And the silent motions of passing death,
And the smell, cold, oppressive, and dank,
Sent through the pores of the coffin plank ;

The dark grass, and the flowers among the grass,
Were bright with tears as the crowd did pass ;
From their sighs the wind caught a mournful tone,
And sate in the pines, and gave groan for groan.

The garden, once fair, became cold and foul,
Like the corpse of her who had been its soul,
Which at first was lovely as if in sleep,
Then slowly changed, till it grew a heap
To make men tremble who never weep.

Swift summer into the autumn flowed,
And frost in the mist of the morning rode,
Though the noonday sun looked clear and bright,
Mocking the spoil of the secret night.

The rose leaves, like flakes of crimson snow,
Paved the turf and the moss below.
The lilies were drooping, and white, and wan,
Like the head and the skin of a dying man.

And Indian plants, of scent and hue
The sweetest that ever were fed on dew,
Leaf after leaf, day after day,
Were massed into the common clay.

And the leaves, brown, yellow, and gray, and red,
And white with the whiteness of what is dead,
Like troops of ghosts on the dry wind past ;
Their whistling noise made the birds aghast.

And the gusty winds waked the wingèd seeds
Out of their birthplace of ugly weeds,
Till they clung round many a sweet flower's stem,
Which rotted into the earth with them.

The water-blooms under the rivulet
Fell from the stalks on which they were set;
And the eddies drove them here and there,
As the winds did those of the upper air.

Then the rain came down, and the broken stalks,
Were bent and tangled across the walks;
And the leafless net-work of parasite bowers
Massed into ruin; and all sweet flowers.

Between the time of the wind and the snow,
All loathliest weeds began to grow,
Whose coarse leaves were splashed with many a speck,
Like the water-snake's belly and the toad's back.

And thistles, and nettles, and darnels rank,
And the dock, and henbane, and hemlock dank,
Stretched out its long and hollow shank,
And stifled the air till the dead wind stank.

And plants, at whose names the verse feels loath,
Filled the place with a monstrous undergrowth,
Prickly, and pulpous, and blistering, and blue,
Livid, and starred with a lurid dew.

And agarics and fungi, with mildew and mould
Started like mist from the wet ground cold;
Pale, fleshy, as if the decaying dead
With a spirit of growth had been animated!

Their moss rotted off them, flake by flake,
Till the thick stalk stuck like a murderer's stake,
Where rags of loose flesh yet tremble on high,
Infecting the winds that wander by.

Spawn, weeds, and filth, a leprous scum,
Made the running rivulet thick and dumb
And at its outlet flags huge as stakes
Dammed it up with roots knotted like water-snakes.

And hour by hour, when the air was still,
The vapors arose which have strength to kill:
At morn they were seen, at noon they were felt,
At night they were darkness no star could melt.

And unctuous meteors from spray to spray
Crept and flitted in broad noon-day
Unseen; every branch on which they alit
By a venomous blight was burned and bit.

The Sensitive Plant like one forbid
Wept, and the tears within each lid
Of its folded leaves which together grew
Were changed to a blight of frozen glue.

For the leaves soon fell, and the branches soon
By the heavy axe of the blast were hewn;
The sap shrank to the root through every pore
As blood to a heart that will beat no more.

For Winter came: the wind was his whip:
One choppy finger was on his lip:
He had torn the cataracts from the hills
And they clanked at his girdle like manacles;

His breath was a chain which without a sound
The earth, and the air, and the water bound;
He came, fiercely driven, in his chariot-throne
By the tenfold blasts of the arctic zone.

Then the weeds which were forms of living death
Fled from the frost to the earth beneath.
Their decay and sudden flight from frost
Was but like the vanishing of a ghost !

And under the roots of the Sensitive Plant
The moles and the dormice died for want:
The birds dropped stiff from the frozen air
And were caught in the branches naked and bare.

First there came down a thawing rain
And its dull drops froze on the boughs again,
Then there steamed up a freezing dew
Which to the drops of the thaw-rain grew;

And a northern whirlwind, wandering about
Like a wolf that had smelt a dead child out,
Shook the boughs thus laden and heavy and stiff,
And snapped them off with his rigid griff.

When winter had gone and spring came back
The Sensitive Plant was a leafless wreck;
But the mandrakes, and toadstools, and docks, and
    darnels,
Rose like the dead from their ruined charnels.

CONCLUSION.

Whether the Sensitive Plant, or that
Which within its boughs like a spirit sat
Ere its outward form had known decay,
Now felt this change, I cannot say.

Whether that lady's gentle mind,
No longer with the form combined
Which scattered love, as stars do light,
Found sadness, where it left delight,

I dare not guess; but in this life
Of error, ignorance, and strife,
Where nothing is, but all things seem,
And we the shadows of the dream,

It is a modest creed, and yet
Pleasant if one considers it,
To own that death itself must be,
Like all the rest, a mockery.

That garden sweet, that lady fair,
And all sweet shapes and odors there,
In truth have never past away:
'Tis we, 'tis ours, are changed; not they.

For love, and beauty, and delight,
There is no death nor change: their might
Exceeds our organs, which endure
No light, being themselves obscure.

1820.

Last Love Poems.

TO EDWARD WILLIAMS.

THE serpent is shut out from paradise.
　　The wounded deer must seek the herb no more
　　　In which its heart-cure lies :
　　The widowed dove must cease to haunt a bower
Like that from which its mate with feignèd sighs
　　　Fled in the April hour.
　　　I too must seldom seek again
Near happy friends a mitigated pain.

Of hatred I am proud, — with scorn content ;
　　Indifference, that once hurt me, now is grown
　　　Itself indifferent.
　　But, not to speak of love, pity alone
Can break a spirit already more than bent.
　　　The miserable one
　　　Turns the mind's poison into food, —
Its medicine is tears, — its evil good.

Therefore, if now I see you seldomer,
　　Dear friends, dear *friend!* know that I only fly
　　　Your looks, because they stir

Griefs that should sleep, and hopes that cannot
    die :
The very comfort that they minister
    I scarce can bear, yet I,
    So deeply is the arrow gone,
Should quickly perish if it were withdrawn.

When I return to my cold home, you ask
    Why I am not as I have ever been.
    You spoil me for the task
Of acting a forced part in life's dull scene,—
Of wearing on my brow the idle mask
    Of author, great or mean,
    In the world's carnival. I sought
Peace thus, and but in you I found it not.

Full half an hour, to-day, I tried my lot
    With various flowers, and every one still said,
    " She loves me —— loves me not."
And if this meant a vision long since fled —
If it meant fortune, fame, or peace of thought —
    If it meant,— but I dread
    To speak what you may know too well :
Still there was truth in the sad oracle.

The crane o'er seas and forests seeks her home ;
    No bird so wild but has its quiet nest,
    When it no more would roam ;
    The sleepless billows on the ocean's breast
Break like a bursting heart, and die in foam,
    And thus at length find rest.
    Doubtless there is a place of peace
Where *my* weak heart and all its throbs will cease.

I asked her, yesterday, if she believed
    That I had resolution.   One who *had*
      Would ne'er have thus relieved
    His heart with words, — but what his judgment
        bade
Would do, and leave the scorner unrelieved.
      These verses are too sad
    To send to you, but that I know,
Happy yourself, you feel another's woe.

                        1821.

SONG.

RARELY, rarely, comest thou,
    Spirit of Delight !
Wherefore hast thou left me now
    Many a day and night ?
Many a weary night and day
'Tis since thou art fled away.

How shall ever one like me
    Win thee back again?
With the joyous and the free
    Thou wilt scoff at pain.
Spirit false ! thou hast forgot
All but those who need thee not.

As a lizard with the shade
    Of a trembling leaf,
Thou with sorrow art dismayed ;
    Even the sighs of grief

Reproach thee, that thou art not near,
And reproach thou wilt not hear.

Let me set my mournful ditty
　　To a merry measure,
Thou wilt never come for pity,
　　Thou wilt come for pleasure.
Pity then will cut away
Those cruel wings, and thou wilt stay.

I love all that thou lovest,
　　Spirit of Delight !
The fresh Earth in new leaves drest,
　　And the starry night ;
Autumn evening, and the morn
When the golden mists are born.

I love snow, and all the forms
　　Of the radiant frost ;
I love waves, and winds, and storms,
　　Every thing almost
Which is Nature's, and may be
Untainted by man's misery.

I love tranquil solitude,
　　And such society
As is quiet, wise and good ;
　　Between thee and me
What difference? but thou dost possess
The things I seek, not love them less.

I love Love — though he has wings,
　　And like light can flee,

But above all other things, .
 Spirit, I love thee —
Thou art love and life ! O come,
Make once more my heart thy home.

1821.

———✦———

A LAMENT.

OH, world ! oh, life ! oh, time !
On whose last steps I climb
 Trembling at that where I had stood before ;
When will return the glory of your prime?
 No more — O, never more !

Out of the day and night
A joy has taken flight ;
 Fresh spring, and summer, and winter hoar,
Move my faint heart with grief, but with delight
 No more — O, never more !

1821.

———✦———

A DIRGE.

ROUGH wind, that moanest loud
 Grief too sad for song ;
Wild wind, when sullen cloud
 Knells all the night long ;
Sad storm, whose tears are vain,
Bare woods, whose branches strain,
Deep caves and dreary main,
 Wail, for the world's wrong !

1822.

TO ——.

ONE word is too often profaned
    For me to profane it,
One feeling too falsely disdained
    For thee to disdain it.
One hope is too like despair
    For prudence to smother,
And pity from thee more dear
    Than that from another.

I can give not what men call love,
    But wilt thou accept not
The worship the heart lifts above
    And the Heavens reject not,
The desire of the moth for the star,
    Of the night for the morrow,
The devotion to something afar
    From the sphere of our sorrow?

                    1821.

LINES.

WHEN the lamp is shattered
The light in the dust lies dead —
    When the cloud is scattered
The rainbow's glory is shed.
    When the lute is broken,
Sweet tones are remembered not;
    When the lips have spoken,
Loved accents are soon forgot.

As music and splendor
Survive not the lamp and the lute,
　The heart's echoes render
No song when the spirit is mute : —
　No song but sad dirges,
Like the wind through a ruined cell,
　Or the mournful surges
That ring the dead seaman's knell.

When hearts have once mingled
Love first leaves the well-built nest,
　The weak one is singled
To endure what it once possest.
　O, Love! who bewailest
The frailty of all things here,
　Why choose you the frailest
For your cradle, your home and your bier?

Its passions will rock thee
As the storms rock the ravens on high :
　Bright reason will mock thee,
Like the sun from a wintry sky.
　From thy nest every rafter
Will rot, and thine eagle home
　Leave thee naked to laughter,
When leaves fall and cold winds come.

1822.

———◆◆◆———

TO ——.

WHEN passion's trance is overpast,
If tenderness and truth could last
Or live, whilst all wild feelings keep

Some mortal slumber, dark and deep,
I should not weep, I should not weep!

It were enough to feel, to see,
Thy soft eyes gazing tenderly,
And dream the rest — and burn and be
The secret food of fires unseen,
Couldst thou but be as thou hast been.

After the slumber of the year
The woodland violets re-appear,
All things revive in field or grove,
And sky and sea, but two, which move,
And form all others, life and love.

1821.

—•◦•—

WITH A GUITAR, TO JANE.

ARIEL to Miranda. — Take
This slave of Music, for the sake
Of him who is the slave of thee,
And teach it all the harmony
In which thou canst, and only thou,
Make the delighted spirit glow,
Till joy denies itself again,
And, too intense, is turned to pain;
For by permission and command
Of thine own Prince Ferdinand,
Poor Ariel sends this silent token
Of more than ever can be spoken;
Your guardian spirit, Ariel, who,
From life to life, must still pursue
Your happiness; — for thus alone

Can Ariel ever find his own.
From Prospero's enchanted cell,
As the mighty verses tell,
To the throne of Naples, he
Lit you o'er the trackless sea,
Flitting on, your prow before,
Like a living meteor.
When you die, the silent Moon
In her interlunar swoon,
Is not sadder in her cell
Than deserted Ariel.
When you live again on earth,
Like an unseen star of birth,
Ariel guides you o'er the sea
Of life from your nativity.
Many changes have been run,
Since Ferdinand and you begun
Your course of love, and Ariel still
Has tracked your steps, and served your will;
Now, in humbler, happier lot,
This is all remembered not;
And now, alas! the poor sprite is
Imprisoned, for some fault of his,
In a body like a grave; —
From you he only dares to crave,
For his service and his sorrow,
A smile to-day, a song to-morrow.

The artist who this idol wrought,
To echo all harmonious thought,
Felled a tree, while on the steep
The woods were in their winter sleep,

Rocked in that repose divine
On the wind-swept Apennine;
And dreaming, some of Autumn past,
And some of Spring approaching fast,
And some of April buds and showers,
And some of songs in July bowers,
And all of love; and so this tree, —
O that such our death may be! —
Died in sleep, and felt no pain,
To live in happier form again:
From which, beneath Heaven's fairest star,
The artist wrought this loved Guitar,
And taught it justly to reply,
To all who question skilfully,
In language gentle as thine own;
Whispering in enamored tone
Sweet oracles of woods and dells,
And summer winds in sylvan cells;
For it had learnt all harmonies
Of the plains and of the skies,
Of the forests and the mountains,
And the many-voicèd fountains;
The clearest echoes of the hills,
The softest notes of falling rills,
The melodies of birds and bees,
The murmuring of summer seas,
And pattering rain, and breathing dew,
And airs of evening; and it knew
That seldom-heard mysterious sound,
Which, driven on its diurnal round,
As it floats through boundless day,
Our world enkindles on its way —

All this it knows, but will not tell
To those who cannot question well
The spirit that inhabits it;
It talks according to the wit
Of its companions; and no more
Is heard than has been felt before,
By those who tempt it to betray
These secrets of an elder day:
But sweetly as its answers will
Flatter hands of perfect skill,
It keeps its highest, holiest tone
For our belovèd Jane alone.

1822.

TO JANE — THE INVITATION.

BEST and brightest, come away!
Fairer far than this fair Day,
Which, like thee to those in sorrow,
Comes to bid a sweet good-morrow
To the rough Year just awake
In its cradle on the brake.
The brightest hour of unborn Spring,
Through the winter wandering,
Found, it seems, the halcyon Morn
To hoar February born;
Bending from Heaven, in azure mirth,
It kissed the forehead of the Earth,
And smiled upon the silent sea,
And bade the frozen streams be free,
And waked to music all their fountains,

And breathed upon the frozen mountains,
And like a prophetess of May
Strewed flowers upon the barren way,
Making the wintry world appear
Like one on whom thou smilest, dear.
Away, away, from men and towns,
To the wild wood and the downs —
To the silent wilderness
Where the soul need not repress
Its music lest it should not find
An echo in another's mind,
While the touch of Nature's art
Harmonizes heart to heart.

Radiant Sister of the Day,
Awake! arise! and come away!
To the wild woods and the plains,
And the pools where winter rains
Image all their roof of leaves,
Where the pine its garland weaves
Of sapless green and ivy dun
Round stems that never kiss the sun;
Where the lawns and pastures be,
And the sand-hills of the sea; —
Where the melting hoar-frost wets
The daisy-star that never sets,
And wind-flowers, and violets,
Which yet join not scent to hue,
Crown the pale year weak and new;
When the night is left behind
In the deep east, dun and blind,
And the blue noon is over us,

And the multitudinous
Billows murmur at our feet,
Where the earth and ocean meet,
And all things seem only one
In the universal sun.

1822.

————◆◇◆————

TO JANE — THE RECOLLECTION.

Now the last day of many days,
    All beautiful and bright as thou,
        The loveliest and the last, is dead,
Rise, Memory, and write its praise !
Up, to thy wonted work ! come, trace
        The epitaph of glory fled, —
For now the Earth has changed its face,
    A frown is on the Heaven's brow.

    We wandered to the pine forest
        That skirts the Ocean's foam,
    The lightest wind was in its nest,
        The tempest in its home.
    The whispering waves were half asleep,
        The clouds were gone to play,
    And on the bosom of the deep,
        The smile of Heaven lay ;
    It seemed as if the hour were one
        Sent from beyond the skies,
    Which scattered from above the sun
        A light of Paradise.

We paused amid the pines that stood
    The giants of the waste,
Tortured by storms to shapes as rude
    As serpents interlaced,
And soothed by every azure breath,
    That under heaven is blown,
To harmonies and hues beneath,
    As tender as its own ;·
Now all the tree-tops lay asleep,
    Like green waves on the sea,
As still as in the silent deep
    The ocean woods may be.

How calm it was ! — the silence there
    By such a chain was bound
That even the busy woodpecker
    Made stiller by her sound
The inviolable quietness ;
    The breath of peace we drew
With its soft motion made not less
    The calm that round us grew.
There seemed from the remotest seat
    Of the white mountain waste,
To the soft flower beneath our feet,
    A magic circle traced, —

A spirit interfused around,
    A thrilling silent life,
To momentary peace it bound
    Our mortal nature's strife ; —
And still I felt the centre of
    The magic circle there,

Was one fair form that filled with love
 The lifeless atmosphere.

We paused beside the pools that lie
 Under the forest bough,
Each seemed as 'twere a little sky
 Gulfed in a world below;
A firmament of purple light,
 Which in the dark earth lay,
More boundless than the depth of night,
 And purer than the day —
In which the lovely forests grew
 As in the upper air,
More perfect both in shape and hue
 Than any spreading there.

There lay the glade and neighboring lawn,
 And through the dark green wood
The white sun twinkling like the dawn
 Out of a speckled cloud.
Sweet views which in our world above
 Can never well be seen,
Were imaged by the water's love
 Of that fair forest green.
And all was interfused beneath
 With an elysian glow,
An atmosphere without a breath,
 A softer day below.

Like one beloved the scene had lent
 To the dark water's breast,
Its every leaf and lineament

With more than truth exprest;
Until an envious wind crept by,
    Like an unwelcome thought,
Which from the mind's too faithful eye
    Blots one dear image out.
Though thou art ever fair and kind,
    The forests ever green,
Less oft is peace in Shelley's mind,
    Than calm in waters seen.

1822.

————◦◦◦————

REMEMBRANCE.

SWIFTER far than summer's flight —
Swifter far than youth's delight —
Swifter far than happy night,
    Art thou come and gone —
As the wood when leaves are shed,
As the night when sleep is fled,
As the heart when joy is dead,
    I am left lone, alone.

The swallow summer comes again —
The owlet night resumes his reign —
But the wild-swan youth is fain
    To fly with thee, false as thou. —
My heart each day desires the morrow;
Sleep itself is turned to sorrow;
Vainly would my winter borrow
    Sunny leaves from any bough.

Lilies for a bridal bed —
Roses for a matron's head —
Violets for a maiden dead —
   Pansies let *my* flowers be :
On the living grave I bear
Scatter them without a tear —
Let no friend, however dear,
   Waste one hope, one fear for me.

                        1821.

LINES WRITTEN IN THE BAY OF LERICI.

SHE left me at the silent time
When the moon had ceased to climb
The azure path of Heaven's steep,
And like an albatross asleep,
Balanced on her wings of light,
Hovered in the purple night,
Ere she sought her ocean nest
In the chambers of the West.
She left me, and I staid alone
Thinking over every tone
Which, though silent to the ear,
The enchanted heart could hear,
Like notes which die when born, but still
Haunt the echoes of the hill ;
And feeling ever — O too much! —
The soft vibration of her touch,
As if her gentle hand, even now,
Lightly trembled on my brow ;
And thus, although she absent were,
Memory gave me all of her

That even Fancy dares to claim : —
Her presence had made weak and tame
All passions, and I lived alone
In the time which is our own ;
The past and future were forgot,
As they had been, and would be, not.
But soon, the guardian angel gone,
The dæmon reassumed his throne
In my faint heart. I dare not speak
My thoughts, but thus disturbed and weak
I sat and saw the vessels glide
Over the ocean bright and wide,
Like spirit-wingèd chariots sent
O'er some serenest element
For ministrations strange and far ;
As if to some Elysian star
Sailed for drink to medicine
Such sweet and bitter pain as mine.
And the wind that winged their flight
From the land came fresh and light,
And the scent of wingèd flowers,
And the coolness of the hours
Of dew, and sweet warmth left by day,
Were scattered o'er the twinkling bay.
And the fisher with his lamp
And spear about the low rocks damp
Crept, and struck the fish which came
To worship the delusive flame.
Too happy they, whose pleasure sought
Extinguishes all sense and thought
Of the regret that pleasure leaves,
Destroying life alone, not peace!

1822.

TO ——.

Music, when soft voices die,
Vibrates in the memory;
Odors, when sweet violets sicken,
Live within the sense they quicken;

Rose leaves, when the rose is dead,
Are heaped for the belovèd's bed;
And so thy thoughts, when thou art gone,
Love itself shall slumber on.

1821.

Adonais;

AN ELEGY ON THE DEATH OF JOHN KEATS.

———•■•———

'Αστὴρ πρὶν μὲν ἔλαμπες ἐνὶ ζώοισιν ἐῷος.
Νῦν δὲ θανὼν λάμπεις ἔσπερος ἐν φθιμένοις.

PLATO. ·

PREFACE.

IT is my intention to subjoin to the London edition of this poem a criticism upon the claims of its lamented object to be classed among the writers of the highest genius who have adorned our age. My known repugnance to the narrow principles of taste on which several of his earlier compositions were modelled, prove, at least that I am an impartial judge. I consider the fragment of " Hyperion " as second to nothing that was ever produced by a writer of the same years.

John Keats died at Rome of a consumption, in his twenty-fourth year, on the —— of —— 1821; and was buried in the romantic and lonely cemetery of the Protestants in that city, under the pyramid which is the tomb of Cestius, and the massy walls and towers, now mouldering and desolate, which formed the circuit of ancient Rome. The cemetery is an open space among the ruins, covered in winter with violets and daisies. It might make one in love with death, to think that one should be buried in so sweet a place.

The genius of the lamented person to whose memory I have dedicated these unworthy verses, was not less delicate and fragile than it was beautiful; and where cankerworms abound, what wonder, if its young flower was blighted in

293

the bud ?　The savage criticism on his " Endymion," which appeared in the *Quarterly Review*, produced the most violent effect on his susceptible mind; the agitation thus originated ended in the rupture of a blood-vessel in the lungs ; a rapid consumption ensued, and the succeeding acknowledgments from more candid critics, of the true greatness of his powers, were ineffectual to heal the wound thus wantonly inflicted.

It may be well said, that these wretched men know not what they do.　They scatter their insults and their slanders without heed as to whether the poisoned shaft lights on a heart made callous by many blows, or one, like Keats's, composed of more penetrable stuff.　One of their associates, is, to my knowledge, a most base and unprincipled calumniator.　As to " Endymion ; " was it a poem, whatever might be its defects, to be treated contemptuously by those who had celebrated with various degrees of complacency and panegyric, " Paris," and " Woman," and a " Syrian Tale," and Mrs. Lefanu, and Mr. Barrett, and Mr. Howard Payne, and a long list of the illustrious obscure?　Are these the men, who in their venal good nature, presumed to draw a parallel between the Rev. Mr. Milman and Lord Byron?　What gnat did they strain at here, after having swallowed all those camels?　Against what woman taken in adultery, dares the foremost of these literary prostitutes to cast his opprobrious stone?　Miserable man! you, one of the meanest, have wantonly defaced one of the noblest specimens of the workmanship of God.　Nor shall it be your excuse, that murderer as you are, you have spoken daggers, but used none.

The circumstances of the closing scene of poor Keats's life were not made known to me until the Elegy was ready for the press.　I am given to understand that the wound which his sensitive spirit had received from the criticism of " Endymion," was exasperated by the bitter sense of unrequited benefits ; the poor fellow seems to have been hooted from the stage of life, no less by those on whom he had wasted the promise of his genius, than those on whom he had lavished his fortune and his care.　He was accompanied to Rome, and attended

in his last illness by Mr. Severn, a young artist of the highest
promise, who, I have been informed, "almost risked his own
life, and sacrificed every prospect to unwearied attendance
upon his dying friend." Had I known these circumstances
before the completion of my poem, I should have been tempted
to add my feeble tribute of applause to the more solid recompense which the virtuous man finds in the recollection of his
own motives. Mr. Severn can dispense with a reward from
"such stuff as dreams are made of." His conduct is a golden
augury of the success of his future career — may the unextinguished Spirit of his illustrious friend animate the creations
of his pencil, and plead against Oblivion for his name!

I WEEP for Adonais — he is dead!
O, weep for Adonais! though our tears
Thaw not the frost which binds so dear a head!
And thou, sad Hour, selected from all years
To mourn our loss, rouse thy obscure compeers,
And teach them thine own sorrow, say: "with me
Died Adonais; till the Future dares
Forget the Past, his fate and fame shall be
An echo and a light unto eternity!"

Where wert thou, mighty Mother, when he lay,
When thy Son lay, pierced by the shaft which flies
In darkness? where was lorn Urania
When Adonais died? With veilèd eyes,
'Mid listening Echoes, in her Paradise
She sate, while one, with soft enamored breath,
Rekindled all the fading melodies,
With which, like flowers that mock the corse be-
      neath,
He had adorned and hid the coming bulk of death.

O, weep for Adonais — he is dead!
Wake, melancholy Mother, wake and weep!
Yet wherefore?   Quench within their burning bed
Thy fiery tears, and let thy loud heart keep
Like his, a mute and uncomplaining sleep;
For he is gone, where all things wise and fair
Descend; — oh, dream not that the amorous Deep
Will yet restore him to the vital air;
Death feeds on his mute voice, and laughs at our
    despair.

Most musical of mourners, weep again!
Lament anew, Urania! — He died,
Who was the Sire of an immortal strain,
Blind, old, and lonely, when his country's pride,
The priest, the slave, and the liberticide,
Trampled and mocked with many a loathèd rite
Of lust and blood; he went, unterrified,
Into the gulf of death; but his clear Sprite
Yet reigns o'er earth; the third among the sons of
    light.

Most musical of mourners, weep anew!
Not all to that bright station dared to climb;
And happier they their happiness who knew,
Whose tapers yet burn through that night of time
In which suns perished; others more sublime,
Struck by the envious wrath of man or God,
Have sunk, extinct in their refulgent prime;
And some yet live, treading the thorny road,
Which leads, through toil and hate, to Fame's serene
    abode.

But now, thy youngest, dearest one has perished,
The nursling of thy widowhood, who grew,
Like a pale flower by some sad maiden cherished,
And fed with true-love tears, instead of dew;
Most musical of mourners, weep anew!
Thy extreme hope, the loveliest and the last,
The bloom, whose petals nipt before they blew
Died on the promise of the fruit, is waste;
The broken lily lies — the storm is overpast.

To that high Capital, where kingly Death
Keeps his pale court in beauty and decay,
He came; and bought, with price of purest breath,
A grave among the eternal. — Come away!
Haste, while the vault of blue Italian day
Is yet his fitting charnel-roof! while still
He lies, as if in dewy sleep he lay;
Awake him not! surely he takes his fill
Of deep and liquid rest, forgetful of all ill.

He will awake no more, oh, never more! —
Within the twilight chamber spreads apace,
The shadow of white Death, and at the door .
Invisible Corruption waits to trace
His extreme way to her dim dwelling-place;
The eternal Hunger sits, but pity and awe
Soothe her pale rage, nor dares she to deface
So fair a prey, till darkness, and the law
Of change, shall o'er his sleep the mortal curtain draw.

O, weep for Adonais! — The quick Dreams,
The passion-wingèd Ministers of thought,
Who were his flocks, whom near the living streams

Of his young spirit he fed, and whom he taught
The love which was its music, wander not, —
Wander no more, from kindling brain to brain,
But droop there, whence they sprung; and mourn
    their lot
Round the cold heart, where, after their sweet pain,
They ne'er will gather strength, or find a home again,

And one with trembling hands clasps his cold head,
And fans him with her moonlight wings and cries;
"Our love, our hope, our sorrow, is not dead;
See, on the silken fringe of his faint eyes,
Like dew upon a sleeping flower, there lies
A tear some Dream has loosened from his brain."
Lost Angel of a ruined Paradise!
She knew not 'twas her own; as with no stain
She faded, like a cloud which had outwept its rain.

One from a lucid urn of starry dew
Washed his light limbs as if embalming them;
Another clipt her profuse locks, and threw
The wreath upon him, like an anadem,
Which frozen tears instead of pearls begem;
- Another in her wilful grief would break
Her bow and wingèd reeds, as if to stem
A greater loss with one which was more weak;
And dull the barbèd fire against his frozen cheek.

Another Splendor on his mouth alit,
That mouth, whence it was wont to draw the breath
Which gave it strength to pierce the guarded wit,
And pass into the panting heart beneath

With lightning and with music: the damp death
Quenched its caress upon his icy lips ;
And, as a dying meteor stains a wreath
Of moonlight vapor, which the cold night clips,
It flushed through his pale limbs, and past to its
eclipse.

And others came . . . Desires and Adorations,
Wingèd Persuasions and veiled Destinies,
Splendors, and Glooms, and glimmering Incarna-
tions
Of hopes and fears, and twilight Phantasies ;
And Sorrow, with her family of Sighs,
And Pleasure, blind with tears, led by the gleam
Of her own dying smile instead of eyes,
Came in slow pomp ; — the moving pomp might
seem
Like pageantry of mist on an autumnal stream.

All he had loved, and moulded into thought,
From shape, and hue, and odor, and sweet sound,
Lamented Adonais. Morning sought
Her eastern watch-tower, and her hair unbound,
Wet with the tears which should adorn the ground,
Dimmed the aërial eyes that kindle day ;
Afar the melancholy thunder moaned,
Pale Ocean in unquiet slumber lay,
And the wild winds flew round, sobbing in their dis-
may.

Lost Echo sits amid the voiceless mountains,
And feeds her grief with his remembered lay,
And will no more reply to winds or fountains,

Or amorous birds perched on the young green spray,
Or herdsman's horn, or bell at closing day;
Since she can mimic not his lips, more dear
Than those for whose disdain she pined away
Into a shadow of all sounds : — a drear
Murmur, between their songs, is all the woodmen
    hear.

Grief made the young Spring wild, and she threw
    down
Her kindling buds, as if she Autumn were,
Or they dead leaves; since her delight is flown
For whom should she have waked the sullen year?
To Phœbus was not Hyacinth so dear
Nor to himself Narcissus, as to both
Thou, Adonais: wan they stand and sere
Amid the faint companions of their youth,
With dew all turned to tears; odor, to sighing ruth.

Thy spirit's sister, the lorn nightingale
Mourns not her mate with such melodious pain;
Not so the eagle, who like thee could scale   .
Heaven, and could nourish in the sun's domain
Her mighty youth with morning, doth complain,
Soaring and screaming round her empty nest,
As Albion wails for thee: the curse of Cain
Light on his head who pierced thy innocent breast,
And scared the angel soul that was its earthly guest!

Ah woe is me! Winter is come and gone,
But grief returns with the revolving year;
The airs and streams renew their joyous tone;
The ants, the bees, the swallows reappear;

Fresh leaves and flowers deck the dead Seasons'
    bier;
The amorous birds now pair in every brake,
And build their mossy homes in field and brere;
And the green lizard, and the golden snake,
Like unimprisoned flames, out of their trance awake.

Through wood, and stream, and field, and hill, and
    Ocean,
A quickening life from the Earth's heart has burst
As it has ever done, with change and motion,
From the great morning of the world when first
God dawned on Chaos; in its steam immersed
The lamps of Heaven flash with a softer light;
All baser things pant with life's sacred thirst;
Diffuse themselves; and spend in love's delight,
The beauty and the joy of their renewèd might.

The leprous corpse, touched by this spirit tender,
Exhales itself in flowers of gentle breath;
Like incarnations of the stars, when splendor
Is changed to fragrance, they illumine death
And mock the merry worm that wakes beneath:
Nought we know, dies. Shall that alone which
    knows
Be as a sword consumed before the sheath
By sightless lightning?—th' intense atom glows
A moment, then is quenched in a most cold repose.

Alas! that all we loved of him should be,
But for our grief, as if it had not been,
And grief itself be mortal! Woe is me!

Whence are we, and why are we? of what scene
The actors or spectators? Great and mean
Meet massed in death, who lends what life must
     borrow.
As long as skies are blue, and fields are green,
Evening must usher night, night urge the morrow,
Month follow month with woe, and year wake year to
     sorrow.

He will awake no more, oh, never more !
"Wake thou," cried Misery, " childless Mother, rise
Out of thy sleep, and slake, in thy heart's core,
A wound more fierce than his with tears and sighs."
And all the Dreams that watched Urania's eyes,
And all the Echoes whom their sister's song
Had held in holy silence, cried : " Arise ! "
Swift as a Thought by the snake Memory stung,
From her ambrosial rest the fading Splendor sprung.

She rose like an autumnal Night, that springs
Out of the East, and follows wild and drear
The golden Day, which, on eternal wings,
Even as a ghost abandoning a bier,
Had left the Earth a corpse. Sorrow and fear
So struck, so roused, so rapt Urania ;
So saddened round her like an atmosphere
Of stormy mist ; so swept her on her way
Even to the mournful place where Adonais lay.

Out of her secret Paradise she sped,
Through camps and cities rough with stone, and
     steel,

And human hearts, which to her aëry tread
Yielding not, wounded the invisible
Palms of her tender feet where'er they fell:
And barbèd tongues, and thoughts more sharp than
    they
Rent the soft Form they never could repel,
Whose sacred blood, like the young tears of May
Paved with eternal flowers that undeserving way.

In the death-chamber for a moment Death,
Shamed by the presence of that living Might,
Blushed to annihilation, and the breath
Revisited those lips, and life's pale light
Flashed through those limbs, so late her dear de-
    light.
" Leave me not wild and drear and comfortless,
As silent lightning leaves the starless night!
Leave me not!" cried Urania: her distress
Roused Death: Death rose and smiled, and met her
    vain caress.

" Stay yet awhile! speak to me once again;
Kiss me, so long but as a kiss may live;
And in my heartless breast and burning brain
That word, that kiss shall all thoughts else sur-
    vive,
With food of saddest memory kept alive,
Now thou art dead, as if it were a part
Of thee, my Adonais! I would give
All that I am to be as thou now art!
But I am chained to Time, and cannot thence de-
    part!

"Oh gentle child, beautiful as thou wert,
Why didst thou leave the trodden paths of men
Too soon, and with weak hands though mighty
    heart
Dare the unpastured dragon in his den ?
Defenceless as thou wert, oh, where was then
Wisdom the mirrored shield, or scorn the spear ?
Or hadst thou waited the full cycle, when
Thy spirit should have filled its crescent sphere,
The monsters of life's waste had fled from thee like
    deer.

" The herded wolves, bold only to pursue ;
The obscene ravens, clamorous o'er the dead ;
The vultures to the conqueror's banner true
Who feed where Desolation first has fed,
And whose wings rain contagion ; — how they fled,
When like Apollo, from his golden bow,
The Pythian of the age one arrow sped
And smiled ! — The spoilers tempt no second blow,
They fawn on the proud feet that spurn them lying
    low.

" The sun comes forth, and many reptiles spawn ;
He sets, and each ephemeral insect then
Is gathered into death without a dawn,
And the immortal stars awake again ;
So is it in the world of living men :
A godlike mind soars forth, in its delight
Making earth bare and veiling heaven, and when
It sinks, the swarms that dimmed or shared its light
Leave to its kindred lamps the spirit's awful night."

Thus ceased she: and the mountain shepherds
    came,
Their garlands sere, their magic mantles rent;
The Pilgrim of Eternity, whose fame
Over his living head like Heaven is bent,
An early but enduring monument,
Came, veiling all the lightnings of his song
In sorrow; from her wilds Ierne sent
The sweetest lyrist of her saddest wrong,
And love taught grief to fall like music from his tongue.

Midst others of less note, came one frail Form,
A phantom among men; companionless
As the last cloud of an expiring storm
Whose thunder is its knell; he, as I guess,
Had gazed on Nature's naked loveliness,
Actæon-like, and now he fled astray
With feeble steps o'er the world's wilderness,
And his own thoughts, along that rugged way,
Pursued, like raging hounds, their father and their
    prey.

A pard-like Spirit beautiful and swift —
A Love in desolation masked; — a Power
Girt round with weakness; — it can scarce uplift
The weight of the superincumbent hour;
It is a dying lamp, a falling shower,
A breaking billow; — even whilst we speak
Is it not broken? On the withering flower
The killing sun smiles brightly: on a cheek
The life can burn in blood, even while the heart may
    break.

His head was bound with pansies overblown,
And faded violets, white, and pied, and blue ;
And a light spear topped with a cypress cone,
Round whose rude shaft dark ivy-tresses grew
Yet dripping with the forest's noonday dew,
Vibrated. as the ever-beating heart
Shook the weak hand that grasped it ; of that crew
He came the last, neglected and apart ;
A herd-abandoned deer struck by the hunter's dart.

All stood aloof, and at his partial moan
Smiled through their tears ; well knew that gentle
      band
Who in another's fate now wept his own ;
As in the accents of an unknown land,
He sung new sorrow ; sad Urania scanned
The Stranger's mien, and murmured : " Who art
      thou ? "
He answered not, but with a sudden hand
Made bare his branded and ensanguined brow,
Which was like Cain's or Christ's — Oh ! that it should
      be so !

What softer voice is hushed over the dead ?
Athwart what brow is that dark mantle thrown ?
What form leans sadly o'er the white death-bed,
In mockery of monumental stone,
The heavy heart heaving without a moan ?
If it be He, who, gentlest of the wise,
Taught, soothed, loved, honored the departed one ;
Let me not vex, with inharmonious sighs
The silence of that heart's accepted sacrifice.

Our Adonais has drunk poison — oh!
What deaf and viperous murderer could crown
Life's early cup with such a draught of woe?
The nameless worm would now itself disown:
It felt, yet could escape the magic tone
Whose prelude held all envy, hate, and wrong,
But what was howling in one breast alone,
Silent with expectation of the song,
Whose master's hand is cold, whose silver lyre un-
    strung.

Live thou, whose infamy is not thy fame!
Live! fear no heavier chastisement from me,
Thou noteless blot on a remembered name!
But be thyself, and know thyself to be!
And ever at thy season be thou free
To spill the venom when thy fangs o'erflow:
Remorse and Self-contempt shall cling to thee;
Hot Shame shall burn upon thy secret brow,
And like a beaten hound tremble thou shalt — as
    now.

Nor let us weep that our delight is fled
Far from these carrion kites that scream below;
He wakes or sleeps with the enduring dead;
Thou canst not soar where he is sitting now. —
Dust to the dust! but the pure spirit shall flow
Back to the burning fountain whence it came,
A portion of the Eternal, which must glow
Through time and change, unquenchably the same,
Whilst thy cold embers choke the sordid hearth of
    shame.

Peace, peace ! he is not dead, he doth not sleep —
He hath awakened from the dream of life —
'Tis we, who, lost in stormy visions, keep '
With phantoms an unprofitable strife,
And in mad trance, strike with our spirit's knife
Invulnerable nothings. — *We* decay
Like corpses in a charnel; fear and grief
Convulse us and consume us day by day,
And cold hopes swarm like worms within our living
    clay.

He has outsoared the shadow of our night ;
Envy, and calumny, and hate, and pain,
And that unrest which men miscall delight,
Can touch him not and torture not again ;
From the contagion of the world's slow stain
He is secure, and now can never mourn
A heart grown cold, a head grown gray in vain ;
Nor, when the spirit's self has ceased to burn,
With sparkless ashes load an unlamented urn.

He lives, he wakes — 'tis Death is dead, not he ;
Mourn not for Adonais. — Thou young Dawn
Turn all thy dew to splendor, for from thee
The spirit thou lamentest is not gone ;
Ye caverns and ye forests, cease to moan !
Cease ye faint flowers and fountains, and thou
    Air
Which like a mourning veil thy scarf hadst thrown
O'er the abandoned Earth, now leave it bare
Even to the joyous stars which smile on its de-
    spair !

He is made one with Nature: there is heard
His voice in all her music, from the moan
Of thunder, to the song of night's sweet bird;
He is a presence to be felt and known
In darkness and in light, from herb and stone,
Spreading itself where'er that Power may move
Which has withdrawn his being to its own;
Which wields the world with never wearied love,
Sustains it from beneath, and kindles it above.

He is a portion of the loveliness
Which once he made more lovely: he doth bear
His part, while the one Spirit's plastic stress
Sweeps through the dull dense world, compelling
    there,
All new successions to the forms they wear;
Torturing th' unwilling dross that checks its flight
To its own likeness, as each mass may bear;
And bursting in its beauty and its might
From trees, and beasts, and men, into the Heavens'
    light.

The splendors of the firmament of time
May be eclipsed, but are extinguished not;
Like stars to their appointed height they climb
And death is a low mist which cannot blot
The brightness it may veil. When lofty thought
Lifts a young heart above its mortal lair,
And love and life contend in it, for what
Shall be its earthly doom, the dead live there
And move like winds of light on dark and stormy
    air.

The inheritors of unfulfilled renown
Rose from their thrones, built beyond mortal
    thought,
Far in the Unapparent.   Chatterton
Rose pale, his solemn agony had not
Yet faded from him ; Sidney, as he fought,
And as he fell, and as he lived, and loved
Sublimely mild, a Spirit without spot,
Arose ; and Lucan, by his death approved :
Oblivion as they rose shrank like a thing reproved.

And many more, whose names on earth are dark
But whose transmitted effluence cannot die
So long as fire outlives the parent spark,
Rose, robed in dazzling immortality.
" Thou art become as one of us," they cry,
" It was for thee yon kingless sphere has long
Swung blind in unascended majesty,
Silent alone amid a Heaven of Song.
Assume thy wingèd throne, thou Vesper of our
    throng ! "

Who mourns for Adonais ? oh, come forth
Fond wretch ! and know thyself and him aright.
Clasp with thy panting soul the pendulous Earth ;
As from a centre, dart thy spirit's light
Beyond all worlds, until its spacious might
Satiate the void circumference : then shrink
Even to a point within our day and night ;
And keep thy heart light lest it make thee sink
When hope has kindled hope, and lured thee to the
    brink.

Or go to Rome, which is the sepulchre
Oh, not of him, but of our joy : 'tis nought
That ages, empires, and religions there
Lie buried in the ravage they have wrought ;
For such as he can lend, — they borrow not
Glory from those who made the world their prey ;
And he is gathered to the kings of thought
Who waged contention with their time's decay,
And of the past are all that cannot pass away.

Go thou to Rome, — at once the Paradise,
The grave, the city, and the wilderness ;
And where its wrecks like shattered mountains
    rise,
And flowering weeds, and fragrant copses dress
The bones of Desolation's nakedness
Pass, till the Spirit of the spot shall lead
Thy footsteps to a slope of green access
Where, like an infant's smile, over the dead,
A light of laughing flowers along the grass is spread.

And gray walls moulder round, on which dull Time
Feeds, like slow fire upon a hoary brand ;
And one keen pyramid with wedge sublime,
Pavilioning the dust of him who planned
This refuge for his memory, doth stand
Like flame transformed to marble ; and beneath,
A field is spread, on which a newer band
Have pitched in Heaven's smile their camp of
    death
Welcoming him we lose with scarce extinguished
    breath.

Here pause : these graves are all too young as yet
To have outgrown the sorrow which consigned
Its charge to each ; and if the seal is set,
Here, on one fountain of a mourning mind,
Break it not thou! too surely shalt thou find
Thine own well full, if thou returnest home,
Of tears and gall.   From the world's bitter wind
Seek shelter in the shadow of the tomb.
What Adonais is, why fear we to become?

The One remains, the many change and pass ;
Heaven's light forever shines, Earth's shadows fly ;
Life, like a dome of many-colored glass,
Stains the white radiance of Eternity,
Until Death tramples it to fragments. — Die,
If thou wouldst be with that which thou dost seek!
Follow where all is fled! — Rome's azure sky,
Flowers, ruins, statues, music, words, are weak
The glory they transfuse with fitting truth to speak.

Why linger, why turn back, why shrink, my Heart?
Thy hopes are gone before : from all things here
They have departed ; thou shouldst now depart!
A light is past from the revolving year,
And man, and woman ; and what still is dear
Attracts to crush, repels to make thee wither.
The soft sky smiles, — the low wind whispers near ;
'Tis Adonais calls! oh, hasten thither,
No more let Life divide what Death can join together.

That Light whose smile kindles the Universe,
That Beauty in which all things work and move,

That Benediction which the eclipsing Curse
Of birth can quench not, that sustaining Love
Which through the web of being blindly wove
By man, and beast, and earth, and air, and sea,
Burns bright or dim, as each are mirrors of
The fire for which all thirst ; now beams on me,
Consuming the last clouds of cold mortality.

The breath whose might I have invoked in song
Descends on me ; my spirit's bark is driven,
Far from the shore, far from the trembling throng
Whose sails were never to the tempest given :
The massy earth and sphered skies are riven!
I am borne darkly, fearfully, afar ;
Whilst, burning through the inmost veil of Heaven,
The soul of Adonais, like a star,
Beacons from the abode where the Eternal are.

1821.

ODE TO THE WEST WIND.

I.

O WILD West Wind, thou breath of Autumn's being,
Thou, from whose unseen presence the leaves dead
Are driven, like ghosts from an enchanter fleeing,

Yellow, and black, and pale, and hectic red,
Pestilence-stricken multitudes : O, thou,
Who chariotest to their dark wintry bed

The wingèd seeds, where they lie cold and low,
Each like a corpse within its grave, until
Thine azure sister of the spring shall blow

Her clarion o'er the dreaming earth, and fill
(Driving sweet buds like flocks to feed in air)
With living hues and odors plain and hill :

Wild Spirit, which art moving everywhere;
Destroyer and preserver; hear, O hear!

II.

Thou on whose stream, 'mid the steep sky's commo-
    tion
Loose clouds like earth's decaying leaves are shed,
Shook from the tangled boughs of Heaven and Ocean,

Angels of rain and lightning : there are spread
On the blue surface of thine airy surge,
Like the bright hair uplifted from the head

Of some fierce Mænad, even from the dim verge
Of the horizon to the zenith's height
The locks of the approaching storm.   Thou dirge

Of the dying year, to which this closing night
Will be the dome of a vast sepulchre,
Vaulted with all thy congregated might

Of vapors, from whose solid atmosphere
Black rain, and fire, and hail will burst: O hear!

III.

Thou who didst waken from his summer dreams
The blue Mediterranean, where he lay,
Lulled by the coil of his crystàlline streams,

Beside a pumice isle in Baiæ's bay,
And saw in sleep old palaces and towers
Quivering within the wave's intenser day,

All overgrown with azure moss and flowers
So sweet, the sense faints picturing them !   Thou
For whose path the Atlantic's level powers

Cleave themselves into chasms, while far below
The sea-blooms and the oozy woods which wear
The sapless foliage of the ocean, know

Thy voice, and suddenly grow gray with fear,
And tremble and despoil themselves: O hear!

IV.

If I were a dead leaf thou mightest bear ;
If I were a swift cloud to fly with thee ;
A wave to pant beneath thy power, and share

The impulse of thy strength, only less free
Than thou, O uncontrollable! If even
I were as in my boyhood, and could be

The comrade of thy wanderings over heaven,
As then, when to outstrip thy skyey speed
Scarce seemed a vision ; I would ne'er have striven

As thus with thee in prayer in my sore need.
Oh! lift me as a wave, a leaf, a cloud!
I fall upon the thorns of life! I bleed!

A heavy weight of hours has chained and bowed
One too like thee: tameless, and swift, and proud.

v.

Make me thy lyre, even as the forest is :
What if my leaves are falling like its own!
The tumult of thy mighty harmonies

Will take from both a deep, autumnal tone,
Sweet though in sadness. Be thou, Spirit fierce,
My spirit! Be thou me, impetuous one!

Drive my dead thoughts over the universe
Like withered leaves to quicken a new birth!
And, by the incantation of this verse,

Scatter, as from an unextinguished hearth
Ashes and sparks, my words among mankind !
Be through my lips to unawakened earth

The trumpet of a prophecy! O wind,
If Winter comes, can Spring be far behind?

1819.

NOTES.

---•-•-•---

NOTE i. p. 1.

THE *Hymn to Intellectual Beauty* is placed first in this book, not only because it pictures Shelley's earliest aspirations, but also because Shelley has not added in this hymn, as he has done in other poems, any " mortal image " to his expression of the Platonic doctrine of the love of the Idea of Beauty. To understand the poem the reader ought to refer to that passage in Shelley's translation of the " Symposium " of Plato which begins — Diotima is represented as speaking : — " Your own meditation, Socrates, might perhaps have initiated you in all these things which I have already taught you on the subject of Love," and continue to the close of the speech of Diotima. See *Essays*, vol. i. pp. 118–122.

NOTE ii. p. 6.

" Shelley . . . was at a loss for a title, and I proposed that which he adopted — *Alastor, or the Spirit of Solitude.* The Greek word, ἀλάστωρ, is an evil genius, κακοδαίμων, . . . The poem treated the spirit of solitude as a spirit of evil." This statement of Mr. Peacock's is supported not only by the poem, but also by the Preface, especially by the words — " The poet's self-centred seclusion was avenged by the Furies of an irresistible passion pursuing him to speedy ruin." See also the lines —

> " The spirit of sweet human love has sent
> A vision to the sleep of *him who spurned
> Her choicest gifts.*"

Note iii. p. 12.

" Her voice was like the voice of his own soul
Heard in the calm of thought."

The *Hymn to Intellectual Beauty* represents the pure Platonic conception of Love, and of that which it loves. In *Alastor*, in *Prince Athanase*, in many of the lyrics, Shelley retreats from this conception, and amalgamating two thoughts in the "Symposium," invents a conception of his own. In that dialogue Aristophanes tells an amusing myth of the original human-being divided into man and woman, and of each part of this man-woman ever afterwards passionately seeking the other. The serious element in this is, " that the loves of this world are an indistinct anticipation of an ideal union which is not yet realized," or perhaps that each human being has its complement, and strives to find it. That is one element in Shelley's conception. The other is taken from the representation made by Diotima of the lover of absolute Beauty seeking for its image in mortal forms, and his loving of these images when found, as one of the steps whereby he ascends to the love of ideal Beauty. Throwing these two together, Shelley forms a new conception. He conceives of the archetypal Beauty, that Beauty which is the model and source of all other beauty, as embodied somewhere beyond this material world in the other half of his own soul. In visions he sees this Being, and pursues her incessantly, but is always driven by a weakness in his nature to try and find her image in real women. His ideal love continually glides back into a desire of realizing itself on earth. He is thus, as he calls himself in *Adonais*, a "power girt round with weakness." *Alastor* records the coming of the Vision, and the agony of not finding it realized. Unable to be content with the love of Ideal Beauty alone, unable to find it realized to the sense on earth, the poet, beaten between and tortured by these two inabilities, dies of the pain. *Epipsychidion* records a moment when he thought that he had found realized in Emilia this "soul out of his soul." Had *Prince Athanase* been finished, it would have recorded the vicissitudes of this pursuit.

The personal element in Love, which is only a step towards the higher Love in Plato, is a distinct part of it in Shelley. And it was his profound feeling of the necessity of this for him that made him create, as part of his idea of Love, an ideal image of his own soul, a heightened, externalized personality of himself, whom he felt in Knowledge, in Woman, and in Nature, and to absolute union with whom, such union as is described in the latter part of *Epipsychidion,* he passionately aspired. But it is best to refer to Shelley himself for this invention, for this addition to the Platonic theory of Love. He expresses it fully enough in his *Essay on Love.* See the sentences beginning " Thou demandest — What is Love? " They illustrate passage after passage in *Alastor* and in the other poems. See, also, verses 3, 4, and 5 of the poem of *The Zucca.*

NOTE iv. pp. 18, 19.

There can be no reason for these unearthly and unnatural scenes, except the wish to illustrate a temper of mind as unearthly and unnatural. They are the image of a mind tossed by the waves of impossible desire, and so maddened that only the quiet of death can follow. And so it is. The gentle stream follows, and the profound forest, and the ideal landscape, evening and death.

NOTE v. p. 25.

" On every side now rose
Rocks which, in unimaginable forms,
Lifted their black and barren pinnacles
In the light of evening, and its precipice
Obscuring the ravine, disclosed above
'Mid toppling stones."

I cannot but think that the easiest explanation of this disputed passage is to read *the* for *its.* The *precipice* is mentioned afterwards in two or three passages, but in these passages it is spoken of as it is seen on the other side of the valley, beyond the gap, where it falls downwards to the plain.

What the poet sees now are, first, the sides of the valley rising with pinnacles of rock; and, secondly, in front 'of him, the towering sides sweeping round and closing up the valley in a precipitous curve, which, because it is between him and the descending sun, obscures the ravine where he is walking. This precipice, which shuts in the valley in front of him, opens its stony jaws ("the abrupt mountain breaks"), is *disclosed*, at first *above*, and afterwards below, as he walks on. He then sees the gate of the hills, and passing through it by the side of the stream, among the toppling stones, beholds the mighty landscape far below, in the light of evening and of the descending moon. But I am inclined to think that *its* is right. *Its* may either be carelessly used, as if he had mentioned the mountain, when he has only mentioned rocks, or, by one of those tortuous constructions, not uncommon in Shelley, *its* stands for *its own* — its own precipice obscuring the ravine.

Note vi. p. 25.

This wonderful description of a vast landscape is one of the many instances in Shelley of Nature presenting herself to him as she presented herself to the landscape-painter Turner.

Note vii. p. 28, last line.

The application of the adjectives has been discussed. But it seems plain enough. It is quite in Shelley's manner, as in the "Ode to the West Wind," in "When the lamp is shattered," and in many other poems, to go back to and bring together his illustrations. Here the poet's frame is a lute, a bright stream, a dream of youth. The lute is still, the stream is dark and dry, the dream is unremembered.

Note viii. pp. 31, 33.

These two poems are inserted here from their striking the same note as the last scene in Alastor.

NOTE ix. p. 40.

This is part of the introduction of *Hellas.* The first and third verses are sung by a chorus of Greek captive women while Mahmud is sleeping, the second and fourth verses by the Indian slave who sits beside his couch.

NOTE x. pp. 42, 43.

This is a splendid example of that highly wrought painting of cloud and sky in which Shelley stands almost alone among English poets. There are fine examples in Wordsworth and Byron, but they have neither the detail, nor the splendor, nor the subtilty of color that Shelley puts into his skies. This might be a description of one of Turner's storm skies. The long trains of tremulous mist that precede the tempest, the cleft in the storm-clouds, and seen through it, high above, the space of blue sky, fretted with fair clouds, the pallid semicircle of the moon with mist on its upper horn, the flying rack of clouds below the serene spot — all are as Turner saw them; but painting cannot give what Shelley gives — the growth and progress of the changes of the storm.

NOTE xi. p. 48.

I have only inserted the *Mask*, and left out its explanation. That explanation, in its two parts, has seemed to me to trouble, as all explanations do, and especially an artist's, the work of art.

NOTE xii. p. 83.

This is another of those pictured skies in which Shelley excels. They are almost the only aspects of Nature which he sees with absolute clearness, and describes with absolute directness. This could be painted from, but then only Turner could have painted it, or would have cared to paint it.

NOTE xiii. p. 93.

" The inmost purple spirit of light, and made
Their peaks transparent."

Nothing can be more accurate. In certain states of atmosphere, when the sun sinks over those hills in autumn, they change as it were into violet vapor, and seem no less transparent to the eye.

In this poem, *Julian and Maddalo*, Shelley employs, he says, a certain familiar style of language. It is not gracefully or easily employed, nor is the language familiar. In the narrative parts it actually resembles the style of Shelley's novels *Zastrozzi* and *St. Irvyne*, and is prosaic beyond anything in Wordsworth.

> " My dear friend,
> Said Maddalo, my judgment will not bend
> To your opinion, though I think you might
> Make such a system refutation-tight
> As far as words go."

That is prose, and bad prose, and it does not stand alone.

In the descriptive parts, the poem is, of course, not familiar, but highly imaginative. In the tale of the Madman, its passion lifts it wholly out of the familiar. Excellent indeed as *Julian and Maddalo* is, its note is peculiar and unequal, nor are its elements kindly mixed. And this partly arises from Shelley having put so much of himself into the Madman, that the character is not separated from his own, that is, from Julian's, with sufficient sharpness. Julian and the Madman grow into one another as we read.

NOTE xiv. p. 111.

It is interesting to compare with *Mont Blanc*, Letter iv. to Peacock. It contains the germ of many of the images used, and of the thoughts expressed in the poem.

NOTE xv. p. 119.

I saw once, from a tower that overlooked two rookeries, this very thing. The moment the sun's disk had fully climbed over the edge of a distant wood, the whole band of rooks, from both their homes, silent before, rose, all the birds together, with a great "hail" into the air, and hovering together for a second or two, streamed down the wind towards the sun.

NOTE xvi. p. 132.

I have put in this extract from *Rosalind and Helen*, that its feebler work may be compared with Shelley's treatment of the same subject, under the influence of passion, in the *Recollection*.

NOTE xvii. p. 134.

This is the same subject as *The Zucca* of the poems. In this form it occurs in an unfinished drama, and is more in the special manner of Shelley than is the poem itself. The subject, thus twice treated, and alluded to also in the Witch of Atlas (p. 210, line 5), grew out of a real incident which is described in one of the Shelley letters.

NOTE xviii. p. 146, lines 15, 16.

This is the second time that Shelley borrows this phrase from Wordsworth; from the *Elegiac Stanzas suggested by a picture of Peele Castle.*

> "Whene'er I looked, thy image still was there;
> It trembled, but it never passed away."

NOTE xix. p. 148.

The poems of the preceding section I have called Poems of Nature and Man, because in them, as in some others elsewhere placed in this book, Shelley has mixed up Nature with human feeling, chiefly with his own feeling. In some of these poems, which I have called *Poems of pure Nature*, he writes of Nature as his special form of Pantheism, if I may call it that, urged him. He writes of her apart from Man, as the outward image of an all-sustaining, all-pervading Love, whom he embodied in the creation of *Asia*. Nay, he sometimes writes of this Love alone, and seems to forget that there is any image of her in the outward world. She is when he conceives her best, alive, and has her own separate pleasures and pains. And below her, and deriving life from her, is *Panthea,* the whole of the phenomenal universe. But he writes also in these poems of certain distinct individualities in Nature, without any reference to a spiritual life in which they are contained. The Cloud, the Apennine, the sphere of vapor sucked by the sun from the forest pool, the Moon, the Earth, have each and all their own distinct life, their own living spirit; be, and have, and do of their own will.

NOTE xx. p. 155.

I have left out the last verse of this song to *Asia,* because it is mixed up with the events of the Drama. The song is, in this book, the better without it. If *Asia* is the embodiment of that Love by which the universe is, and who, in loving, makes the universe, this song seems to conceive that there is a something behind and greater than this Love; a central source of Being and Power — the *Demogorgon* of the *Prometheus Unbound.* Yet to call Demogorgon the central source of being, would say more, perhaps, than Shelley meant. If he had been asked himself what he meant, he might have replied, I conceive of a vast Perception, and no more. Nevertheless, the Thought and the Song may be compared with Goethe's conception of *the Mothers* in the second part of Faust, and of Faust's descent to find them.

NOTE xxi. pp. 158, 164.

The last stanza is omitted of the Echo Song.

At page 164 the answer of the Earth to the first stanza of the Moon's song to him is omitted, and also the long series of stanzas which follow the Earth's, " It interpenetrates my granite mass," partly because they are mixed up with the ethical end of the Drama, partly because they are, if one may dare to say so, less good than the rest.

I have changed the common punctuation at the end of the line, " Hangs o'er the sea, a fleece of fire and amethyst," because it seems plain that Shelley meant the Moon to take up the answering song, and to carry out herself that which the Earth was about to say. In the same way the Earth takes up and finishes for the Moon what she was about to say after the lines

> " When the sunset sleeps
> Upon its snow " —

so that each toss to and fro their thoughts of each other. The concluding lines which follow the verse, " Through isles for ever calm," seem to me to spoil, by their fierceness of note, those that precede them. I have, therefore, as one may in selections, been bold enough to leave them out.

Note xxii. p. 181.

These few poems which are apart from those on Nature, and on Man, and on Shelley's phases of passion outside his home, are called *Poems of Home Life*, for want of a better title. At page 196, though the Eton remembrances are interesting, the new matter lately discovered is not inserted.

Note xxiii. p. 201.

Whom or what Shelley meant by his *Witch of Atlas* is scarcely worth asking. She keeps her own secret. But I have sometimes thought that its germ may be found in the line in *Mont Blanc* —

> " In the still cave of the Witch, Poesy ; "

and her birth from Apollo, and the beasts that come to her as to Orpheus' song, and many other things, fit that Witch.

Note xxiv. p. 227.

Shelley translates his title in the line —

> " Whither 'twas fled *this soul out of my soul ;* "

and the word *Epipsychidion* is coined by him to express the idea of that line. It might mean " something which is placed on a soul," as if to complete or crown it. Or it might be, and more probably was, intended by Shelley to be a diminutive of endearment, from *Epipsyche.* There is no such Greek word as ἐπι-ψυχή. But Epipsyche would mean "a soul upon a soul," just as Epicycle, in the Ptolemaic astronomy, meant "a circle upon a circle." Such a "soul on a soul" might be paraphrased as "a soul which is the complement of, or responsive to, another soul," *i.e.,* to the soul of the poet, so that each soul seeks to be united with that other to be in harmony wherewith it has been created. This idea, many suggestions of which may be found in Plato, seems most clearly expressed in the lines near the end of the poem beginning —

" One passion in two hearts."

As in the Vita Nuova, Dante writes sometimes of Beatrice herself, and sometimes of the absolute Love and Wisdom whom she represents, and at other times seems to write of both together, as if the earthly and the heavenly passion were wrought into one, so here Shelley (pp. 229–33) speaks now of Emilia alone, and now of that Epipsychidion whom he feels through her, and who is veiled in her. The phrases change from being personal and passionate to being impersonal and passionate. The image and the thing imaged are frequently fused into one. Yet in the end, he ascends through Emilia to the "Divinity of the world of his own thoughts." Who that was he describes —" There was a Being whom my spirit oft." It is the Spirit of the *Hymn to Intellectual Beauty.* " Her spirit was the harmony of truth." Then he describes the search for her, repeating the motive and the story of *Alastor.* In the midst of this we come on that thought, not contained in Alastor, which is found in the notes to *Prince Athanase.* He meets " one whose voice is venomed melody." This is the image of sensual Love of Beauty — Aphrodite Pandemos — and the description of this lower love may be compared with that dwelt on in Shakspere's later sonnets to which Shelley, afterwards speaking of this poem, refers. ·

Shelley now turns away from his youthful experience in *Alastor* to speak of how he sought to find in mortal women the shadow of that celestial substance of his Epipsychidion.

The one "who was true (p. 233), but not true to him," is Harriet Grove. I conjecture that the " comet, beautiful and fierce," is that woman of whose love for Shelley we have so many hints, and who swept, as it were like a comet, across the orbit of his life in London, Switzerland, and Naples. Mary Godwin is the Moon of the passage. I imagine that the lines which tell of her only speak of the first years of his union with her, and that the " storms which then lashed the ocean of his sleep" image the troubled feelings which we find in the lines written to her in 1814, and the misery he felt on hearing of his wife's death. In that case, " She, the Planet of that hour," who was " quenched," and who is not represented as in any way one of the images of his ideal soul, would be the only allusion to Harriet Westbrook, and one sufficiently obscure not to be unbecoming. The strange thing is that, under the symbolism of the text, Mary Godwin — and here the later experience of his married life enters the poem — is certainly represented as not having sufficiently kindled or warmed his life. When the earthquakes broke up the "death of ice," she, the white Moon, smiled all the while, ignorant as she was at Naples of the passion that then, as is thought, made him dejected. There are other passages in his poems that support the view that though he was happy in his marriage he was not contented. Then Emilia is described, " Soft as an Incarnation of the Sun," in whom at last he finds life. For a short space Shelley mingles together Sun and Moon, bright regents of his life, in alternate sway, and then the Moon and Mary disappear. The rest of the Poem, though it seems especially personal, is not intended to be so. He slips again and again into phrases of personal passion, because of his " error of seeking in a mortal image the likeness of what is perhaps eternal," but he is always striving, in intention, to speak only of the vision of his youth, of her who is his second soul, the spiritual substance of all his ideals, of all the Knowledge and Love and Beauty and Nature which he perceives. Of this Emilia is only the shadow. And the Ionian Isle and all else are meant to be impalpable; images of an immaterial world. He says that no keel has ever ploughed the sea-path to the island. It is itself cradled 'twixt Heaven, Air, Earth, and Sea, and is never visited by the scourges that afflict the earth. The passionate description of his life there with Emilia is the description of Shelley at last united to that other far-off half of his being, and the incorporation of the two into one is as ideal as the rest. It is love reaching its perfect aim, but it has clasped its reality so wholly in the immaterial world of pure thought, that he, with that weakness, as he thought it, which unfitted him for continuance in this etherial region, cannot live in it save for a moment. Earth claims him again.

> " Woe is me!
> The wingèd words on which my soul would pierce
> Into the heights of love's rare Universe
> Are chains of lead around its flight of fire —
> I pant, I sink, I tremble, I expire!"

(Compare some lines in the last verse of the *Ode to the West Wind.*)

The fault of the poem as an exposition of the Platonic theory of Love, even with Shelley's addition thereto, is perhaps the very root of its excellence as poetry. It *is* mixed, consciously or unconsciously, with some love for the woman herself, and this love rising through the intellectual imagery and setting it on fire, redeems it from the cold abstractness of the philosophy, and makes it passionate poetry. Yet the passion for Emilia was truly an ideal one. Shelley himself compared it, when it had died in another and less ideal love, to the love of Ixion for the cloud, and he could not look with much pleasure on this poem, its offspring. He had not then enough of love to absorb or to give substance to his ideal philosophy. Of this idealism of love *Epipsychidion* was the last result. He expressed it all in that poem, and finished with it. Whatever love came afterwards was real, for a woman herself, not for her as the shadow of a spiritual substance. "It is a part of me," said Shelley, speaking of this poem, "which is already dead." There is not a trace of this philosophy of Love in the poems written to Mrs. Williams. It is true that the verses, 3, 4, 5, I have already alluded to, in *The Zucca* (1822) of the Poems, were written after *Epipsychidion*, and describe, more clearly than elsewhere, his imagined love. But they are verses that look back to what has been rather than on what is. At their beginning, the past tense, *I loved*, is used, and even when the present tense is used, the things said have the note of the past.

The main motive of the poem is again taken up with different coloring and imagery in the fable, *Una Favola*, which has been published by Mr. Garnet in his *Relics of Shelley*. That *Fable* is dated 1820, but I should conjecture from its peculiar note, and from its being written in Italian, that it was composed after his meeting with Emilia Viviani. At any rate many of its images and expressions are repeated in *Epipsychidion*. The cave where death and life are, and their flight, the obscure forest into which Emilia comes, are both in the *Fable*, and many other things. So, also, he who cares for *Epipsychidion* would do well to read the first canzone of Dante's *Convito*, the last stanza of which is translated by Shelley as an introduction to this poem.

NOTE xxv. p. 249.

"The author has connected many recollections of his visit to Pompeii and Baiæ, with the enthusiasm exerted by the proclamation of a constitutional Government at Naples. This has given a tinge of picturesque and descriptive imagery to the introductory Epodes, which depicture the scenes, and some of the majestic feelings permanently connected with the scene of this animating event.

"'*The viper's palsying venom.*' The viper was the armorial device of the Visconti, tyrants of Milan." — *Shelley's Note*.

NOTE xxvi. p. 252.

I have printed this, as also "Life may change, but it may fly not," at p. 261, without the divisions made by the alternating semichorus.

Note xxvii. p. 260.

This is the close of *Prometheus Unbound.* It has been included in this book, not for the sake of its poetical quality, which is inferior to other passages in the Drama which might have been inserted, but for its importance as a declaration, not only of what Shelley thought Man would become, but also of how he thought Man should act now in order to arrive at the Golden Age. The two last verses embody the main motives of the *Revolt of Islam.*

Note xxviii. p. 262.

The *Sensitive Plant* is inserted in this place as an introduction to the love poems which belong to Mrs. Williams, because Shelley said that Mrs. Williams was the exact antitype of the lady depicted in it. The *Sensitive Plant* is, of course, Shelley himself, "companionless," as he makes himself in *Adonais*, "desiring what it has not, the beautiful."

Note xxix. p. 278.

" Wild wind, when sullen cloud
Knells all the night long."

We may compare in order to explain the term —

" As the last cloud of an expiring storm
Whose thunder is its knell." (*Adonais.*)

"Bare woods, whose branches stain" must be *strain*, as many have conjectured. All the things spoken of are sounding. The wind moans, the cloud knells, the caves and sea wail, and there are few sounds so in tune with the tempest of this poem as the groaning of branches straining in a storm.

Note xxx. p. 284.

I have left out the lines which, however interesting personally, are out of harmony with the rest of the poem.

NOTE xxxi. p. 286.

The four lines omitted by Shelley in the *Recollection* deserve insertion here.

> " Were not the crocuses that grew
>   Under the ilex tree
> As beautiful in scent and hue
>   As ever fed the bee ? "

NOTE xxxii. p. 293.

The Greek motto is translated elsewhere by Shelley.

> " Thou wert the morning star among the living,
>   Ere thy fair light had fled ;
> Now, having died, thou art as Hesperus, giving
>   New splendor to the dead."

NOTE xxxiii. pp. 305, 306.

The *Pilgrim of Eternity* is Byron. *Ierne* is Ireland, and her *lyrist*, Moore.

No analysis of Shelley's nature can excel or equal the self-description of the three verses of p. 306. Leigh Hunt is the last of the mountain shepherds alluded to, p. 307.

The lines —

> " And his own thoughts, along that rugged way
> Pursued, like raging hounds, their father and their prey."

are Shelley's reminiscence of two lines in a poem of Wordsworth's.

> " And his own mind did like a tempest strong
> Come to him thus, and drove the weary wight along."

It is interesting to compare them. They speak volumes of both poets.

NOTE xxxiv. p. 311.

" And flowery weeds and fragrant copses dress
The bones of Desolation's nakedness."

Nothing but the bones are there now; and what have we gained?

NOTE xxxv. p. 314.

" This poem was conceived and chiefly written in a wood that skirts the Arno, near Florence, and on a day when that tempestuous wind, whose temperature is at once mild and animating, was collecting the vapors which pour down the autumnal rains. They began, as I foresaw, at sunset, with a violent tempest of hail and rain, attended by that magnificent thunder and lightning peculiar to the Cis-alpine regions.

" The phenomenon alluded to at the conclusion of the third stanza is well known to naturalists. The vegetation at the bottom of the sea, of rivers and of lakes, sympathizes with that of the land in the change of seasons, and is consequently influenced by the winds that announce it." — *Shelley's Note.*

It is characteristic of Shelley's pleasure in repeating an image or a thought that pleased him, that he makes use of this " phenomenon " at least three times in different poems.

NOTE xxxvi. p. 293.

The lines from Moschus with which Shelley prefaced the *Adonais* were accidentally omitted in the text. I insert them here, with a translation made of them by Professor Mahaffy.

Φάρμακον ἦλθε Βίων ποτὶ σὸν στόμα φαρμακοειδές.
πῶς τευ τοῖς χείλεσσι ποτέδραμε κ'οὐκ ἐγλυκάνθη;
τίς δὲ βροτός, τοσσοῦτον ἀνάμερος ὡς κεράσαι τοι
ἢ δοῦναι λαλέοντι τὸ φάρμακον, οὐ φύγεν ᾠδάν;

Bion, a potion came to thy mouth which soothed like a potion.
How did it touch thy lips and not change its bitter to sweetness?
Who so savage of men as to mix or to give thee the poison
Even as thou didst speak ? Fled he not from the voice of thy
singing?

INDEX OF FIRST LINES.

333